They were wt brought them

"You're beautiful,

"You don't mean th

"Yes, I do. I've always thought so. Since the first moment I saw you. But I know you can't see me as someone on your level," Finn said.

She laid her hand on his arm, the movement gentle and the touch uncharacteristically intimate. "Don't say that. I'm not what you think I am. I want to be like everybody else, to get married and have children. I want what everyone else has...."

"You can have it."

"It's not that simple."

"Yes, it is. Or it could be. It's a beautiful night, you're a beautiful woman and I'm asking."

"Asking?"

"You to marry me." Finn held his breath. "I want you to be my wife...."

Dear Reader,

Welcome to another month of wonderful books from Harlequin American Romance! We've rounded up the best stories by your favorite authors, with the hope that you will enjoy reading them as much as we enjoy bringing them to you.

Kick-start a relaxing weekend with the continuation of our fabulous miniseries, THE DADDY CLUB. The hero of Mindy Neff's *A Pregnancy and a Proposal* is one romantic daddy who knows how to sweep a woman off her feet!

Beloved historical author Millie Criswell makes her contemporary romance debut with *The Wedding Planner.* We are thrilled to bring you this compelling story of a wealthy bachelor out to find himself a bride...with a little help from the wedding consultant who wishes she were his only choice!

We've also got the best surprises and secrets. Bailey Dixon has a double surprise for Michael Wade in Tina Leonard's delightful new Western, *Cowboy Be Mine.* And in Bonnie K. Winn's *The Mommy Makeover,* a dedicated career woman is suddenly longing for marriage—what *is* her handsome groom's secret?

With best wishes for happy reading from Harlequin American Romance...

Melissa Jeglinski
Associate Senior Editor

The Mommy Makeover

BONNIE K. WINN

HARLEQUIN®

TORONTO • NEW YORK • LONDON
AMSTERDAM • PARIS • SYDNEY • HAMBURG
STOCKHOLM • ATHENS • TOKYO • MILAN • MADRID
PRAGUE • WARSAW • BUDAPEST • AUCKLAND

ISBN 0-373-16812-8

THE MOMMY MAKEOVER

Copyright © 2000 by Bonnie K. Winn.

This edition published by arrangement with Harlequin Books S.A.

® and TM are trademarks of the publisher. Trademarks indicated with ® are registered in the United States Patent and Trademark Office, the Canadian Trade Marks Office and in other countries.

Visit us at www.romance.net

Printed in U.S.A.

ABOUT THE AUTHOR

A hopeless romantic, Bonnie K. Winn naturally turned to romance writing. This seasoned author of historical and contemporary romance has won numerous awards, including having been voted one of the Top Ten Romance Authors in America, according to *Affaire de Coeur*.

Living in the foothills of the Rockies gives Bonnie plenty of inspiration and a touch of whimsy, as well. She shares her life with her husband, son and spunky Westie terrier.

Bonnie welcomes mail from her readers. You can write to her c/o Harlequin Books, 300 E. 42nd St., New York, NY 10017.

Books by Bonnie K. Winn

HARLEQUIN AMERICAN ROMANCE

Prologue

The incomparable Houston skyline dazzled beneath the mammoth windows of the sixtieth-floor office. Resembling glitzy, gift-wrapped packages, the tall glass skyscrapers mingled with older, more stately stone buildings. Like the city itself, it was a courtship of old and new. But Katelyn Amhurst had little time to dwell on the dynamic view, even less to consider courtships.

She glanced skeptically at her longtime assistant, Daniel. They had gone beyond ''boss'' and ''employee'' years earlier. Daniel saw himself as a cross between mother confessor and drill sergeant. While Katelyn viewed him with tolerant affection, she often wished he would ease up on his compulsive need for control. ''I want to stop smoking,'' she told him, ''but—''

''I thought you wanted to beat this thing,'' Daniel interrupted persuasively, flipping back his precision-cut blond hair. It was his one vanity. Katelyn knew Daniel was currently pursuing a cute brunette in accounting. No doubt the extra grooming was for her benefit.

Katelyn concealed a grin. She wished someone would keep his attention so he would quit harping about her love live. Or rather lack of it. ''I don't know, Daniel. Subliminal tapes? Isn't that a little simplistic?''

Offended indignation gripped his thin features. "When have you ever known me to be simple?"

"Point taken. Not that I haven't hoped…"

He took a deep breath as a long-suffering expression descended on his face. "The tape will do wonders for you. In fact, I'd say it'll turn your life around."

"It's a subliminal tape, not a brain transplant," she replied, still not reaching for the cassette.

Daniel anticipated her next request and handed her the day planner, which had been buried beneath a foot-high stack of folders. "Or a personality transplant," he muttered beneath his breath.

"What? Oh, thanks. I was looking for that."

He sighed quietly. "I know."

She flipped open to the mind-boggling schedule of meetings, appointments and other commitments. "I have the Franklin dinner tonight. Did you hire a new limo service?"

"Yesterday," he replied, rolling his eyes. "Now, are you going to let a pack of cigarettes control you, or do you want the tape?"

Katelyn frowned. She'd mapped out her life with the precision of a Rand McNally atlas. From her Ivy League education and brilliant advertising career to her equally well-thought-out decision to skip both marriage and children. Despite Daniel's efforts to convince her otherwise, she knew that latter decision was wise. She had everything in her life under total control. Except the one habit she couldn't quite kick—smoking. If Daniel's tape might work…why not? Casually, she took the tape and tossed it on top of her desk.

Head bent, she missed the smirk on Daniel's face. When she glanced up, she met guileless blue eyes. "You won't regret this, Katelyn." He slipped the tape into a Walkman. "Just be sure to listen to it."

"I'm not in the habit of forgetting things," she reminded

him, putting the tape player in her purse. Her razor-sharp mind was legend—terrifying her underlings and impressing her superiors. But she and Daniel had worked together too long for him to be intimidated.

"No, but you *are* in the habit of resisting doing what you don't want to do," he retorted.

She squared her shoulders. "You make me sound like a willful child."

"I'd rather think of you as an intelligent adult."

"Ahem." She studied his expression, searching for sarcasm. "Well, thanks. I think."

"And, Katelyn?"

"Yes?"

"The tape only works if you *really* want it to."

"I *really, really* want to quit smoking. Okay? Now, I'd better run. I'm meeting with Grayco in…" She glanced at her wristwatch and let out an uncharacteristic oath. "Fifteen minutes. I'll take a cab, but tell the new driver to pick me up there after the meeting."

"Your wish is my command," Daniel replied as she gathered everything in an efficient flurry and headed to the door.

She glanced back. "I don't know about that. Sometimes I'm not sure just *who's* in charge."

DANIEL MERELY smiled in reply, watching the whirlwind of contained energy she created as she issued orders, signed documents thrust at her and kept a constant path to the elevator.

His gaze focused on her purse, knowing it contained the tape. Not the one on smoking, as she supposed. No, the tape resting innocently in her purse was actually entitled, *Embrace Your Femininity*. Its subliminal message implanted suggestions designed to turn even the most ruthless barracuda into an old-fashioned, loving wife and mother. It also emphasized the rapidity of the biological countdown Katelyn claimed didn't affect her. Everything about the tape was designed to push a woman straight into marriage and motherhood.

Something Daniel truly believed Katelyn needed.

She lived, breathed, and consumed her work.

Her work and nothing else.

Daniel knew that Katelyn limited her dating to only ''safe'' men—ones who were neither threatening nor potential mates. Katelyn had convinced herself she would be happy living alone. She reminded Daniel of his older sister, Cindy. She had believed a career would keep her warm at night as well. Now, Cindy was sad, bitter and inescapably alone.

Having come to regard Katelyn almost as a sister, Daniel didn't want her to have the same fate.

Chapter One

Finn Malloy was hot. Figuratively and literally. Houston's muggy heat was wilting his ever-so-proper chauffeur's uniform and Katelyn Amhurst's tardiness was doing the same to his normally even temperament.

The fact that she was a half hour late didn't faze him— he knew executive meetings weren't conducted by a stopwatch. Even an hour late didn't bother him, but Katelyn had surpassed two hours and still wasn't in sight. Finn wondered if she was even inside the damned building. Standing next to his car, he stared at the skyscraper and a mile-high wall of reflective glass stared back, giving no hint of who was inside.

Having not met the lady yet, Finn didn't know if she was the type who habitually miscalculated the length of meetings, didn't know how to manage time, or simply had no consideration for the poor slob of a driver waiting out in the heat.

He hoped she knew his clock started ticking when he pulled up in front of the building, not when she took a notion to step outside and into his limo. His operation might be a one-man show, but he maintained the same billing rates the big boys did.

Eventually he hoped to add at least one more car to his fleet. *Fleet!* Hah! Finn doubted anyone referred to a solitary limo as a fleet. But, every building started with a single piece of lumber or brick. And Malloy Enterprises was starting with this sole vehicle—one that the bank owned more of than he did, at the moment.

He glanced at his wristwatch and groaned. Two and a half hours. Maybe he should call her office and see if there'd been a change of plans. They had his cell-phone number, but maybe she was the type who suffered from the ten-broken-fingers syndrome, too.

Finn reached into his pocket for the phone, then paused. A woman was heading in his direction, but she couldn't be the corporate crusher. No woman who moved like that could be a barracuda of the business world.

Her long hair, caught in a severe barrette, resembled a red flame in the sunshine, though he could see it was actually a combination of blond, gold, brown and red. High cheekbones competed with a sensual mouth for dominance in her arresting face. But his eyes really lingered on her lush figure, the long legs that stretched out endlessly, capped by ankle-breaking high heels.

No, it wasn't in his stars to drive around a ripe morsel like that. With those long legs, she'd sashay right past his car…

"You, there. Look alive. I'm in a hurry."

He stared blankly at her. Could it be?

Katelyn tapped her briefcase against the discreet limo logo on the car door. "You *are* the new driver, aren't you?"

Finn straightened up, clearing his throat, hoping to clear the confusion as well. "Yes, ma'am. I'm Finn Malloy."

Delicate brows arched upward as eyes of indeterminate color barely scanned him. She wore her indifference like the raw silk power suit that hugged her curves. "Fine. As I said, I'm in a hurry. I have to be at the River Oaks Country Club in less than an hour, but first we need to stop at my condo.''

She was in a hurry. That was rich. After he'd waited in the heat for more than two hours. ''Guess your meeting ran overtime,'' he commented, opening the door for her.

She grunted an unintelligible reply.

Seeing neither an explanation nor apology stirring, he closed her door and opened his own. He pulled away from the curb, the long car gliding effortlessly into the already crowded street.

Hearing a click, then smelling the distinctive aroma of a freshly lit cigarette, Finn frowned. ''Ma'am. This is a no-smoking car.''

Watching in the mirror, he saw the displeasure cross her face before she inhaled deeply, then rolled down her window and stubbed out the cigarette.

He couldn't make any exceptions. Too many passengers wouldn't ride in a car that even faintly smelled of cigarette smoke. But she didn't complain. He guessed she knew the tide had turned against smokers—especially since it was becoming more and more difficult to find places to smoke.

Glancing again in the rearview mirror he saw that she had donned a pair of seriously dark-rimmed glasses and was absorbed in a deep stack of papers. Apparently, she was up to her neck in work. Hell, he could cut her some slack. She probably hadn't enjoyed being in a meeting that ran over by two hours any more than he'd enjoyed waiting for her. ''So, you the one who got stuck doing homework?''

''Hmm?'' she responded after a moment without looking at him, her head still bent downward.

''The papers. Are you the only one who had to stay after school?''

She finally glanced up, annoyance clouding her features. ''School? You must be confused. I work for Ellington Advertising. I would have thought you'd know that from your dispatcher.''

"Right." He'd have to remember that if he ever hired a dispatcher. Apparently, her job description didn't include having a sense of humor.

He let the silence build in the car for a few minutes, but he wasn't the sort of person who was comfortable with silence for long. "So, you got a big night planned at the country club?''

"Um," she replied, once again not bothering to lift her head.

She was a real live one, he thought with disgust. She might look like a million bucks, but her conversation wasn't worth two cents. Still, he persevered. "Gotta go home and change first, huh?''

"Ummm.''

At this rate he could talk himself to death.

"Guess you want to knock 'em dead.''

At this she did glance up. He met her frosty eyes in the rearview mirror. "I assure you it is not my intention to 'knock 'em dead,' nor is what I wear any of your concern.''

Frosty? Make that Antarctica frigid. He was surprised that ice hadn't formed on the windows, despite the exterior heat. "No, *ma'am.*''

Her eyes narrowed suspiciously before she returned them to her work.

Finn reached over to fiddle with the radio knobs, considering choosing a hard-rock station he knew would blast her prim little behind right off the seat. Instead he inserted a richly melodic Rachmaninoff tape that seemed to suit anyone he'd ever driven. He preferred it to the icy silence.

He rapped his fingers against the wheel in time to the music as he navigated through the growing traffic. Choosing to forego the freeway, knowing it would be snarled during commuting hours, he swung off onto a little-known alternate route. Of course, the ice princess lived in the trendy Galleria area. He could have guessed that without the information provided by her assistant.

Accustomed to her rigid silence, he nearly jumped when she spoke. "Where *are* we?"

"Headed to your condo."

"Via Guatemala?" she questioned, staring out at the unfamiliar neighborhood.

He laughed, even though he doubted she meant to be funny. "Not quite. This way we'll miss most of the traffic. Don't worry. I know this city better than most people know their lovers."

There was a momentary silence and he guessed she wasn't comfortable with his point of reference.

"Be that as it may, Mr...."

"Malloy," he supplied. "Finn."

"Mr. *Malloy,*" she continued, ignoring his first name. "I prefer to not be driven through hell's half acre. Safety is just as important a consideration as traffic."

"You said you have to be at the country club in an hour. If I took the freeway, we wouldn't even be at your condo in an hour."

"Mr. Malloy, are you deliberately trying to be difficult?"

He grinned into the mirror, meeting her eyes, which now looked to be a cloudy gray. "No, but I've been told it's one of my natural talents."

"I doubt I'd term that a talent."

"There are enough yes-men in the world. Don't you get a charge out of something different?"

"I don't get a *charge* out of risking my life to travel home."

"You're not in any danger. Besides, I can protect you if we run into trouble."

"I'm not impressed with muscles, Mr...."

"Malloy," he supplied again. "Finn."

And again she ignored his first name. "...Malloy. I'm impressed with efficiency."

"And you don't think a person can have both?"

"It hasn't been my experience. Now, Mr. Malloy, I have work to do."

"Hey, sorry lady."

Meeting her gaze in the rearview mirror, he had the impression she was silently counting to ten. "My name is Ms. Amhurst. I trust you can remember that."

"Probably every bit as well as you can remember mine," he replied pleasantly, his grin taking the sting out of his well-placed barb.

She harrumphed in reply and turned her attention back to her work. And despite a few more tries at conversation on his part, she didn't respond. It was as though she'd set her hearing to the off position. When he pulled up in front of her condo a short time later, she didn't comment on the remarkably quick time he'd made, nor anything else for that matter. Instead, she moved those delicious-looking legs of hers inside at warp speed.

"Yes, ma'am, I'll be fine outside in the heat. No, I don't need anything cold to drink—even if I have been waiting hours for you, without so much as a sip of water. Don't give it another thought." His words rang in the empty parking lot and he glanced upward at the windows he guessed were hers. Firmly drawn blinds covered the glass—no surprise there. He hadn't met such an uptight woman in... He doubted he'd ever met such an uptight woman.

Finn was tempted to step back into the car to turn on the air-conditioning but he had a hefty gasoline bill to keep an eye on. He figured she'd be quite a while, even though she said she needed to be at the country club soon. He just hoped she didn't intend to set another lateness record.

Having parked in the shade, Finn opted for pulling his cap over his eyes as he leaned against the limo's immaculate fender. Settled in for a lengthy wait, he was startled when he heard the tapping of high heels only fifteen minutes later, followed by her voice, already barking orders.

"Let's get moving, Malloy," she ordered, grinding out a cigarette beneath one shoe.

Apparently if she dropped the "Mister" she could remember his name, he thought wryly. "Yes, ma'am."

He offered a mock salute, before turning to open the rear door. But then he took a look at her—a really good look. She'd swept all of that marvelous hair up, revealing a long, shapely neck. A diamond necklace winked from between ample cleavage and a thigh-high slit in her long form-hugging gown flashed those incredible legs. He guessed she dressed to impress and intimidate. Nose in the air or not, she was one hot package.

Until he looked into her eyes. No longer seeming to be gray, they were the same rich blue as her gown—and as frosty as the rest of her glacial expression.

Finn stared at her curiously. "Do you have on different colored contacts?"

She glared at him. "I don't wear contacts."

"Then your eyes really do change color?"

"Yes. Not that it's any of your concern. You're paid to drive, Malloy, not ogle."

"Sorry about that, Ms. Amhurst. You're not like most of the clients I drive," he replied, stifling his instinctive response.

"Perhaps I'll request a more experienced driver next time," she told him as she slid inside. "One who's accustomed to all types of clients."

Neat trick if you can manage it, he thought, wondering what she'd think if she knew he was Malloy Enterprises's solitary employee. He was owner, operator, driver, dispatcher, accountant and salesman. Which reminded him that he needed this contract—more than he needed to antagonize *Ms.* Amhurst. "I'm in the process of getting that experience, ma'am. I appreciate your patience."

She harrumphed before settling back in the seat.

With uncharacteristic silence he headed toward the country club. He could almost hear her unspoken surprise. It was nearly as much fun keeping her in suspense as actually needling her. She could believe he was bowing to her wishes, and at the same time he wouldn't be antagonizing the hand that fed him.

Within minutes, they pulled up to the gatehouse of the prestigious River Oaks Country Club where entry was permitted only to a select few. But his passenger's impeccable credentials shot them past the guard in moments.

Finn stopped in front of the massive entryway and opened the passenger door. Despite her standoffish manner, he couldn't help admiring Katelyn's elegant appearance. Silhouetted against the soft-pink aged brick, she looked as though the ornate building had been designed strictly as a backdrop for her. Then she broke the spell.

"Be here precisely at twelve."

"Or my limo will turn into a pumpkin?" he responded with a charming smile intended to break the ice.

She gave him a long-suffering look. "Don't be late, Malloy."

He tipped his hat and then saluted. "No, ma'am."

She turned, obviously dismissing him and he watched her walk inside, enjoying the gentle sway of her hips, the occasional flash of long legs.

"Knock 'em dead, Cinderella," he muttered. Glancing at his watch, he realized he had time to go home and try to get a grip on things. With several hours of paid time to do as he pleased, perhaps driving the ice princess wouldn't be so bad after all.

KATELYN FELT the dull, throbbing beginnings of a head-ache. Resisting the urge to rub her temples until she was safely out of sight, she smiled heartily at the executives from the Franklin Group as they left the dining room.

While the dinner hadn't run overly long, it had been an excruciating four hours. The subtle balance between business and flirtation made her feel like she'd walked a tight-rope all night. She knew it was part of being a woman in a male dominated executive world, still she wished she could simply concentrate on business and restrict the an-noying male/female thing to her personal life. Katelyn gri-maced at her last thought. As though she had time for a personal life.

She escaped to the smoking room and enjoyed one lei-surely cigarette, waiting until she was certain the men from the Franklin Group were gone.

Katelyn sighed. Time to find her irksome new driver. Why couldn't he just be one of the many bland, quiet little men who'd usually been her drivers? No chatter, no double entendres to deal with. He'd learn, like previous ones, that she took no guff. He'd either straighten up or lose the firm's contract. With that thought in mind, she stalked toward the limo. Luckily for him, he was there on time, early in fact since it was only eleven-forty-five. And, he was at atten-tion. Perhaps he just made a bad first impression or had been gripped with nervous chatter.

"Malloy," she greeted him, knowing she wasn't ever likely to forget his name again. It should have been easy to remember. He wore his Irish heritage like an ID badge. Wavy, black hair, sapphire-blue eyes, and a tall, muscular physique. And if she was in the mood to notice, a rugged, handsome face as well. But she wasn't in the mood. Had she thought he could have been nervous? No, that wasn't his problem. He didn't lack an iota in the confidence de-partment.

''Ma'am,'' he replied, without as much of his earlier cockiness.

Good, perhaps he's learning, she thought as he opened the passenger door.

Katelyn slid inside, leaning her head back against the seat, grateful the long evening was nearly over. As Finn opened his door, she straightened up, not willing to have anyone witness her fatigue. It was a sign of weakness, something she couldn't tolerate.

As her head became level, she met three curious pairs of eyes. Since their heads barely reached the top of the seat, she could only assume they were very small children.

''Malloy?''

''Uh, these are my kids.'' He tapped the first one's head. ''This is Jenny—she's five. And the matching monsters are the twins—Erin and Eric. They're three.''

Katelyn's eyes moved between him and the children. ''But what are they doing *here?*''

''Ah. Another baby-sitter quit. Since it was the middle of the night, I couldn't get another one on such short notice.''

Katelyn refused to disguise her impatience or distaste. ''Your personal problems are not my concern. I expect you to remedy the situation immediately.'' She snapped out the order with all the compassion of a drill sergeant.

''What do you suggest? That I toss them out on the sidewalk until I've driven you home?''

Three woeful faces stared at her and she resisted the urge to squirm. ''Of course not. But you have until tomorrow to take care of—'' she glanced at the children ''—it. If not, expect your firm to lose our contract. There are plenty of chauffeuring firms. I don't need…'' She looked again at the winsome trio. ''Complications. You read me?''

''Like the Marine handbook.''

While she wondered at his odd reply, he buckled the kids

into seat belts. From her vantage point they literally disappeared from sight. Relief filled her along with a nostalgic tugging that had attacked her more often than she wanted to admit. Her friend, Stefanie, insisted that it was her biological clock.

But Katelyn refused to believe her. Even though in the few still, quiet moments she allowed herself, Katelyn wondered at her decision to forego marriage and children. Wondered what it would be like to have a little moppet of her own.

Then she would remember her mother—how she'd never had time for her. Career-driven, she had left Katelyn's upbringing to nannies and housekeepers. It wasn't a fate she was willing to inflict on another generation. So, she pushed aside the urges, ignored the ticking of her biological clock and concentrated on the satisfaction her career gave her. She knew she wasn't cut out to be one of the stay-at-home mommies, content to drive a minivan, spend her days wiping running noses, and exist in her husband's shadow. No, she was too smart for that.

One of the children started to whine at that moment and Katelyn was immediately grateful for her own generous share of common sense.

She saw Finn reach over to soothe the child, speaking in a gentle voice as he did. Soon the whimpers quieted, but Katelyn wondered when the next protest would erupt. Now fully alert, despite her fatiguing evening, she was too anxious to stay quiet.

"So, Malloy, why isn't your wife home with the kids? Does she work evenings?"

There was a small moment of silence, then she heard him clear his throat. "I lost my wife when the twins were born."

Katelyn felt an immediate sense of remorse for probing at such a painful subject. "I'm sorry. I didn't know—"

"You couldn't," he replied shortly.

"Hmm, right." Katelyn knew when she was in uncharted territory and retreated back into silence.

Finn apparently caught the message because he was quiet as well, driving them swiftly through the night. It didn't take long to reach her condo. After she'd exited the limo, Katelyn glimpsed the children through Finn's open door. Sleeping, they looked like little angels. But she suspected that was an illusion.

"I have a nine-o'clock meeting at the Republic Bank Building. Be here at eight sharp in the morning."

Once again he tipped his hat. "Yes, ma'am."

FINN WATCHED HER walk inside, but he was almost too tired to appreciate the view. He turned to the car just as Erin woke up crying. Her wails woke her twin brother and Jenny was only a few moments behind. He guessed by the time they got home and he managed to get them to sleep, half the night would be gone. And he'd have to be up early to find a baby-sitter for the day, not to mention a permanent one.

Eight o'clock sharp, huh? He might be there at eight, but he sure as hell wasn't going to be sharp.

The drive home was just enough time for the children to deeply fall asleep. Finn tried not to waken them as he carried each one inside. The twins were the easiest. Although they fretted a bit, they settled back to sleep fairly quickly. Jenny, however, was more difficult.

"I had a dream, Daddy," she muttered, clinging to him as he tried to put her to bed.

Patiently, he pushed the damp hair away from her forehead. "What did you dream about, sweetie?"

"I dreamed I called and called, but no one was there, Daddy."

Pain clenched Finn's heart. He agonized over the time

he had to leave the children with sitters. No doubt it was stealing their sense of security. "I'm here now."

Jenny had taken her mother's death hard. Still little more than a baby herself, she had sobbed for her mother. In those first days, Jenny had cried herself to sleep each night in exhaustion. Finn had always picked her up to soothe her, but inevitably Jenny's cries would waken the twins. Physically, it wasn't possible to hold a toddler and two newborns at the same time. Despite a succession of housekeepers, there simply wasn't enough time for the children. That was why Finn had started his limo service, in the hopes of spending more time with them. He stroked her soft, dark hair. "It's okay, sweetie. Daddy's here."

She hiccuped a remaining half-cry. "I miss Mommy."

Despite her young age, Jenny had clung to the memories of her mother. Finn had learned the hard way that a traumatic event such as death could remain even in a young child's memory. Emotion clogged his throat. "I know, honey. I miss her, too." Finn watched as Jenny settled down a bit, wishing fate hadn't been so unkind to their family.

"Daddy, are we ever going to have a mommy again?"

This time the pain felt worse. Finn knew the children needed a mother. Housekeepers and babysitters were no substitute. And he couldn't spend as much time with the children as they needed—he had to earn a living. But he was neither inclined nor eager to try the dating scene. And when was there time? As it was, he was running constantly to try and stay on top of things. Any woman who wandered into their chaotic household would no doubt leave shrieking.

He met Jenny's questioning eyes. "What makes you ask about a mommy now?"

Jenny lifted small shoulders in a half-shrug. "Brianna's mommy is real nice. She makes cookies in the oven, not from the store. And she knows which clothes Barbie wears and she knows how to fix Brianna's hair into really pretty braids.''

Finn sighed. All the things he couldn't do. ''But I bet she can't rebuild an engine.''

Jenny scrunched her face in girlish disdain. ''Icky. Why would girls want to know that?''

Why indeed? ''Maybe we could try that hair thing. Braids, eh?''

''Uh, huh. French fried braids.''

Finn drew his brows together. ''Braids that look like French fries?''

''Daddy! They don't *look* like French fries, they *are* French fried.''

Finn looked at her in puzzlement. What the heck were French fried braids? He wasn't sure which one of them was confused, but he was fairly certain one of them was. ''Tell you what, Jen. I'll figure out how to make them, okay?''

''Okay,'' she replied reluctantly. Then she lifted large expressive eyes, instant reminders of his late wife, Angela. ''But it's still not the same as having a mommy.''

Of course not. As hard as he tried, Finn could never replace her mother. There was one thing he could never overcome. He wasn't a woman.

Exhausted, Finn hoped that Jenny would fall asleep soon. He would be lucky if he managed to grab even a few hours' sleep before his early morning assignment. And he guessed his new boss would have little tolerance if he showed up late. She might look dynamite, but unfortunately she was as equally explosive.

Jenny curled her hand trustingly in his and Finn resigned himself to staying by her side. Perhaps Ms. Amhurst would wake up on the right side of the bed in the morning. She couldn't be as tough as she appeared.

Chapter Two

Katelyn rechecked her watch, drummed her fingers over the wine-colored leather of her briefcase and then tapped her shoe impatiently. Five minutes after eight. Hadn't she told that cocky driver to be there at *precisely* eight o'clock?

She took another drag on her cigarette as she looked out of the glass double doors of her lobby and saw Malloy's limo pulling into the circle drive. Quickly ditching the cigarette, she pushed open the lobby doors and strode outside. Malloy leapt from the car, but she was faster, yanking open the rear door herself.

"You're late," she greeted him, slamming her briefcase on the seat beside her as she slid inside.

"Good morning," Finn replied, wondering if the woman had replaced her Cheerios with ice cubes or, possibly, ground glass.

She merely glared in response.

Finn considered telling her it was nothing short of a miracle that he'd shown up at all, considering he'd had to find a baby-sitter, put out all his domestic fires, and then turn an hour drive through traffic to her condo into thirty-five minutes. And all of that had been accomplished on almost no sleep. But, he suspected she wouldn't care. It was his job, after all, and his messy personal predicaments were none of her concern.

He pulled out of the driveway. "We'll get there in plenty of time," he assured her.

She grunted in reply and opened her briefcase.

Finn grasped the thermos in the seat beside him, then lifted it so that she could see. "Coffee?"

He could see she looked tempted.

"There are cups in the bar—creamer and sugar, too. Normally, the coffee's back there, along with donuts and bagels, but I had a pretty full morning trying to line up a sitter. We can swing by Shipley's Donuts or the bagel place—"

"Coffee's fine," she cut him off, taking the thermos. "In the future, don't stock donuts or bagels. I prefer power drinks. Daniel can give you a supply. But for now, as I said, I don't want to be late."

"You won't be," he replied, determined to make it downtown in record time if he had to drive over the rooftops of the cars in his way.

"So you said. But we had a late start."

God, she was a thorny woman. It was no wonder she was over thirty and single. He pitied the man who decided to get close to her.

Finn glanced into the rearview mirror and saw that she was deep into her work already. Then again, maybe she wouldn't surface often enough from her briefcase to be a bother.

He might be old-fashioned, but he thought a woman should get at least equal joy from her home and family. He suspected the ice princess would be appalled at such a thought.

Still, he tried again to talk with her. "So, another big meeting this morning?"

"Ummm," she replied, obviously not paying any attention to him.

"Will this one last as long as yesterday's?"

"Ummm," she repeated.

"Same old thing?" he asked patiently, already knowing her answer.

"Ummm," she said, as though on automatic pilot.

"Just another boring day dancing naked on conference room tables, eh?"

"Ummm."

He waited patiently for a few moments.

"What did you say?" she asked suspiciously, finally looking up from her work.

"I asked if this meeting might run long like yesterday's."

"Oh. I don't know. It shouldn't, but few creative meetings can be accurately predicted."

"Everyone thinks their brainchild is best," Finn surmised.

Katelyn glanced up in surprise. She hadn't thought the man capable of such perceptiveness. "Precisely. And it's difficult for the client to remember they're paying us to be creative."

"Probably because it's hard for them to accept that their ideas aren't any good," Finn guessed. "Or to remember that's why they need you. If they were creative geniuses they'd have their own ad agency, instead of hiring one."

"Right again." Katelyn frowned. She didn't want to believe the man was intelligent—it went against her picture of him. Purposely she turned her attention back to her notes. This campaign was a killer. She didn't need any distractions—like wondering if hunky limo drivers had brains.

Finn tried to stifle a yawn. Between the kids keeping him up late and then having to get up early, he was dead tired. Looking ahead into the traffic, he realized the line of cars in front of him had come to a dead stop. He hit the brakes hard and heard a distinct thud. Since he'd managed to avoid hitting the car in front of him and the car behind had stopped a safe distance away, it hadn't come from outside. Which left his passenger.

Craning his neck around, Finn looked in the back but didn't see her. Doubting she'd bailed out, he stared straight down—into Katelyn's furious face. Crumpled into a heap, she was wedged on the floor between the seat and the bar.

"Where did you learn to drive? Beirut?" Katelyn asked as she pulled herself up and onto the seat.

"Didn't you have your seat belt on?"

"Are you suggesting that your erratic driving is somehow *my* fault? Because my seat belt wasn't fastened?"

"Of course not. But you should have it on." Finn held up a hand to stave off her protests. "For your own safety. Sorry about the quick stop. I'm a little tired this morning. Guess my reflexes aren't up to par."

"Mr. Malloy, my firm hired you to drive. I suggest you get your reflexes back on line." She palmed the goose egg forming on her forehead. "Or I'll be forced to find another firm."

Finn swallowed his automatic response and his jaw ticked with the effort to keep it still. Not trusting himself to speak, he clamped his lips tightly together as he shoved a tape into the player.

The truth was, he needed this contract desperately. This morning was a glaring example. As a single father, Finn relied on the flexibility of having his own business. He also needed a steady contract that would guarantee to cover the limo payment, insurance and costs. And most of those contracts went to the bigger firms. It was a miracle that he'd gotten the call from Ellington. He couldn't blow the job because the ice princess was a pain. He supposed her orderly life didn't have any messy complications. Certainly nothing as unpredictable as children.

As promised, Finn delivered her to the Republic Bank

Building ahead of schedule—a full ten minutes early. But even though he pointedly glanced at his watch as she exited the car, she didn't comment.

"Did Daniel give you today's schedule?" she asked instead.

"He faxed it to me."

"Then you know I have a steady stream of meetings all day."

"Yes."

"Fine. It'll be a full day, then."

"So it seems," he replied, managing a reasonably charming smile.

She looked at him, searching for sarcastic undertones, then decided to let it go. Gripping her briefcase, she headed inside the building for meeting number one.

Finn watched her walk away, thinking she was true to form. He wasn't any more significant to her than the dozens of strangers crowding the sidewalk. In fact, if the limo could operate on automatic pilot he doubted she would miss his presence.

Clamping on his hat, he set the alarm on his watch for two hours from now, then climbed inside the car. If he was going to do battle with the ice princess, he had to get some z's.

STEFANIE LANGSTON paused in front of Daniel's desk, perching her slim, elegant body on the one empty corner, languidly swinging her impressive legs. Daniel smiled in appreciation as he rapidly concluded his phone call.

"This must be my lucky day," Daniel told her as he hung up the phone, his eyes resting on her beautiful face.

She smiled, raising her brows ever so slightly. "Of course, dear boy."

Then they both grinned, accustomed to this banter.

"She in?" Stefanie asked, referring to Katelyn.

"Yep. And your timing's exceptional. She should be off this conference call any minute now."

Stefanie nodded, then her expression grew thoughtful. "That's good."

Daniel picked up on her changing mood. "Something wrong?"

Again she nodded. "You remember that talk we had a while back? About how Katelyn's been all work and no play?"

Daniel nodded cautiously. Although he and Stefanie had an easy, friendly rapport, he didn't want to confide his plan to her.

"Well, I think it's getting worse. I asked her the other day if she'd met anyone interesting and she told me she'd stopped looking." She met Daniel's eyes. "And that can't be good. In fact, I can't remember the last time Katelyn was excited about someone she was dating."

"True," he agreed. "And she's not acting much like herself anymore."

"I read you, Daniel. She's edgy, impatient, and I think she's forgotten how to laugh." Stefanie narrowed her eyes knowingly. "But I don't have to tell you. She can't be a lot of fun to work for these days."

That much Daniel was willing to admit. "You're right. I'm worried about her."

"Me, too." Stefanie pulled her perfectly arched brows together. "Frankly, I think she needs to meet someone new, someone she can't dismiss. Someone who could turn into a significant other."

Daniel looked at her in surprise. "*You're* advocating marriage?"

"Okay, so I'm no Betty Crocker, but Katelyn's not like me. I grew up with all the traditional trappings and I know it's there if I choose that road—" She grinned wickedly in self-derision "—or not. But Katelyn thinks she's not cut out for the serious stuff, and I disagree. Otherwise, she wouldn't be reexamining her decision to remain married only to her career.''

Daniel hadn't counted on an ally in Stefanie. "So you think she might need a push in the right direction?''

Her eyes lit up. "Precisely.'' She adopted her best mock alluring expression. "I knew I liked you, Daniel.''

"It's mutual. And who better to nudge her in the right direction than us?''

Stefanie grinned. "Exactly. We can be discreet, thoughtful…'' she paused with a wicked grin. "And pushy.''

Katelyn's office door swung open. "Hey, Stef. What're you doing here?''

"I thought I'd kidnap you for lunch.''

Katelyn automatically glanced at her watch. "I wish I could, but I don't have time for lunch today.''

"Maybe dinner then?''

Katelyn shook her head. "I'm booked tonight, too.''

"Hot date?''

Katelyn laughed cryptically. "Date? What's that? Nope, this is strictly business.'' As she spoke, Katelyn reached for the stack of messages on Daniel's desk.

As she did, Stefanie exchanged a look with Daniel.

"Okay, I sense a brush-off when I hear it,'' Stefanie replied.

"It's not that, Stef, really. You know you're my dearest friend and I'd love to spend an evening with you. Let me grab my planner and we'll set up something. Maybe next week?''

"Sure.''

"Actually, I have about five minutes before the next meeting. Come into my office. There's just enough time for a cup of coffee.''

Stefanie trailed behind Katelyn, turning slightly before

entering the office. She caught Daniel's gaze, cementing their alliance.

KATELYN RELAXED in the dark interior of the car, relieved that the last meeting of the day was finally over. The nagging heartburn that had been erupting since her five-o'clock meeting was now a full-fledged fire in her stomach. Digging in her purse for an antacid, she fervently wished for a cigarette. At that moment, her fingers came across the Walkman Daniel had given her.

Maybe the tape could really work. Lord knew she needed to drop this irksome habit. It was getting to be easier to sneak a marching band into most places than a cigarette. Even the car her firm paid for was off-limits. It was beyond annoying. Not to mention the fact that she had so far failed to control this one aspect of her life.

With that thought she put the headphones on. As with any subliminal tape, she really didn't understand it, but she was so tired. And the beginning just seemed to drone on about the benefits of listening to subliminal tapes. Still, she found herself relaxing, her head nodding as she leaned back in the seat. Maybe if she just closed her eyes for a minute...

"The freeway's closed, we're going to have to take Memorial Drive," Finn told her.

When she didn't reply, he sat in silence for a few moments. But silence had never been his strong suit. "That okay with you, Ms. Amhurst?"

Still no reply.

"Hey. You alive back there?"

Stopping at a red light, he craned his head back and saw that she was fast asleep. Even in sleep, she was an enigma. Although signs of weariness creased her face, she was also incredibly alluring. Asleep, she possessed a quality not visible while awake—a touch of vulnerability. Finn wondered if it was a trick of lighting or his own imagination.

But then her lips formed a quiet sigh. Inexplicably, the sound moved him. It shouldn't. Katelyn Amhurst was a rigid power freak. Still, the fleeting glimpse made him pause. How much of that was genuine? Was there another Katelyn beneath the corporate killer?

The car behind him honked. Pulling back from the thought, Finn accelerated. The movement caused the papers resting on the front seat to fall to the floor. He had picked them up from the back seat, intending to sort them. Katelyn had emptied her briefcase between meetings. He guessed some of the papers might be ones Katelyn needed, but they were mixed with bits of trash.

Stopping at the next light, he reached for the papers, his hand closing over a small piece of cardboard. He started to drop it on the seat when he noticed that it was the inner paper from a cassette tape. He scanned it quickly: "Embrace Your Femininity." Startled, he glanced back at Katelyn. No wonder she looked a tad vulnerable. But that was no doubt temporary. As the light changed, he slipped the label into the glove compartment.

A few minutes later, as they arrived at her condo, Finn made enough noise to ensure that Katelyn woke up. When he opened her door, she looked groggy but together, even remembering to remove the headphones.

As she dropped the Walkman into her purse, Finn cleared his throat, wondering about the tape label he had just seen. "So, what are you listening to?"

"It's supposed to help me stop smoking."

Right. Finn cleared his throat, stemming his reaction. "And is it working?"

"This is the first time I've listened to it."

That explains a lot. "Guess you have to listen to it over and over for it to really work."

"I suppose so."

"No better time than when you're in the car."

She struggled to contain a yawn. "Uh-huh. Seven-thirty tomorrow morning." She eyed him balefully. "Not seven thirty-five."

He saluted, not completely squelching his grin. "Yes, ma'am."

Katelyn hefted her briefcase as she slung her purse strap over her shoulder, then turned toward her lobby door.

Finn watched her for a moment. "Good night."

"'Night," she muttered around a yawn.

He grinned despite her lukewarm reply. Whistling, he started up the car and turned onto the still busy street. He had thought this job was going to be a real pain. Suddenly, it looked very interesting.

Chapter Three

"Dammit, Malloy. You're late again."

"Six minutes, Ms. Amhurst. And I was caught in traffic."

"I thought you knew your way around the traffic."

He sighed, rolling his eyes heavenward. "There was a major accident, life-flight was involved. Short of hiring my own helicopter, I was stumped."

"People blame everything on the city's traffic," she groused.

"You'll have to admit it's a definite factor living in Houston."

"The only thing I *have* to admit is that I have a meeting I *must* be on time to." She reached for one of her power drinks. "Malloy, the difference between a successful person and one who wishes he were, is the successful person *would* hire the helicopter."

Finn pursed his lips, considered a variety of answers and settled for the most benign one he could manage. "I'll have to remember that."

She quirked her eyebrows and he noticed that today her eyes were greenish—reflecting the color of her tailored suit. He'd never met anyone before whose eyes changed color so dramatically. They could reflect her clothing, her background, or even the moods of the sky.

He drove rapidly toward the downtown skyline, determined to make sure she wasn't late for her meeting. And he arrived with five minutes to spare. Once again she didn't comment on the accomplishment.

Instead she handed him a sheet of paper. "Here are some changes in today's schedule. And the Woodruff meeting is vital. If I don't make that one, heads will roll, including mine…" Katelyn paused, making certain she had his attention. "And yours."

He accepted the sheet and scanned the location of the Woodruff meeting, nearly groaning. It was going to be held in one of the new buildings that had popped up in the Intercontinental Airport area.

One of the unique aspects of Houston was the number of mini-downtown areas that had cropped up all over the huge expanse of the city, each with their own skyline and unique set of problems. This one's problem was location. While a thriving, growing area, it was inescapably situated near the city's northern airport—a traffic nightmare at best, an unnavigable stretch of car-covered concrete at worst.

Two major freeways headed toward this particular airport and both of them could clog in an instant, and stay clogged for hours. Especially at the time Katelyn's meeting was scheduled—three o'clock. At that hour it would be a nightmare to drive toward the airport. The roads would be filled with a mass of commuters and airport-bound travelers.

If there was a snag they could be stuck in a gridlock for hours. Since it was a major portion of his job to monitor the traffic and make sure his limo didn't get caught in any of those snags, he knew exactly whose head would *really* roll if they didn't make the meeting.

When Finn delivered her to the lunch meeting, Katelyn reminded him again about the importance of the Woodruff meeting. "I'll be through at two. That should give us an hour to get there. Enough time?"

"If the freeway gods are on our side," he replied, fervently hoping they would be.

Finn opted for a sandwich in the car as he listened to his traffic-band radio. The first hour passed safely enough. He called one of his connections at a local radio station and got the latest scoop from the eye-in-the-sky helicopter report. Both freeways, northbound I-45 and I-59, were traveling at normal speeds.

"Kyle, this one's important," Finn told his friend. "If there's a change, can you call me on the cell in time to form an alternate plan?"

"Man, other than taking to the airways, there's not an alternate if anything happens to both freeways."

Finn tried to relax. "But what are the chances of something happening on *both* freeways?"

"This is Houston, man. They could both get wiped out in a torrential flood. Terrorists could blow them up. A tornado could hit 'em both or—"

"Don't cheer me up, Kyle. Just call if something happens."

Finn hung up, wishing the bad feeling in his gut would go away. He upped the volume on his radio and listened. Five minutes later his feeling became reality. An ammonia tanker had overturned on I-45 and they were closing the entire freeway. As he listened, details spilled from the radio with sickening accuracy. The lethal gas had the potential to kill anyone in the area and even the surrounding neighborhoods were being evacuated.

Finn found himself crossing his fingers as he thought about the remaining freeway. Then he remembered his own words to Kyle. What were the chances of both freeways being closed?

At that moment his cell phone rang. Misgiving filled him as he answered. Kyle's words completed the scenario. A petroleum tanker that had been routed off I-45 took a steep curve on I-59 and overturned. Because of the possible flammability, combined with the chemical mix of the ammonia spill, that freeway had been closed as well. And, Kyle confirmed, every arterial and side street was jammed to the hilt.

"Only two strikes, man, but I guess you're still out," Kyle sympathized.

Katelyn's words replayed themselves in Finn's thoughts. *The successful person would hire the helicopter.*

"Not quite, Kyle. I've got *three* strikes, remember."

"And *two* freeways."

"You've got connections with the helicopter companies, haven't you?"

"Yeah. We use 'em for backup when our copter's down."

"Can you get me one in less than an hour?"

"That's a tall order. With the freeway blocked, they'll be swamped."

"That's why I need your connections, Kyle."

Finn heard a long sigh. "You got it. I'll call you back in ten."

The phone clicked off and Finn hoped his friend could deliver.

The next ten minutes crawled by. When the phone rang, he grabbed it. Kyle didn't keep him in suspense. "We got it."

Finn breathed a sigh of relief, not doubting for a moment that Ms. Amhurst would indeed fire him if they failed to make the meeting. Too much was riding on this contract to let that happen. He took down the directions Kyle gave him and floored the car. He didn't have long to reach the heliport and return.

LESS THAN AN HOUR later, Finn and the pilot from Armadillo Airlines touched down at the helipad atop the building

Katelyn's lunch meeting had been held in. The helicopter's dispatcher had reached Katelyn at the meeting and told her to meet them on the helipad atop the building.

Finn spotted Katelyn before they landed, her distinctive hair shining in the sunlight, her tailored suit plastered against her body by the powerful draft of the copter blades.

She strode up to the helicopter as Finn climbed out. "Malloy, what the hell is this all about?"

Instead of answering, Finn lifted her into the helicopter, ignoring her protests. By the time he explained the entire situation, she would be late to her appointment and he valued his head. "You've got a meeting to make. And this is the only way you're going to get there. Both the freeways are closed and the side streets aren't moving. The *successful* person knows it when she sees a good thing."

For once Katelyn didn't seem to have a rapier-sharp retort.

Finn climbed in beside her and buckled in. Katelyn had a strange look on her face, but she was quiet as the pilot took off. It didn't take long to cross the city. Beneath them, stacks of unmoving cars littered the freeways and jammed the roads as far as they could see.

If Finn hadn't been convinced before that the helicopter was the only way to reach their destination, he was now. The pilot landed efficiently on the helipad atop the Woodruff Building and Finn climbed out. He waited for Katelyn to follow, but she didn't move. Climbing back inside, he saw that she was still in her seat, her hands gripping the armrests.

The pilot glanced at her sympathetically. "Not everybody likes traveling by whirlybird."

Finn hadn't noticed before, but she was as white as parchment. And her hands were nearly bloodless as she gripped the armrests. "Ms. Amhurst."

Nothing.

"Ms. Amhurst, we're at the Woodruff Building."

Silence.

"Katelyn?" He angled his face so that his eyes met hers. Now they were a dark blue-gray. And they were terrified.

"Katelyn, it's okay. We're on the ground." He glanced back behind him. Actually they were on top of a thirty-story building and the rooftop wasn't as generous as he would have liked.

She looked at him blankly.

Finn carefully pried her fingers from the armrest, then gently pulled her forward in the seat. "Katelyn, we're going to step outside. You'll be on level ground."

She didn't resist as he lifted her down and out of the helicopter. The pilot waited patiently as they slowly cleared the area. As they reached the door leading inside the building, Katelyn slumped. Finn grasped her elbow and led her through it.

The cool rush of the air-conditioning was a welcome relief and seemed to reach her as his voice hadn't. Still, he led her to a bench near the window.

She hid her shaking hands beneath her briefcase. "I guess I should have mentioned that I'm not real comfortable riding in small aircraft—and I suppose now that includes helicopters."

Not comfortable. That was one way to put it. Scared senseless was another. "Why don't we see if they have some vending machines and get a cup of coffee?"

"I'm fine," she insisted, her face still pale.

"Well, I'm not. I'd like a cup of coffee. That was a pretty hair-raising ride."

She glanced at her watch. "We *are* fifteen minutes early."

Seeing that she looked relatively steady, Finn stood and punched the elevator button.

When it arrived, Katelyn joined him. As the doors slid

closed, she looked at him. "It seems you're a quick study, Malloy."

"You *did* say the successful person would hire the helicopter."

"I didn't know you'd take that literally," she muttered.

"Changing your stand on what defines the successful person?"

"No." Katelyn admitted as she shuttered her expression. "And I won't underestimate you again."

His sudden smile took her by surprise. Impossibly white teeth, eyes as blue as the ocean depths, the rugged features... Combined, they were enough to take her breath away. Telling herself it was her fright from the helicopter ride that had robbed her breath, she shored up a returning smile.

"That looks real good on you," he said, his eyes not leaving hers.

Flustered, she brushed at an invisible bit of lint on her sleeve. "What does?"

"The smile. Looks like it belongs there."

Remarkably, she felt her cheeks warming. She felt embarrassed and glanced away. "You've seen me smile before."

His lips twitched. "Oh?"

For a moment she was tempted to huffily freeze. Then the humor of the situation struck her. "It really is absurd, isn't it? It was *my* brilliant idea to hire a helicopter."

He nodded, his smile growing bigger. "I have to agree with you. Frankly, I would never have thought of hiring a helicopter on my own."

Sheepishly she grinned. "When I put my foot in it, I do it big-time."

His expression gentled. "Maybe that's why you're such a success."

Uncharacteristically, she glanced down, pretending to study her shoes. "Is that how you see me?"

"You're smart, talented and doing what you want. Isn't that success?"

Katelyn lifted her gaze. "Lately I've been wondering about that. I decided a long time ago that I wasn't cut out for marriage and kids but now…"

"Now?" Finn prompted.

She shrugged. "I've wondered if maybe I'm missing out by not having children. Sounds silly, doesn't it?"

But he didn't look amused. "I don't think so. My kids are everything to me. As hard as it is being a single parent, I wouldn't trade them for anything. I know I'm no corporate whiz, but my life's richer than if I had Trump's fortune."

"You really mean that, don't you?" she questioned, boggled by the concept, moved by his sincerity.

"With everything that's in me. Children are our dreams, our future."

The biological clock she'd fervently tried to ignore chimed insistently. "But we can fashion a different sort of future."

"What kind of future would that be?" Finn asked. "Do you really care who takes your job when you retire? Is that the legacy you want to leave the world? Frankly, I doubt that anyone on their deathbed wishes they had spent more time at work."

The words chilled her, but Katelyn recognized their truth. "Are you saying what I've done will mean nothing if I don't have children?"

"Of course not. I *am* saying that love and family are enduring."

"Perhaps not everyone is cut out to be a parent," she said quietly, revealing one of her hidden fears.

"That's true enough," he admitted. "But if your intentions are good, love will get you over the rough spots."

She considered this. "But what if you have no idea what kind of parent you'll be?"

"If you've given it that much thought," he replied softly. "I'd say you have the makings of a good mother."

Unexpectedly, she felt warmed by his words. He probably didn't know the Dow Jones from the S & P, but he had a wisdom all his own. And she liked the kindness she saw in his eyes. Over the years that quality had lessened in importance. It occurred to her that might have been unwise.

She realized Finn could be right. Success had many definitions. And she wasn't entirely certain hers was the right one.

FINN LOOKED at the fallout on the front lawn of his house and groaned. A tricycle was perched in the shrubbery and an open umbrella was suspended in the crepe myrtle tree. A pot of begonias was tipped over, dirt and flowers spilling across the porch. The twins must have been especially inventive today. One three-year old was a handful. Two of them far exceeded a simple doubling of the equation. Together, Eric and Erin could climb, grab, push, and pull down most anything they chose. Worse though, two small minds invented some incredible feats. And from the evidence on the lawn, it looked like they had come up with a corker.

It was terribly quiet. He wondered if this latest exploit had pushed Mrs. Phillips over the edge. She was an older woman whose patience and energy were diminishing rapidly as she cared for three young, active children. But she had been blessedly dependable. And the steady stream of sitters that had preceded her had all flaked out in one fashion or other.

Mentally crossing his fingers, Finn pulled open the front door. It was equally quiet inside. Uneasily, he glanced around, not seeing Mrs. Phillips or the children. He called out, but no one answered.

Worried, he walked rapidly to the patio door and slid it open. But what he saw made him want to slam the door shut.

Mrs. Phillips was covered in white foam and the twins were both orange, from head to toe, as was their dog, Snuffles. Finn could smell paint thinner and soap. And he could see water rushing from the hose, drenching Jenny.

He walked closer. "Mrs. Phillips?"

She turned, her face darkening to an ugly red beneath the odd foam. "It's about time you got here," she snarled.

Oh, this was bad. Very bad. "What happened?"

Mrs. Phillips turned an accusing glare on the twins. "Those two…two…they painted each other and the dog with your industrial day-glow safety paint!"

"She said we could paint!" Erin defended, looking strangely like a glowing alien.

"With *your* paints!" Mrs. Phillips screeched. "With normal children's watercolors. Who in the world would have thought they could climb up to the paint in the garage?"

"What is that goop all over you?" he asked, knowing there wasn't a satisfactory answer to her question.

Balefully, Mrs. Phillips stared at Jenny. "This one decided to spray me with the fire extinguisher."

"She said the house was on fire!" Jenny protested.

"I *said* you kids could get in trouble as fast as a house afire. And that's when she turned on the water hose as well." Mrs. Phillips gestured downward at her soaked shoes. The leather was obviously ruined. "As though I hadn't already had enough water for today. The twins filled the bathtub without telling me and it ran over, flooding the bathroom. Your upstairs carpet will never be the same, not to mention my sanity!''

Finn swallowed his amusement. If the poor woman didn't look so aggrieved, he would have pointed out the inherent humor in the situation. But, clearly, she wouldn't be in the mood to hear it. He doubted he would be either if he had been covered in foam and water. ''I'm sorry, Mrs. Phillips. I know this has been a bad day—''

''Bad day? Mr. Malloy a bad day was two weeks ago when the twins filled my tote bag with shampoo, *after* emptying it from the bottle. Or last week when they poured the cake batter in the toaster. Or even two days ago when they poured sugar on the couch and filled the aquarium with ketchup.''

''It made the water red!'' Eric offered.

Mrs. Phillips glared at him.

''Of course I'll replace your shoes and tote bag, Mrs. Phillips. And I'll try not to be late again.''

''Doesn't matter if you are,'' she stated.

''It doesn't?'' he asked uneasily.

''Nope. Because I quit. I would have left hours ago, but I'm not the kind of person to abandon young children.'' She took a deep, exasperated breath. ''Even ones like this.''

Finn glanced between the sitter and his children, who didn't look particularly remorseful. ''Surely we could work something out. The kids like you and I'm sure they weren't deliberately trying to provoke you.''

''If this wasn't deliberate, I'd hate to be on the receiving end when they are. Nope, I felt sorry for you, being a widower and all, but enough's enough. What these kids need is a mother. Someone who can keep them in line.''

Glumly, Finn resigned himself to the inevitable. They had lost yet another sitter, which meant he would have to scramble to find one for the next day. ''If you'll give the total of the damages to the agency, I'll make sure you're reimbursed.''

She swiped at the foam still coating her clothes, then tossed down the rag she had been using to try and clean the paint from the twins. ''Mr. Malloy, you haven't got that much money!'' Stalking toward the house, she punctuated her exit with the squishing creaks of her waterlogged shoes.

He flinched when she slammed the patio door hard enough to rattle the glass. Then he turned his gaze on his children. A trio of angelic expressions greeted him. So Mrs. Phillips thought they needed a mother. That was hardly a surprise. It was a logical conclusion. But it wasn't the kind of decision based on logic.

''Daddy, Miz Pipps was *mad!*'' Jenny told him, reaching her arms toward him.

Disregarding her soggy state, he picked her up. ''You guys have to take it easy on the sitters. I'm running out of willing ones.''

''You could just stay home with us,'' Jenny concluded with childlike reasoning.

He pushed the wet hair from her eyes. ''I wish it were that easy, sweetie.''

''Up!'' Erin demanded, holding up paint-covered arms. Next to her, Snuffles wagged his orange tail, flicking the paint on Finn's pants.

He sighed as he picked her up, knowing his clothing was already ruined. ''Okay, my little alien.''

''We're hungry,'' Jenny added.

''Didn't you have dinner?'' Finn asked in dismay.

Jenny shook her head. ''I don't think Miz Pipps likes us anymore.''

That was an understatement. ''It's okay, sweetie. I'll order a pizza. I wonder if they'll deliver turpentine with it.''

''Turptine,'' Eric repeated several times, enjoying the new word.

And a new baby-sitter, Finn added silently. He would have to find one by morning. Coupled with cleaning up the twins, that would mean another late night. Yet he couldn't be late for Ms. Amhurst. Feeling like a wishbone being pulled apart, Finn wondered again how he was going to make it all work.

KATELYN RECHECKED her makeup in the hand mirror, then fiddled with the bow of her chiffon blouse. It had been an impulse buy the previous day. The frothy confection in the store's window had caught her attention and, uncharacteristically, she'd popped inside and bought the blouse without even trying it on. Its soft lines weren't her usual style, but something about the very feminine item appealed to her. Along with the flowered broomstick skirt she'd also purchased. All sorts of different things seemed to appeal to her lately. It probably had something to do with quitting smoking, she decided.

The delighted saleswoman had given her a generous sample of a floral scent she insisted suited her as well. And somehow that morning it had. Katelyn rechecked her hair, having left it long and loose in soft waves. Her briefcase rested on the limo seat, still unopened, but she couldn't bring herself to dive in as usual. It was such a delightful day—in fact she'd been humming all morning.

The limo turned into the circular drive of the Allen Center buildings and she sighed. She couldn't remember the last time she'd been tempted to play hooky. And now she could think of little else. But discipline had been ingrained since she was a child. She exited the car, fussing a bit with her unaccustomed skirt.

"You look real nice this morning," Finn commented.

Katelyn couldn't stop the soft smile that bloomed across her face. "Um…thank you."

It was part of the subtle metamorphosis she seemed to

be undergoing. She smiled more often, although she tried to quash the reaction.

"You're welcome," he replied.

"That'll be all. My meeting should be done by eleven."

HE WATCHED as, instead of striding briskly inside, Katelyn strolled slowly, stopping to admire a cart of cut flowers and speak with the vendor, purchasing a single daisy.

She turned, the light striking her face. For a moment Finn saw her strictly as a woman. For some inexplicable reason he was drawn to her in a way he hadn't felt since his wife's death. It wasn't just chemistry. Sure, Katelyn Amhurst was a knockout. But he'd known other beautiful women. And he didn't even know what it was about Katelyn. Her strength, combined with a scant touch of vulnerability, was compelling.

As he watched, the president of Katelyn's firm fell into step beside her. Now, that man was in her league. Finn felt his own jaw tighten. It wouldn't be wise to forget that Katelyn was in a league totally her own. One to which he didn't stand a chance of gaining admittance.

FROWNING, Daniel flipped through his planner. He had allowed two weeks to pass since giving Katelyn the first tape. He had seen minor changes in her. But at the slow rate of progress she was making, Katelyn would be too old to have children by the time she wanted them.

The door to his office opened. "Hi, Daniel." Mary, the brunette from accounting, was becoming more than just someone to date. Their relationship had evolved into an exclusive one.

He smiled, momentarily distracted. "I thought you were swamped with budget forecasts."

She shrugged prettily. "I couldn't concentrate on them.

Had my mind on our date last night." She glanced at his open planner. "Busy?"

"Not exactly." Needing a woman's viewpoint, Daniel had told Mary about the tape. Initially it had raised her feminine hackles until he had explained his reasoning. "I'm thinking about the plan with Katelyn—it's taking a lot longer than I anticipated."

Mary drew her brows together. "I don't think the tapes are supposed to work overnight."

Daniel's expression was glum. "I'm afraid that as slow as it's going, Katelyn will get tired of listening to the Stop Smoking tape before she has a chance to meet someone."

"Hmm. Maybe you need to try a different tape," she suggested.

"Different?" Daniel echoed.

"More intense—to the point. Perhaps one that advocates marriage."

"She's not dating anyone right now," Daniel objected.

"But you said the tapes work slowly. Perhaps another one could get her thinking along the lines of marriage so that she'll be open to meeting someone new."

"Someone suitable," Daniel agreed. "Katelyn makes a point of always dating men who aren't any more interested in marriage than she is."

"And maybe the tape could change that," Mary suggested. "Normally I would feel obliged to defend my fellow woman, but lately I've been warming to the idea of commitment myself."

Pleased, Daniel met her gaze. "You are, huh?"

She nodded. "And without the help of a tape."

"Too bad Katelyn's not as bright as you." He closed the planner, pushing it aside. "Want to go shopping on your lunch hour?"

She smiled. "For tapes?"

Daniel grinned. "I have an ulterior motive."

Mary tilted her head. "Which is?"

"Katelyn benefits with the tape..."

Mary dimpled prettily. "And?"

"And I get to spend time with you."

Chapter Four

Katelyn adjusted her sunglasses as she examined the magazines on the newsstand rack. Bypassing *Newsweek, Time* and the *Wall Street Journal,* her attention wandered toward the bridal magazines. Katelyn wasn't sure why she had been so drawn to them in the last few weeks, but she picked up nearly half a dozen different ones. After paying for them, she stuffed the magazines in her briefcase, not wanting anyone to see them.

Certainly not her driver. Malloy would get too much enjoyment out of watching her moon over bridal magazines. She could tell he wasn't accustomed to women like her—women who valued their careers. She suspected most of his dates were the type who wanted to step in and mother his children. At that thought she felt an unexpected pang. She'd been thinking more and more about children lately, wondering what she was missing out on. It had begun with that unexpectedly frank talk with Malloy after the helicopter episode. But now she didn't know why her feelings seemed so out of control.

Oh, it was probably a full moon, she told herself.

That, or the alarm had been activated on her biological clock.

Strolling outside, she met Malloy's level stare as he leaned against the limo fender. She wished he wouldn't always *look* at her. It was as though he saw right through her skin and into her mind. She wasn't sure just what was going through her mind these days and she didn't need any thought-voyeurs examining her uncertainties.

As she approached him, he whisked open the door and perversely she wished he wasn't so efficient. Realizing how ridiculous the thought was, she slid inside.

"Ready for your dinner meeting?" Finn asked as he took his place behind the wheel.

"I'd like to go home and put on something else."

She'd been doing more of that lately—changing her schedule unexpectedly. "Right." He concentrated on navigating into the traffic, then glanced into the rearview mirror. "Something special tonight?"

Katelyn glanced up, her eyes a golden green this evening "It's a work meeting, but I don't have to look as though I've worked all day."

He wasn't sure there was a logical or tactful reply to that. "Uh-huh. You expect to be late tonight?"

"I expect to be climbing the walls by nine." She sighed wistfully. "But unfortunately I don't expect to be rescued from the clutches of boredom by a white knight."

Finn glanced cautiously at her. Maybe even corporate types gave into feminine whimsy. She had been acting softer lately. Finn thought she'd just become accustomed to him.

Wondering how long she expected the dinner meeting to last, Finn glanced in the rearview mirror as he started to ask. But what he saw halted his words. He blinked to make sure he was seeing straight.

Katelyn was reading, but not the expected stack of paperwork. Instead she was immersed in a bridal magazine. So immersed she didn't even notice him watching her.

What was going on with her? Briefly Finn remembered the tape label he'd found. As quickly, he dismissed it. For all he knew, the tape had been one about using femininity for corporate power. Or it could have been exactly what she'd said—one to help her stop smoking.

"So, how's quitting smoking going?" Finn asked, curious why she was behaving in such a different manner.

"What? Oh, okay I guess," she replied. "I haven't really thought about it that much."

He glanced back in the mirror, seeing the unexpectedly wistful expression on her face. "Something else on your mind?"

She hesitated. "It probably would sound silly."

"Try me."

"Well, ever since we talked about children, I've just had this nagging feeling…" Katelyn paused. "I keep wondering what it must be like—to have these miniature people—ones so much like yourself." Her words ended on a deprecating laugh. "I guess I sound crazy."

"Not in my opinion," Finn replied steadily as he stopped for a red light. Their eyes met in the rearview mirror. "Would you rather ignore those feelings and spend the rest of your life regretting what could have been?"

Her gaze remained connected with his. "Do you have any? Regrets, I mean."

"Of course. But not about my kids. But I would regret it like hell if I'd decided against having them."

"I want that, too," Katelyn replied, surprising them both. "The certainty, I mean. I want to be absolutely sure I'm doing the right thing."

Surprised, Finn studied the woman he'd thought was totally certain about everything. "And you're not sure now?"

She shook her head. "I thought I was, but now things aren't as clear. My feelings seem muddled. Like about having children. I was so sure about my decision. And now…"

"You have doubts?"

"More than just doubts." Katelyn's voice changed, infused with a tone Finn had never heard her use. ''Something inside tells me you're right. I don't want to wake up someday and wish I'd done things differently.''

The light changed and the car behind them honked impatiently. Finn tore his gaze from the rearview mirror, breaking their connection. But his thoughts remained on her words. Was it possible Katelyn not only wanted children, but could possibly even be good with them? He hadn't considered her in this light. Briefly he remembered the vulnerability she had exhibited while sleeping. He had dismissed that for the most part. But could he be wrong? Was the barracuda really a woman beneath her prickly surface?

Glancing again in the rearview mirror, Finn decided it was worth consideration.

DANIEL USED his key to enter Katelyn's condo. He often housesat for her, watering the plants and picking up her mail when she was out of town. But his mission today was different.

While the last tape he'd given Katelyn had accelerated the process, it still wasn't working as quickly as he expected. Realistically, Daniel knew he couldn't expect her to listen to the tapes indefinitely. Happy in his own relationship with Mary, he wanted Katelyn to find a potential mate as well.

Not only would she be happier, so would he. He sensed that it was her frustration in recent months that had made her edgy, unusually testy. Even though her behavior wore on his nerves, he was genuinely concerned about Katelyn. Having climbed to an enviable position of power, she would find it difficult to relinquish her career for a husband and children. Daniel knew that without outside intervention, Katelyn would grow more frustrated and unhappy.

Again, Daniel thought of his sister, the bitterness she

couldn't escape. He intended to make sure Katelyn had a different choice.

Although the last tape he'd purchased had advocated marriage, this one practically guaranteed that it would push the listener into holy wedlock. It worked primarily on a woman's natural desire to procreate. Katelyn should soon be brimming with desire for a husband and children.

Daniel had exchanged this newest tape for the one in her cassette recorder, but he wasn't certain she would listen to it enough for it to work. So, he'd purchased a second tape.

Walking into her bedroom, he spotted the stereo system. It was a separate unit that Katelyn had bought to bring an air of romance to the room. However, she had confessed that the unit hadn't been used in a long time.

But Daniel had a better use for the neglected stereo.

He slipped the tape in the proper slot, adjusted the volume and then for the pièce de résistance, set the timer. Every night the stereo would turn on at a predetermined time. As she slept, the tape would play repeatedly.

Grinning, Daniel realized Katelyn would be after her perfect mate in a flash. He just hoped the man she chose was ready. Because a determined Katelyn could put a steamroller to shame. And after listening hundreds of times to the tape, she was going to be one determined hunter.

IT HAD BEEN an interesting three weeks for Finn. His relationship with Katelyn had altered dramatically. It began changing when she had discussed her uncertainty about having children. Since then, the rigid ice princess persona had lessened until it completely disappeared. Instead of treating him like a faceless employee, Katelyn had actually been kind, even interested in hearing about his life and goals. In other circumstances, he would have said they were becoming friends. But that was a loaded description.

Because even though Finn knew Katelyn was his boss,

he still found her enormously attractive. But, now that she had started acting like a regular human being, he realized it went beyond just a physical attraction. The intelligence in her eyes drew him along with a grudging admiration for all she had accomplished. He had witnessed her drive and determination and knew it equaled that of only the most dedicated. Most male executives would have difficulty keeping up with her and would be hard-pressed to duplicate her success.

While her breakneck pace hadn't slowed appreciably, Katelyn was acting softer, more open-like. Even her clothing choices were changing, going more and more often from dynamic power suits to soft, clingy dresses, wispy blouses and flowered skirts. Instead of pulling her hair back in severe styles, it now hung loose in silky waves.

What was even more puzzling was her uncharacteristic behavior. Katelyn had paused several times to longingly watch children. Once they had passed a church with a wedding in progress and he could have sworn he saw the glint of tears in her eyes. It was baffling, but Finn guessed her actions could be attributed to her biological clock. Apparently she had reached a point in her life where she was questioning the choices she had made. It wasn't that uncommon. For once, Finn could see the definite advantages of female hormones. They appeared to be making a complete transformation in Katelyn.

As he completed the thought, Finn spotted her. She was strolling out the revolving door of a glassy skyscraper, long, burnished hair peeking out of the flowered hat she wore. She looked particularly attractive today. But it struck him that she was like an entirely different person—in appearance, attitude, and behavior. It wasn't like her to stroll instead of walking at a near running pace.

As she approached, he swung open the rear passenger door.

"Hello, Finn. I hope you haven't been waiting too long." It was another of her changes. She no longer felt compelled to address him as Malloy.

"Actually, I just got here a few minutes ago. The meeting didn't go as long as you'd thought. Is that a good sign?"

"Sometimes you don't have to keep beating a dead horse. It's smarter to simply bury it and get on with the next race."

Puzzled, Finn shut the door and got into the car himself. Adjusting the rearview mirror, he studied her face. "I'm not sure exactly what that means."

"The client didn't like the presentation. So, why should I keep trying to sell it? I'll simply work up another campaign."

Simply? Finn knew that Katelyn had spent weeks on the presentation she was now dismissing. A good portion of her success was her unrelenting determination to sell her ideas, dominating meetings with her forceful presence. "And it doesn't bother you that so much work went into it?"

Katelyn shrugged "There's not much I could do about it. I'll just have to think of something fresher. Life's too short to get caught up in the things you can't change. It's much wiser to concentrate on the ones you can."

Finn's gaze remained on hers. As baffling as her behavior was, he couldn't stem his fascination. "And is there something new you plan to concentrate on?"

A dreamy smile slid over her lips. "Perhaps."

Shaking his head, Finn pulled out of the circular driveway and into traffic. He couldn't help wondering what that purposely vague response meant.

Tonight's meeting was being held northwest of the city in a secluded club. While it boasted of a first-class golf course and a four-star restaurant, it wasn't a convenient location since it required a drive through snarled traffic routes. It would have been wisest to take a helicopter to the club, but Finn didn't want to suggest it. He vividly remembered Katelyn's terror in the copter. It wasn't something he wanted to subject her to again.

Finn expertly navigated through the traffic. It didn't take long to reach the loop. From there he took an exit which put them on a farm road, out of the gridlock.

Katelyn leaned forward. "Finn, do you know much about the Lakeview Club?"

"Not much beyond the obvious. It's near a lake. Food's supposed to be good. And it's got a decent golf course. But it's a little bit off the beaten track."

"That's okay," she replied, surprising him. "It looks like a nice drive."

So it was. They wound through the lush greenery that marked the Gulf Coast. First-time visitors often compared the succulent landscape to a cultivated rain forest. The humidity and frequent rain kept plants green year round. Beyond that, trees and plants grew rapidly because of the natural hothouse effect of the environment. And from the air-conditioned comfort of the limo, it was like journeying through a tame jungle.

Having made good time, Finn soon arrived at the Lakeview Country Club. The lines of the lovely Greek revival building emulated those of fine antebellum plantation homes. Even the dusky-pink brick looked authentically aged. But like many things in the often still raw city, it was an upstart. No landed gentry had once owned the fields surrounding the club. But that was part of the lure of Houston. New and old could compete as equals.

Once past the guardhouse, Finn pulled into the circular drive. Only yards from the huge double-door entrance, Finn heard Katelyn's cell phone ring. Then he heard her side of a brief conversation.

She clicked the phone off. "That was Daniel. Tonight's meeting has been postponed."

"Great timing," Finn observed wryly.

"Exactly what I was thinking."

"No reason you still can't have a nice dinner," he suggested. "It might even taste better knowing you don't have a meeting for dessert."

"Hmm," she mused. "That sounds good. But only on one condition."

Finn dearly hoped she didn't intend to have him drive all the way to her condo to fetch something. "And what would that be?"

"That you join me for dinner."

Finn managed to keep his jaw from dropping. But it was a monumental effort. "Excuse me?"

"I'd like you to join me for dinner. We've driven to north Timbuktu. I'm sure you're hungry. I know I am. And as you just suggested, I could still enjoy a nice dinner."

"Actually I was just going to grab a hamburger," he hedged, knowing the prices would shatter his carefully structured budget.

"My treat," she urged with a smile. "Don't tell me you're going to let a lady eat alone?"

Glancing back at her, he knew she could have company with a snap of her perfectly manicured fingers. But Finn had the sense not to rebuff good fortune. After all, it was only one evening. He was sure that, despite her recent changes, Katelyn would be back to one hundred percent business by the next day. But for now...why not enjoy?

Nodding, he emerged from the car, tossing his hat inside, then opening her door. "Ms. Amhurst, you're right. I'd be a fool to let you eat alone."

Her lips edged upward in a slightly provocative smile. "It sounds ridiculous for you to keep calling me Ms. Amhurst. My name is Katelyn. After all, I call you Finn."

But she was the boss. Acknowledging that, he decided to let her call the rules. "All right, Katelyn, whatever you say."

Taking his arm, she wagged the fingers of her other hand at him. "Now that could be a dangerous offer."

Lifting his eyebrows, he studied her changeling eyes. He wasn't sure what was brewing there, but he sensed that it could be downright volatile. Still, it wasn't like him to ignore a challenge, subtle or otherwise. "I'll let you be the judge of that."

Smiling at him, she leaned a touch closer as they passed through the doors into a massive entry hall. The ceiling soared at least two full stories. Descending from the high arch was an ornate crystal chandelier, which sparkled as though lit by the sun itself.

A crisp, tuxedo-clad maitre d' escorted them to the perfect table. While the huge windows offered a magnificent view of the lake, the table was also tucked into an alcove of sorts. It was at once both private and expansive. An exquisite solitary calla lily rested in the cut-crystal vase, surrounded by humble but winsome violets.

Finn eyed the romantic setting with some trepidation. He didn't want Katelyn to suddenly remember he was the mere chauffeur and decide to cancel her contract because he was overstepping his bounds.

"You know, Ms. Amhurst—"

"Katelyn," she insisted. "Remember?"

"I do, but—"

"Relax, Finn. I only want to have dinner with you."

"I just thought you'd rather dine with one of your friends."

She frowned, her expression sad. "I only have one real friend and she's as busy as I am. Guess that doesn't say much for my social skills."

Although Finn wasn't ill at ease in the surroundings, he

was still uncomfortable about becoming too familiar with Katelyn. Bottom line, her contract could launch his dreams. But at the moment, he couldn't help noticing she looked vulnerable again. "One good friend is worth a dozen you can't really count on."

"You think so?" she asked seriously, as though truly valuing his opinion.

He nodded. "Sure. We all have acquaintances, but in a pinch I'd rather have one good friend I can count on, than a dozen acquaintances."

Katelyn tilted her head, studying him. "You're really very wise, you know."

"Now that's not something I expected to hear."

She frowned. "Why not?"

"You're a very accomplished executive. I'm driving a limo. Need I say more?"

She blinked. "A lot more. Are you ashamed of what you do?"

"Of course not," he defended, thinking of his plans to enrich his children's lives.

"Then why can't I consider you wise?"

Finn found himself smiling. "No reason, I suppose."

The waiter approached, handing Finn a wine list. But Katelyn waved it away. "A bottle of your best champagne, please."

Finn looked at her in surprise. "Are we celebrating something?"

"Quite possibly. Don't you like champagne?"

"Yes, but…" Glancing into her eyes, he felt like Scrooge prepared to crush Christmas. "Actually, I love champagne."

"Good." Her smile dazzled. "I'm thinking about changing my life, so I believe champagne's in order."

Finn felt an uncomfortable pit of foreboding lodge in his gut. Was she about to do something that could cost him his contract? Maybe she'd decided to marry a boyfriend. Although Finn didn't know when she had time for a social life. She spent more time with him than anyone else. "What kind of change?"

"I'm still thinking about it. How about you, Finn? What kind of changes would you like to make?"

"Winning the lottery wouldn't hurt."

Disappointment clouded her eyes. "Is that it? Just money?"

Meeting her eyes, he saw a genuine need for the truth. Resigned, he sighed. "Not really. Sure, money would make things easier. But what I want is to improve my children's lives, give them the time and attention they need. I've gone through half a dozen housekeepers and baby-sitters in the last month and I'm about at my rope's end."

"Why don't you get married?" she suggested, her eyes wide with interest.

"Just like that? Seems to me I remember needing a partner for that to work."

She sipped her champagne. "My problem, too." Katelyn lifted her eyes, dark now against the approaching twilight. "But you're a good-looking man. You shouldn't have any difficulties attracting a mate."

Finn sucked in his breath, feeling an immediate reaction to her words. "I could say the same for you."

Before she could reply, a waiter stopped to freshen their glasses.

Katelyn wrinkled her nose after sipping the champagne. "The bubbles tickle."

He found her unexpected behavior amusing, yet oddly endearing. "Don't tell me that's a surprise."

She leaned forward. "Between you and me, the only time I ever drink champagne is with a bunch of stuffed shirts at celebratory business occasions. It's not quite the same."

"Stuffed shirts, huh?"

"Dreadful bores," she confided.

"Unlike you?" he parried.

Sudden hurt infused her face. "Is that how you really see me?"

Instantly ashamed of the taunt, he reached out for her hand. "No, of course not. Just wanted to needle the boss.

She glanced down at their joined hands. "Is that the only way you think of me? As the boss?"

Uncomfortably Finn edged his hand back. "Not exactly. But it is our primary relationship."

Katelyn sighed, then emptied her glass. "You're right. I suppose." She held out her glass.

Automatically he refilled it. "That's not a bad thing, Ms....Katelyn. And lately, we've gotten to be...well, sort of friends."

She smiled wanly. "Not exactly a ringing endorsement."

Finn filled his own glass. The evening was proving to be a diplomatic minefield. "We haven't known each other long enough to really develop a friendship."

Katelyn brightened. "You're right. I hadn't thought about it that way."

It was amazing how Katelyn's smile transformed her face, Finn thought. While always dynamite looking, the smile brought softness to her features, revealing true beauty.

They sipped champagne after ordering dinner. Katelyn looked longingly at the musicians and then at the dance floor. "Would you like to get to know me better?"

Finn resisted choking on his drink with supreme effort. "Excuse me?"

"I know it's not proper form, but would you dance with me?"

Finn thought of all the reasons he should delicately refuse, but caught by the power of her incredible gaze, the reasons dissipated. Instead he rose, holding out his hand.

The evocative swing music of the big band era had enjoyed a resurgence in popularity. Holding Katelyn as the notes of the slow, sultry song resonated through the room, Finn could certainly understand why.

Although he cautioned himself to hold her a proper distance away, the instant their bodies connected, he felt the flash. A micro burst of concentrated heat, the warmth was nearly a visible thing. Tainting the air with the scent of adrenaline, awareness was like a visible thing. It thrummed between them, its beat awakening the blood, inciting the senses.

Disregarding caution, Finn pulled her a bit closer. Any resistance he expected was nonexistent. Instead, Katelyn welcomed the connection, releasing a breathy sigh that muddled his senses.

Swaying to the music, Finn vaguely realized they weren't moving around the room. Instead, they remained mesmerized, taking only a few token steps.

When the song ended, they remained in place, parting with great reluctance. Glancing down at her, Finn saw the betraying leap of Katelyn's pulse at the hollow of her throat. Then he met her eyes. Unmasked, they had taken on a dark blue hue, reflecting her emotions. Emotions, Finn suspected, comprised primarily of passion.

Needing to douse those thoughts, Finn led Katelyn back to the table. While they only picked at the food, the champagne seemed to disappear almost on its own.

Katelyn met his eyes, her own signaling the need that had flared between them. "One more dance?" she asked, her voice husky.

"One more," he agreed, knowing that they would have to return to normality the following day.

But nothing about the dance suggested that return. Instead, as Finn reached for Katelyn, she fused against him. The need he had seen in her eyes whispered to his own. He had been alone for three long years. He had almost forgotten the softness of a woman, the provocative lure of her scent.

Even Katelyn's lips seemed to tremble with an invitation all their own. When they parted with a gentle indrawn breath, he disregarded caution. His mouth sank deeply against hers. Caught up in her returning ardor, he tasted the flavor of passion. More intoxicating than the champagne, the blatant romance of the setting, or the siren notes of the music, her hunger demanded a response.

But Finn knew the restaurant wasn't the place to respond. Instead he pulled her through the French doors to the dusky courtyard. Outside, the moist air was scented with gardenias and honeysuckle, carried in on the breeze of the languid twilight. Thousands of miniature white lights wound through the branches of surrounding crepe myrtle trees while music spilled from the dining room.

Vaguely, Finn recognized the sound of nearby conversation. Pulling his gaze from Katelyn, he belatedly realized they had stumbled into a wedding reception. He began to guide them back inside.

But Katelyn put a restraining hand on his arm. "Wait. Look, they're about to cut the cake."

As they watched, the young couple fed each other the traditional piece of cake. With eyes for only each other, it was both sentimental and sensuous. The groom kissed his bride, then led her to the middle of the dance floor. Along with the guests, Finn and Katelyn watched the young couple dance in the spotlight, their eyes fastened only on one another.

"It's so terribly romantic," Katelyn breathed.

As other couples began to join the newlyweds, Finn held

out his hand. Katelyn moved into his arms, her face both dreamy and yearning.

When the dance ended, they approached the champagne fountain, Katelyn's gaze repeatedly returning to the bride and groom until the crowd swept them out of sight.

Amazed, Finn saw a tear glint in her eyes. "If I didn't know better, I'd think you want to get married."

"Don't say that." Katelyn protested. "I'm not what you think I am. I want to be like everybody else, to get married and have children." She gazed at the newlyweds. Then she spoke, her voice blurred with champagne, subliminal conditioning and emotion. "I want what they have."

"You can have it."

"It's not that simple." She clutched her champagne glass, nearly tipping over at the sudden movement.

Finn reached out to catch her. "Yes, it is. Or it could be."

She watched his arms on hers with fascination. "It could?"

"It's a beautiful night, you're a beautiful woman, and I'm asking." Finn took a deep breath, surprised by the words that came rushing out of his mouth. But even more surprising, he found he didn't regret them.

"Asking?" she questioned.

"You to marry me." He held his breath. "I want you to be my *wife*."

"Your *wife?*" He could see the key word clicking. "You really want to marry me?"

"Yes."

She batted her eyelashes. "Then, I guess you have a bride in your arms."

He was speechless a moment. She had actually accepted his impetuous proposal! A dozen reasons why they shouldn't do this came to mind. But was he an absolute idiot? Katelyn was a beautiful, talented woman who wanted to take on his family. Was he crazy to argue?

She reached up, tracing the line of his lips. "Finn?"

They stood a mere breath apart. He felt his common sense melt beneath the heat she caused. "We can't get married tonight."

"Oh, but we can," she insisted, her full lips curving impishly.

"We can't get a license here so soon—"

"No, but we can in Vegas."

"Vegas?" he asked incredulously.

"The corporate jet is sitting at the airport. I know it's free tonight. We can be in Vegas and back before you know it."

"You want to fly all the way to Vegas? What's the rush?"

Katelyn reached for his hands. "If we don't do it now, we'll think of a million reasons why we shouldn't."

"Maybe that would be wise."

Her changeling eyes darkened mysteriously, lending no clue of their true color. "Do you want to be alone, Finn?"

The answer to that was as telling as the crush of their bodies as he pulled her close. Disregarding reason, he tasted the desperation in her kiss.

Chapter Five

There was cotton in Katelyn's head. Along with a jackhammer, a hydraulic drill, and apparently all the dwarfs in Snow White's house. In fact the dwarfs seemed to be crawling all over her body.

"She's awake!" one of them announced. "She only *looked* dead."

Disoriented, Katelyn wondered if she was still in the middle of a dream. Opening one bleary eye, she couldn't imagine where else she might be, because nothing looked familiar. Especially the three small children crawling all over her. She considered pinching herself to see if she was awake, but she couldn't imagine inflicting any more pain.

Just then, the bedroom door burst open and Finn breezed in. Quickly crossing the room, he dropped a kiss on her forehead. "Morning, Katie."

"No one calls me Katie," she informed him. Then the realization that it was Finn who had blithely kissed her hit her like a tank. "Where *am* I?"

Finn looked slightly chastised, but there was a definite twinkle in his roguish blue eyes. "Don't tell me you can't remember?"

Her own eyes narrowed suspiciously. "Remember what?"

"Our wedding, Mrs. Malloy."

Katelyn suddenly felt faint. Luckily the bed was still beneath her. Luckily? Had they shared this bed? Horrified, she stared at him, remembering her own impulsive suggestion. Had she been seized with a burst of insanity?

Finn pointed to the dresser littered with slightly wilted flowers. "I saved your bouquet. And I brought in the rest of our wedding cake. Of course, the kids have already been into that."

At the reminder of his children, Katelyn stared at them and was rewarded by six curious eyes that stared back steadily. "But how...why..." She held up a hand to her painful head, regretting the champagne she had consumed.

"I know you met the kids once, but that was some time back. The twins are Erin and Eric. I know they look a lot alike, but when Eric had his first haircut, Erin insisted on a matching one. I figure she'll grow out of it by the time she reaches puberty. And their older sister is Jenny."

Katelyn looked at the children blearily. But it was the marriage part she was trying to grapple with. She turned back to Finn. "I think we need to talk."

His eyes flickered with something that looked briefly like pain before he closed his expression. "You're probably right."

However, Katelyn was not particularly concerned with his feelings at the moment. Instead she was trying to guess why she'd agreed to marriage. The more she tried to reason it out, the worse her head throbbed. Clearly she couldn't handle even a reasonable amount of champagne. Finn and the kids kept staring at her and she wished she could simply disappear. Since that wasn't possible, she tried for the next best thing. "Where..." She stared down at the kids. "Where would my clothes be?"

Finn gazed at her steadily. "In the closet."

Of course. If you got married, you shared a closet. Even if you'd temporarily lost your sanity when it happened. The twins chose that moment to shriek in tandem and Katelyn wondered if her head was going to fly through the ceiling.

"Okay, guys, let Katelyn get dressed." The kids jumped off the bed and scampered toward the door. "After you're dressed, we can talk." Hesitating, Finn turned back. "The kids are thrilled you're here."

Katelyn rubbed her aching head "They are?"

His gaelic blue eyes darkened. "They've been hoping for a mother."

Katelyn could swear he'd injected a touch of Irish brogue into his words and she doubted he'd ever even laid eyes on the emerald isle. Still, he'd managed to make her feel incredibly guilty. But the children would simply have to understand it was a crazy mistake. The romantic setting, stumbling in on a touching wedding, too much champagne…somehow all that had combined with the clanging alarm on her biological clock. And she had overreacted. On a far grander scale than ever before, but still a correctable mistake. Glancing up, she saw that Finn was watching her, waiting for her reply. "Kids are resilient. By tomorrow they'll have forgotten all about me."

"They can't talk about anything else," he replied quietly.

She paused, considering his words. "Really?"

"You can't blame them." His expression was somber. "After all it's not every day children think they've got a new mother."

Katelyn could only stare at Finn's back as he left the room. Surely the children hadn't gotten their hopes up so quickly. The maternal urges she'd recently experienced twinged again. She certainly didn't want Finn's children hurt because she'd acted impulsively.

Stumbling into her clothes, Katelyn stared at her face in the mirror. She touched it to make sure it was real, then gave into the urge she'd been having to pinch herself. Flinching, she realized this was no dream.

What could she possibly have been thinking? Marrying her driver? True, she'd been thinking a lot about marriage lately, but she didn't recall considering Finn Malloy a potential groom.

Looking across the room, she saw the bouquet. Drawn by the flowers, she picked them up, turning the bouquet slowly in her hands. She remembered Finn's thoughtfulness in choosing the violets. She also remembered the hope she had seen in his eyes.

Still, what had possessed her to elope with him? True, she hadn't been immune to his rugged good looks. From day one his easy, cocky grin and roguish eyes had suggested far more than a simple willingness to drive. But that was hardly reason to marry someone. Even a handsome, strapping man like Finn Malloy. A man who had stirred her blood like no other.

A warm feeling flooded her, much like the ones she'd been experiencing the last few weeks. *Married.* A wife and mother—two words that had been giving her warm fuzzies for weeks. All sorts of soft, bubbly emotions tumbled through her. A ready-made family. Children to cuddle, a husband to lavish attention on.

Thinking of June Cleaver breakfasts, she left the bedroom and searched for the kitchen, ready to share that first perfect morning. She passed the dining room and saw the remains of the wedding cake. A swinging door connected the dining room to what she assumed was the kitchen. Trying to shore up her courage, she plastered a smile on her face and pushed open the door.

And entered chaos.

The twins were running wildly around the middle of the kitchen while Finn tried to wipe something sticky from their faces. Jenny was heaping cereal in a bowl that overflowed onto the counter. And a dog of indecipherable origins darted between them, scavenging for the overflow.

As she considered backing out the same way she entered, Finn spotted her. "The baby-sitter's late. It'll be difficult to talk until the kids have eaten breakfast."

"Sure," she responded weakly, not realizing how difficult it was to feed three small children. There was so much *mess.* "I'll just grab some coffee."

"Mugs are over there." Finn pointed to one of the cupboards. "Coffee's hot."

The telephone rang just then, adding to the noise level. Finn seemed to grow a third arm, managing to grab the phone while still wiping faces.

"What?" he barked into the phone. "Now's a hell of a time to call me. No, I'm not worried about the language I use in front of my children. I'm more worried about leaving them in the care of incompetents like you!" He slammed the receiver back into its cradle. "Great," he muttered. "Jenny, take the twins to watch cartoons."

Jenny climbed from her stool, herding her brother and sister out of the kitchen.

"Problem?" Katelyn asked tentatively, wondering how Finn coped with all this.

"That was the baby-sitter I had lined up for today. The regular one quit last night when we got home so late. And this one has decided that her numerology chart doesn't favor taking the number sixty-two bus to get here today."

"Just like that?" Katelyn asked in surprise.

"Yep, just like that," he replied grimly.

The phone rang again and Finn swore beneath his breath.

"Maybe she changed her mind," Katelyn suggested hopefully.

"Don't count on it." He ripped the receiver from the cradle, his greeting a barely controlled snarl. Then his voice changed. "Sorry, it's been a real hectic morning." He listened again, his face first registering surprised delight, then gradual disappointment. "Can I get back to you?" he finally asked. This time he replaced the receiver slowly, his mind clearly still on the conversation.

Katelyn couldn't stand the suspense. "What is it?"

"That was the Mathison Foundation. I put in a bid for their contract some time ago. I never dreamed I would get it—the hours are perfect, the money even better."

"Then why the long face?"

"I don't have a baby-sitter," he reminded her.

"Oh." She thought for another moment. "Does this mean you plan to give up the contract with my firm?" She was surprised at the disappointment which flooded her as she asked the question. She had come to look forward to her time with Finn. She hadn't realized he had planned to end that.

"I was hoping to juggle both jobs for a while," he replied. "There's not much chance of that if I can't show up today."

Katelyn took a deep breath. "I could watch the kids."

He looked at her skeptically. "I don't think so. They're a handful and then some."

She straightened her spine defensively. "Are you suggesting I can't handle three small children?"

"I'm saying that anyone who isn't used to kids would have a hard time coping."

Without knowing it, he had just pushed one of her most sensitive buttons. She never wanted to admit she was unable to do something. "And what makes you so sure I'm inexperienced?"

"Aren't you?"

"Don't most teenage girls baby-sit?" Katelyn squirmed, not quite meeting his gaze. "I told you about my neighbor's baby, didn't I?" Behind her back, she crossed her fingers.

"I guess you did. Still…"

''You don't want to lose the contract.''

''No, I don't. But I also don't want you doing this because you feel guilty.''

Katelyn's defenses twitched again. ''Guilty?''

''Just because you've gotten cold feet about this marriage is no reason—''

''Cold feet?'' she retorted.

He shrugged. ''Or whatever you want to call it. Last night at the club the idea of being married and having kids probably sounded as romantic as the setting. But now, in the harsh light of day…''

''Are you suggesting I'm *afraid* of marriage?'' she countered icily.

He shrugged again. ''Maybe afraid isn't the right word, but you've got to admit it was a pretty crazy thing to do.''

She nodded stiffly. ''Impulsive perhaps.''

''And I'll understand if you want an annulment. You didn't know what you were getting into when I suggested this.''

Another direct hit. Finn had just managed to push nearly all her remaining buttons. First, she was no coward. Second, it galled her to have him point out that she was backing out of something she'd agreed with. If she took the easy out he was offering, it would be an admission of failure—another button. And something she never tolerated. ''I didn't ask for an annulment.''

Finn blinked, staring at her in surprise. ''You don't look real thrilled by all this.''

Katelyn straightened her shoulders. ''As I said, it *was* impulsive. That doesn't mean we shouldn't give it a try.''

''You want to be a wife and full-time mother?'' he questioned doubtfully.

Belatedly, she remembered the children. With her aching head, it was a wonder she could remember anything. ''Well…'' she hedged.

"When I thought of marrying again, I pictured the kids having a mother. To be honest, that was very important to me."

"Oh," she managed. A full-time wife and mother? She had a career to think of. But more and more people were working from home, basing themselves close to family. Of course, she would still have to conduct meetings and presentations in the office. But that should be a snap. Calling on her customary decisiveness, she met Finn's gaze. "It shouldn't be a problem. Now, don't you have a phone call to make?"

He glanced around the disorganized kitchen. "I hate to leave you with all this."

Nonchalantly, Katelyn shrugged. "No problem."

A few minutes later, his phone call completed, Finn prepared to leave. She blinked as he casually kissed her goodbye. "See you later, Katie."

"Katelyn," she murmured, rubbing her cheek where he'd kissed her, the warm imprint lingering.

Then the door shut behind her and she began to doubt the wisdom of her decision. For a wild moment she considered running after him. Instead she turned and faced her charges. Back from watching cartoons, Jenny was pouring milk into the overflowing cereal bowl and Katelyn heard the splash of it hitting the counter before she could call out a warning. As she watched, milk formed a fast-running river from the bowl, over the counter and onto the floor where the dog lapped at it happily.

"Don't do that, dog," Katelyn ordered.

The dog ignored her.

"His name is Snuffles," Jenny informed her.

"We want milk!" one of the twins demanded.

"Yes, milk!" the other chimed in loudly.

Katelyn winced as their voices pierced her growing headache. She knew one twin was a boy and the other a girl, but for the life of her they looked identical. No doubt as they aged that would change, but at the moment the dark-haired, dark-eyed toddlers looked remarkably similar.

Jenny righted the milk carton, but the last of the spillage still dripped onto the floor.

Katelyn briefly closed her eyes. Breakfast was a meal that was either delivered to her office by one of her assistants or eaten in a civilized restaurant. Neither experience had prepared her for serving breakfast to three children. In fact nothing in her experience had prepared her for any sort of meal preparation. She was quite an expert on caterers and had a list of premier chefs most hostesses would kill for. But somehow that didn't seem to suit suburbia.

So what did kids eat anyway? Judging by Jenny, lots of cereal. Katelyn rummaged in the cabinet until she found two bowls, filled them with the cereal Jenny had left on the counter and then poured milk into the bowls. Rather pleased with herself, she put the cereal in front of the twins.

And simultaneously their faces crumpled.

Helplessly, Katelyn watched them, and turned to Jenny. "What's wrong with them?"

"They don't like Cocoa Crinkles."

Katelyn's head throbbed harder. "Couldn't you have told me that?"

"You didn't ask."

Katelyn wondered if this was five-year-old logic or if the child had an attitude. Wishing to believe the former, she took a deep breath. "So, what do they like?"

"Milk to drink. And eggs."

"Eggs?" Katelyn repeated with dismay. They had to be cooked.

"Uh-huh."

Katelyn decided to start with the easy part. She found two glasses and reached for the milk carton. And found it held less than half of one glass. Between what Jenny had spilled and what she'd poured into the other two cereal bowls, the carton was empty. Opening the refrigerator, it didn't take long to see there wasn't any more milk. *Juice.* They could drink juice.

Searching the freezer, she found a can of frozen orange juice. It took her a while to thaw the juice, but she finally had it ready and filled two glasses.

"Here we go. Instead of milk, we'll have juice."

Both twins stared unhappily at the juice, not reaching for the glasses.

"Now what's wrong?" Katelyn asked.

"They don't like orange juice," Jenny informed her around a spoonful of cereal.

"Why didn't you tell me?"

"You didn't ask."

Five-year-old logic, she told herself. Not attitude. Searching through the pantry, Katelyn found apple juice. This time she asked Jenny, who replied that they liked apple juice. She took down two more glasses, realizing they were accumulating quite a collection of dirty glassware. She filled the glasses and put them in front of the twins. But they just stared at her.

"Now what?" Calling on all her patience, she kept her voice even. "Jenny, I thought you said they liked apple juice."

"They do, but they won't drink out of regular glasses. You have to put it in their cups—the ones with lids and a straw."

"Why didn't you…" Katelyn didn't finish the question. She already knew the answer.

Digging around in the cabinet, she found the cups, made sure they were the right ones and then filled them with juice. This time the twins reached for them with sticky little hands and drank deeply.

One, she thought perhaps the girl, lowered her cup. "Milk."

"No, it's juice," Katelyn replied.

"That means he wants milk," Jenny interpreted.

"But we don't have any milk."

The little boy's face screwed up. "Milk."

"But we don't have any," Katelyn repeated.

Eric's wobbling lip turned into a full-fledged tremble, then he started to cry.

Katelyn stared helplessly at Jenny. "But there isn't any more milk."

Jenny shrugged. "They want milk."

As if on cue, Erin added her wails to her brother's.

Katelyn appealed to the distraught children. "I don't have my car here. There's no way to get to the store."

They only cried harder.

Katelyn's head throbbed in double-time. Worse, she couldn't stand to see them so miserable.

Grabbing the telephone, she dialed information. "Hello, yes. Could you give me the number of a grocery store near..." She paused, having no idea where she was. Quickly she asked Jenny the address and repeated it to the operator. "I don't care *which* grocery store—just one that sells milk."

Armed with a telephone number, she dialed the store. She did some quick figuring—three kids could probably drink a lot of milk and she probably should get some extra. When the clerk answered, Katelyn requested that they deliver a dozen gallons of milk. She was put on hold and a manager came on to politely explain that they didn't make deliveries. Eric chose that moment to cry even louder.

Katelyn clutched the receiver. "Look, I'll give you one hundred dollars if you'll deliver the milk."

There was a pause on the other end of the phone. "Is this some kind of prank?"

Katelyn put on her best corporate voice. "Does this sound like a prank?" She held the phone in the twins' direction, letting their loud cries stream into the phone. Then she added her own demand. "Now, will you please deliver the milk?"

"You sure there's a hundred in it?" the man asked suspiciously.

"If you get here in the next fifteen minutes, I'll make it a hundred and fifty."

The man rapidly took down the address. Katelyn replaced the receiver. "Okay, guys, milk is on its way."

The twins didn't take a break, still crying.

"It won't do any good to keep crying. It won't get the milk here any faster."

They weren't impressed. Katelyn turned to Jenny. "What have I forgotten to ask?"

Jenny shrugged. "I dunno."

"Eggs—we'll do the eggs," she said desperately.

Eric hiccuped and Katelyn took that as a positive sign.

Searching the refrigerator, she found a carton of eggs. Now what to do with them? She glanced around the kitchen and her eyes fell on the microwave. People cooked all sorts of things in microwaves. Why not eggs?

She took four eggs from the carton, figuring that should be plenty. Remembering what someone had once told her, she put the eggs on a plate and shoved them into the microwave. Now, how long to cook them? She thought three-minute eggs sounded good, and there were four eggs. Twelve minutes. That should do it. She set the timer and started the oven. She wondered why she'd always thought this cooking business was so difficult.

"Okay. They'll be done in a few minutes. Until then…" What did kids like? She searched her throbbing mind. Peanut butter and jelly! Kids loved that. She found the ingredients in the refrigerator and a loaf of bread on the counter.

Hey, she was doing great. It didn't take long to assemble the sandwiches. She made two, then remembered Jenny. "Would you like a peanut-butter-and-jelly sandwich, Jenny?"

"I'm full."

"Okay. Erin, this will give you something to nibble on until your breakfast's done."

"I'm Eric."

"Okay, Eric." She put a sandwich in front of him. Then she turned to the other twin, handing her a matching sandwich. "Then I guess it stands to reason you must be Erin."

"Uh-huh."

Already sticky fingers reached for the sandwiches. Their small hands had some trouble gripping the whole sandwiches and it occurred to Katelyn that perhaps she should have cut them in half. But, the twins were already squishing the sandwiches into more compact squares. Oh, well, probably tasted the same either way, she reasoned.

Since the kids had stopped crying, Katelyn chose this golden moment to phone her office. Although Daniel sounded as though he was in amused shock, he caught her up on the morning mail and messages. Then he said he would send over a duplicate work setup—a desk, computer, video-conferencing equipment, fax and copy machines. He also assured her that he would order additional phone lines to be installed.

Pleased, Katelyn replaced the receiver and turned back to the kids. Her mouth opened in shock. The twins were literally covered in peanut butter and jelly—from their well-smeared hair to the tops of their tiny tennis shoes.

"What in the world?"

Jenny glanced at her brother and sister. "Daddy never gives them peanut-butter-and-jelly—he says it's a disaster."

Katelyn silently counted to ten. "Looks like Daddy's

right.'' She stared dubiously at the twins. ''Maybe I should just turn a hose on you guys.'' She paused, hearing the strangest sound. ''What *is* that?''

As she glanced around the kitchen, her gaze narrowed on the microwave. Just then a huge popping sound erupted from it, escalating quickly into what sounded like an explosion. Part of her thought she should open the door and see what was happening. The other part of her wanted to grab the kids and escape. Did microwaves kill?

The last sane cell in her brain reminded her that she could pull the plug. Doing so, she held her breath. The awful noise continued for a moment, then finally hiccuped to a halt. Staring at the wide-eyed children, Katelyn swallowed and gathered her courage, cautiously opening the door of the microwave.

Seemingly hundreds of pieces of fragmented eggshells plastered the interior. Splotches of raw and partially cooked egg were splattered over the entire surface, and starting to congeal. As she watched, one clump of egg and shell dropped from the roof of the microwave and landed in a sad heap on the plate.

''I don't think you're supposed to put them in there with the shells still on,'' Jenny offered. ''Or cook them so long.''

''I don't suppose you could have told me that.''

''You didn't—''

''Ask. I know.'' Katelyn sighed. ''Maybe next time, you could just tell me, whether I ask or not.''

Jenny shrugged. ''Adults say that, but then they don't always want to hear stuff.''

Katelyn felt a pang. ''Doesn't your daddy listen to you?''

''Daddy *always* listens. Baby-sitters don't.''

Ah, the motherless thing Finn had talked about. ''We'll have to work on that. But, for now, do you have any ideas on how to cook the eggs?''

"Put water and eggs in a pan, and cook them on the stove."

That didn't sound like brain surgery. Katelyn found a pot, one big enough to catch any fallout. After filling it with about a gallon of water, she put it on the stove. Then she reached for the eggs. This time she wasn't making the same mistake.

Carefully, she cracked open the eggs and dropped them into the pot. They just sort of sat there in the water, but she guessed they would look better once they started cooking. She squinted at the motionless water. Maybe she should have waited until it started boiling.

Just then the doorbell rang. The man from the grocery store stood on the porch, several bags at his feet and in his arms. "Your milk."

"Oh, right, please come in." She gestured to the bags. "That's *all* milk?"

"Yep."

Maybe twelve gallons was more than she realized. Oh, well, they'd eventually drink it. She led the way to the kitchen and the man unloaded the plastic jugs onto the counter.

Retrieving her purse, she quickly counted out his money. "I appreciate your delivering the milk. The kids really wanted some."

He glanced between the three children and twelve gallons of milk. "Apparently."

After he left, Katelyn turned to the twins. "Your milk's here!"

"Full," Erin announced.

"Me, too," Eric echoed.

As they scampered down from the table, Katelyn wondered which mess she should clean up first—the twins, the microwave, or the milk. She supposed the kids would be okay for a little while. The microwave, on the other hand, looked like it was in danger of possible meltdown.

Fifteen minutes later, Katelyn was still scraping eggshells from the microwave's interior and she'd hardly made a dent in the mess. Having heard water splashing for a few minutes, Katelyn sighed. She hoped it wouldn't rain all day. It rained frequently in Houston, but she just didn't need a gloomy day. The thought had barely formed when she realized that it was still bright and sunny in the kitchen. Moving over to the window, she looked outside and saw that it wasn't raining. Then where was the sound of water coming from?

Pushing open the swinging door, Katelyn was hit with a blast of cold water. Shaking her head to clear the water from her eyes, she was horrified to realize that it was coming from a lawn sprinkler. But what was a lawn sprinkler doing in the middle of the living and dining room?

Eric and Erin spotted her, screeching as they darted in and out of the water.

"What are you two *doing?*" Katelyn shrieked.

"Hose," Erin announced.

"I can see that!" Katelyn had a sickening feeling as she remembered her words. *Maybe I should just turn the hose on you guys.* Could three-year-olds take everything that literally?

Right now she had to turn the water off before the whole place was soaked. "How did you get that thing in here?"

Eric pointed to the open patio doors. "From outside."

Katelyn ignored the rush of water that splashed her as she grabbed the hose and dragged it back outside. Locating and then wrenching off the outside faucet, Katelyn wondered why she'd thought motherhood would be comprised of warm, tender moments. So far, it only seemed messy— she reached up to touch her dripping hair—and wet.

The twins had trailed outside and were looking mournfully at the disconnected sprinkler. Katelyn realized they were both sopping wet. "Do you guys know how to get dressed?"

Both their heads bobbed up and down.

"Then go upstairs and put fresh clothes on. Do you know where your sister is?"

"Watching TV," one of them replied.

She really was going to have to figure out which twin was which. First she had to sop up the water in the living room. After emptying nearly the entire linen closet, she still could have used more towels. But it occurred to her that she should check on Jenny. Katelyn had to wander through the entire house, but she found Jenny curled up in front of the TV in the den.

"Jenny? What are you doing?"

The child gave her a long-suffering look. "Watching TV."

"But shouldn't you be doing something else?"

"This is what most baby-sitters want us to do."

Katelyn frowned. It hardly seemed like a stimulating activity for a child. "I think we can find something else for you to do."

Jenny sighed and clicked off the remote control. "Okay."

As they walked back into the living room, Jenny glanced around. "Where are the twins?"

"Changing clothes."

"By themselves?"

Katelyn paused. "Isn't that a good idea?"

Jenny shrugged and rolled her eyes. Katelyn grew a little uneasy. "Maybe we should check on them."

Together they went upstairs. "Why don't you show me where their room is?" Katelyn suggested.

"Okay." Jenny led the way. When they reached the twins' room Katelyn heard Jenny's startled screech. Entering the room on her heels, Katelyn issued a gasp of her own. There were clothes everywhere. On the beds, the floor, on top of the toy box. It was as though the dresser had exploded. In fact, every drawer was pulled out, the few remaining contents pulled free and dangling loosely.

The closet was just the same. All of the clothing had been ripped from the lower bar and a chair had been dragged over so that little hands could reach the top of the closet as well.

In the midst of the mess, Eric and Erin stood, wearing a startling combination of clothing—purples, greens and oranges, all mixed as though designed for a clown.

But for the moment, Katelyn had concerns greater than good taste. "Why did you take out *everything?*"

The twins stared at her as though she'd spoken in Russian. Before Katelyn could try again, the doorbell rang.

She didn't know whether to be relieved or annoyed to find her first delivery from the office. For once, Daniel had been *too* efficient. Somehow, bringing anything else into this chaos seemed rather idiotic.

Still she supervised the deliverymen, directing them to put her desk in the alcove off the dining room. Once they had brought in the computer and office machines, the sheer amount of stuff started to seem overwhelming.

"Are we an office now?" Jenny asked as she watched the fax machine come in.

"No, of course not. These things are for my work," Katelyn tried to explain.

"Are *you* an office?" Jenny questioned with five-year-old reasoning.

"No. I'm in advertising."

"Abertising?"

"Like commercials," Katelyn explained.

"You're a *commercial?*" Jenny questioned. "On TV?"

"No, it's not—"

The doorbell rang again. It was a serviceman to put in the extra phone lines and Katelyn wondered just what arms Daniel had twisted to get same-day service. But then, it was no less than she expected from her assistant.

"Are you sure we're not an office?" Jenny questioned again.

"I know this all seems a little unfamiliar right now, but it won't for long." Katelyn glanced up as she answered, seeing the twins following the phone man around. "Jenny, we have to do something to keep the twins busy while the men are here."

"We could make cookies," Jenny suggested.

Great, cooking again. "I don't know. I'm not what you'd call real familiar with baking."

"I know how to make cookies," Jenny replied. "And the twins could put the sprinkles on them."

Katelyn saw that the twins were trying to "help" the phone man and she wavered. "Are you *sure* you know how to bake cookies?"

"Yes I'm *sure.*"

"I guess it's okay." Katelyn searched what was left of her mind. The oven? Should she let Jenny use an oven? "I'll light the oven, though."

"Okay. But all you do is turn the knob."

"Fine. But humor me and let me turn the knob."

Jenny shrugged, and Katelyn realized the gesture was a major component of the child's conversational skills.

Still, Katelyn turned the oven on, feeling she was handling some responsibility. As the kids started taking ingredients out of the pantry, she wondered if she should supervise.

"Ma'am. If you want five extra lines we'll have to reroute the existing lines," the phone man interrupted. "We might have to do some rewiring."

Katelyn was torn. Should she supervise the kids or make

certain the serviceman didn't rip Finn's house apart? She glanced at the ruined microwave, the peanut-butter-covered table and the milk on the counter. Practicality ruled. The kitchen was already destroyed, might as well save the rest of the house.

"Jenny, you're in charge. Be careful and call me if you have any problems."

"Ma'am, the phone lines—"

"I'm coming."

The doorbell rang.

The phone man glared at her and Katelyn gestured an apology. It occurred to her that assistants were more valuable than she realized. Who knew there were so many details to be dealt with?

The doorbell rang insistently again.

A deliveryman with the copier shoved a clipboard at her.

After signing her name, Katelyn tried to decide where she should put the machine. It occurred to her, belatedly, that perhaps she should have thought this out *before* having everything sent over.

The phone man was looking apoplectic so Katelyn went with him to decide where to reroute the lines. Nearly an hour later, she emerged.

The deliveryman had the copier hooked up, but he had a peculiar look on his face. "Is your wiring good?"

"As far as I know. Why?"

"Don't you smell smoke?"

"Smoke? *Smoke!*"

Chapter Six

Katelyn ran toward the kitchen. She hit the swinging door and pushed it open. Smoke was spilling out of the oven, filling the room. She searched for Jenny and saw that she was perched on a stool at the counter, which was now completely littered from one end to the other.

Another quick glance showed that the twins were anchored to either side of the table. A table covered in chocolate chips, raisins, colored crystal decorating sugar, and a conglomeration of nearly everything else in the pantry.

All three children were covered in cookie dough.

And Katelyn was speechless.

Until the smoke detectors started screeching.

In tandem with the automatic sprinklers that rained water down all over the kitchen.

A crazy thought burst through her brain. *At least the outside sprinkler in the living and dining room isn't such a big deal now.*

The kids started jumping up and down, delighted with the downpour.

At that moment the copier deliveryman poked his head into the kitchen. ''Jeez, lady.''

Katelyn stared at him between straggling strands of wet hair plastered to her face. ''Please tell me the sprinklers didn't go off in the rest of the house.''

"Not yet. But, I don't think your service agreement covers that if they do."

"Terrific."

"Your copier's up and running."

"Thanks."

"No problem. Uh, good luck, lady."

"I'll need it," she muttered under her breath. "And then some."

FINN STUMBLED over the cord to a copy machine, wondering at the rapidity with which Katelyn had had the equipment delivered. He thought she was going to see how things went. Apparently she didn't do things in half-measure. Maybe the day had gone so well she had decided the marriage might work after all.

Was the television on? It sounded as though a half dozen phones were ringing and he only had two lines.

Sniffing, he smelled a scorched odor. But, he wasn't completely surprised—he hadn't expected Katelyn to be a gourmet chef. The fact that she was actually in his kitchen was nothing short of miraculous.

Smiling for the first time that day, he strolled further inside, wondering what was making that squishing sound. It almost felt like the carpet. Maybe Katelyn had found time to get it cleaned. She really was something.

Feeling a sense of renewed hope he pushed open the door to the kitchen, ready to greet his new bride. "Katie, I'm home!"

But he doubted she heard him above the din. Eric and Erin sat in the middle of the floor, their wails competing with the rest of the chaos. A fax machine was shooting out papers with frightening speed and the ringing sound he heard was coming from newly installed phones.

For a moment he wondered if someone had pulled every single thing in the pantry and cabinets out onto the counters and table. And for some unknown reason, doused them all with water. In between were several incredible messes, starting with the microwave and ending with pans of burnt-looking lumps. And Snuffles was sniffing each one.

Finn blinked, then tried to refocus. And when he did, he saw what looked to be nearly a dozen gallons of milk lined up on the counter as well. What in the world?

In the middle of it all, Katelyn hovered over an electric fry pan, one hand holding a stack of papers that appeared to be coated in applesauce, her other hand wrapped in a soggy-looking towel. A towel whose sogginess matched the rest of Katelyn. What had happened to her? And his house?

Jenny spotted him first. "Daddy!" She ran toward him, flinging herself in his arms. Automatically he hugged her back, belatedly realizing that Jenny was covered in peanut butter and jelly. And now he was, too.

"Hey, honey," he greeted her, crouching down to her level.

"We made cookies," she announced.

That and a nuclear bomb, it seemed. One Katelyn had apparently set off in his kitchen. "Did you save me one?"

"We saved lots. They're well…well…"

"Done," Katelyn supplied.

"Yeah. Well-done. Do you like well-done cookies, Daddy?"

The twins launched themselves at him, too. "They're the best—but not before dinner, okay?"

Jenny pointed to the counter. "I'm making dinner now."

Peanut butter and jelly sandwiches? Most of which appeared to be applied to the counter.

"I'm making grilled cheese sandwiches for dinner," Katelyn added. She held up one hand. "But so far the pan's winning."

Finn gently untangled himself from the children and rose. Glancing at the stove, he saw the huge pot he used to cook stew and chili in. Curious, he looked inside. Big globs of what looked like egg floated in more than a gallon of water.

Moving next to Katelyn, he looked into the electric fry pan, seeing charcoal-colored sandwiches. Melted cheese oozed into the pan, where it stuck and burned. Apparently it had been a culinary disaster day.

Carefully, he took the stack of papers from Katelyn's uninjured hand. "Let me see what you did to your hand."

She held up the towel-wrapped limb. "It's no big thing."

He unwrapped the towel. A fiery red welt striped the palm of her hand, obviously a painful burn. "How'd you do this?"

"I didn't know that the pan came on by itself after you plugged it in. I thought there'd be an on/off switch."

"There's a temperature control."

"Which was set on four hundred and fifty degrees," she replied ruefully.

He winced. That had to hurt. Clearly she hadn't put anything on the burn other than the wet towel. Finn reached into the kitchen drawer and pulled out a first-aid kit, then urged her toward a kitchen chair.

He reached for the injured hand, feeling the softness of her skin before he carefully turned her hand over. He applied a burn ointment and heard her release a small gasp of relief. The wound must have been stinging badly.

As he wrapped her hand in soft gauze he noticed the tired shadows under her eyes. Knowing she had drunk too much champagne the night before, he guessed her head still felt like it could implode at any moment. And from the evidence in the kitchen, he suspected *she* might be close to exploding.

He gestured to the milk on the counter. "Do we have a milkman I don't know about?"

"I guess I bought a little too much. I did freeze a couple of gallons, though."

Frozen milk. That ought to be tasty. Finn wasn't sure he wanted to know why or how so much milk had landed on the counter.

"Why don't you go take a break?" he suggested. "I'll bathe the twins and put them to bed."

Katelyn didn't protest. "It *has* been a long day."

Finn didn't remind her that it was just past six and that compared to her normal working days, this one was only half over.

As she staggered out of the room, Finn's gaze zoomed in on his children. "So, we've been busy, haven't we?"

Giggles met his words.

"Just as I thought. All right, you heathens. Upstairs with you. You too, Jenny. After the twins' baths, you're next."

Eric pounded on the floor. "Submarines!"

"You, my little man, are going underwater, but I'm not sure it'll be in a submarine."

Lifting his son in the air, Finn planted him on his shoulders. Eric promptly fisted handfuls of Finn's thick hair. Finn glanced affectionately at his children, but despite his parental prejudice, he knew the three were a handful. And Katelyn had already burned one hand. He wondered if she'd be willing to risk another.

She was probably ready to tell him she had misjudged the situation. No doubt she was phoning right now to have the office equipment retrieved. Or maybe she had already rushed out the front door for freedom. He remembered the taste of her kiss, the feel of her body pressed close to his. And hoped like hell she wouldn't bail out on them.

FINN TURNED OFF the overhead light, flicking on the softer lamp light. Curled in the middle of his bed was his new "bride." While he hadn't minded giving up his bed on their wedding night, now he wondered at their future arrangements.

Certainly she deserved a good night's rest—he didn't begrudge her that. She'd obviously had one hell of a day. But his thoughts hadn't really progressed past the last impression of holding her in his arms.

But even then, he hadn't really appreciated how she would look lying in his bed. Her soft, damp hair spread across his pillow as her generous chest moved gently in rhythm with her even breathing.

Again, he remembered the feel of her breasts crushed against his chest, her hips aligned with his, her softness, the heat that had flared between them the night before.

FINN SIGHED heavily and she woke suddenly with a start. "I didn't mean to fall asleep."

"It looks as though you needed the rest."

"I can't imagine why I'm so tired." Katelyn reached a hand toward her head. "But I know now I can't handle more than a glass or two of champagne."

Finn hid his grimace. Apparently their wedding night was going to be postponed again. "Taking care of a family is just as exhausting as corporate scheming."

"I did more than scheme," Katelyn retorted.

"You'll find you need that unlikely quality to be a mother and wife," Finn replied. "Or the kids will take advantage of you."

Her eyes lit suddenly as though she remembered something vital. "I didn't get a chance to give you your paper and slippers," she told him as she scrambled off the bed.

Paper and slippers? Where in the world had that come from? Uncomfortably, Finn realized he didn't want her to relinquish her independence. While he hadn't appreciated her high-handed airs, he didn't want the complete opposite either.

"Katie, didn't you have some faxes to read?" he asked

to distract her. "They seem to have had a run-in with the applesauce."

"So did the twins. I guess they were curious about all the paper coming out of the machine." She frowned. "I do have a pile of e-mail to read."

"Any applesauce in the computer yet?" he questioned, hoping to see a smile.

"No, just peanut butter. The repairman's coming tomorrow."

"I doubt you got much work done today," he said sympathetically, not wanting to dwell on the wrecked house.

"I guess that depends on what you call work," Katelyn replied wryly.

"Is being a mother somewhat of a surprise?"

Despite her fatigue, Katelyn's face softened. "A mother?"

"Well...taking care of the kids."

Katelyn's weary face changed subtly. "Where are the children?"

"Bathed and in bed."

She yawned. "That sounds good."

Which brought up the bed issue. After her day, could he take this one step farther? He felt an arrow of guilt stab him. He supposed not.

Finn pushed a hand through hair thoroughly mussed by the twins. "I've got some paperwork to do. Why don't you make it an early night? Take advantage of one of the few times the kids are all in bed at a decent time."

"I really should get some work done." Absently she rubbed her forehead.

"You'd get more done tomorrow if you give that headache a chance to go away," Finn countered.

"I don't know...."

He could tell she was close to being convinced. The Katelyn Amhurst of relentless corporate days wouldn't have had a doubt—she would have insisted on reading each fax and e-mail.

But this seemed to be a different Katelyn. ''You'll have a full day with the kids tomorrow. You'll need all the energy you can get.''

''Maybe just this once....'' She longingly eyed the bed.

Seeing her give in to the temptation and curl up on the bed, he regretfully edged out the door.

Down the hallway, in his office, Finn threw himself into the well-worn chair. He glanced at the dilapidated couch on the far wall—another long night. And he still wasn't sure what future nights would bring.

WARILY, Katelyn opened her eyes. The throbbing in her head was gone. She remembered the room from yesterday, although everything that had transpired in the last forty-eight hours still seemed like a dream. And from what she remembered of yesterday, it was probably better to keep it that way.

Somewhere she heard phones ringing and suspected they were her office lines. Tempting as it was, she couldn't keep her head buried beneath a pillow all day. Groaning, Katelyn guessed it was time to make breakfast as well. And where was her new husband? The other pillow was crumpled up, an old habit of hers. Had she crumpled it after he'd gotten up? Or had he slept in their bed at all?

Dressing quickly in jeans and a T-shirt she had instructed Daniel to send over, Katelyn realized she had to retrieve the rest of her clothing. Luckily, Daniel could also arrange that.

She and Finn should have discussed permanent living arrangements before they'd gotten married. Why had she been in such a rush? And why did she have such a strong urge to locate Finn's slippers? Nearly as strong an urge as the one she had for a cigarette. It was almost as though she'd been programmed to get married in a hurry. She remembered the subliminal tape to help her stop smoking and nearly laughed aloud. It *was* working, but it was hardly a miracle cure. No, she hadn't been programmed, that was certain.

Shaking her head, she left the bedroom and made her way the kitchen. Pajama-clad toddlers were clutching their cups of milk while Jenny was sipping juice.

"Morning, Katie. Coffee?" Finn offered.

"Yes, please." Katelyn noticed that most everything had been returned to the cabinets and pantry. But the sticky mess that littered the counters was almost worse.

Finn smiled wryly as he followed her gaze. "Maybe I should have left it covered up."

"Things just seemed to get out of hand yesterday. Today should be easier." She wasn't sure why she thought so, but it seemed important to establish that fact. Katelyn glanced at the twins. One flashed her a toothy grin.

Certain this one was the boy, she smiled back. "Morning, Eric."

Finn cleared his throat. "That's Erin. I know the matching haircuts make it confusing. I guess we're lucky Eric didn't want really short hair."

"Oh."

Checking his watch, Finn quickly finished his coffee. "I'm supposed to be at the new job early. Do you have any meetings scheduled today?"

She shook her head. "I told Daniel to clear my calendar for a few days so I can get things in order."

Finn took a deep breath. "You're still willing to try?"

"Why shouldn't I be?"

"You're not just a baby-sitter to the kids." Finn hesitated, not wanting to press the issue, but knowing he had to. "They'll see you as a permanent figure in their lives. So, if you've reconsidered, tell me now. The longer the kids view you as a mother, the harder it will be if you leave.''

Katelyn visibly puffed up. ''I know the house is a wreck, but it was my first day with them. I'm not a quitter!''

''I thought you had experience with kids.''

Again she puffed up, her words barely escaping clenched teeth. ''All right. So I exaggerated. But I'm perfectly capable of learning how to deal with the children. Yesterday just didn't go as I expected.''

He hoped not. Although the children were messy, they were okay. He wasn't sure the house could take much more though. ''Everything new takes getting used to.''

Katelyn drew her brows together. ''Just because I had one rough day doesn't mean I'm ready to quit.''

Finn grinned. ''You've got guts, Katie.''

She glanced around the destroyed room. ''It looks like they're spread out all over this kitchen.''

His gaze followed hers. ''I feel guilty leaving you with all this. And the agency still doesn't have a sitter to send.''

''It's okay. You have your new job. Things will even out once we get into a routine.''

''Right.'' Finn drained the last of his coffee. ''I won't be late.''

Katelyn gazed at him wistfully. Part of her wanted to go with him, to take her career back in hand. Daniel had assured her yesterday that he could shuffle her meetings and set up video conferences, but now she wondered. She had spent years building her career—she didn't want to lose what she'd accomplished. True, she'd been restless lately, but restless enough to give up a lifetime's achievement?

''How's your new contract working out?'' she asked, inexplicably curious, somehow resentful of anyone else Finn drove rather than her.

''Great. The guy's pretty laid-back.''

Katelyn swallowed her reaction, relieved that his primary passenger wasn't female. "Hmm."

Finn hesitated, looked at her longingly, then bent to kiss her cheek. Katelyn shivered beneath the warmth of his lips. Instantly she wondered again if he'd shared her bed. Reaching out, she snagged his arm, intending to find out.

Chapter Seven

Finn glanced at the hand she placed on his arm, then met her gaze. Katelyn opened her mouth to ask.

And the sound of five ringing phones cut her off.

"Sounds like duty's calling," Finn told her ruefully. "And mine is, too. See you tonight, Katie."

"But…"

He gestured at the insistently ringing phone and smiled as he left.

"Can I answer the phone?" Jenny asked.

"I think I'd better." Katelyn glared at the multi-line phone. Great timing. The fax machine spit something at her as well.

She glanced around at the still-chaotic kitchen. The limit of her homemaking skills might only consist of menu planning and maintaining a well-organized list of cleaning companies and caterers, but there was no reason not to take advantage of those skills. Retrieving her day planner, Katelyn made a few calls, including one to a cleaning service.

"Hungry," one of the twins announced.

"You know, I am, too," Katelyn agreed. "What do you say to going out to eat?"

"For breakfast?" Jenny asked.

"Sure. It'll be fun." Inspiration struck. "I think McDonald's serves breakfast."

"McDonald's?" Jenny asked.

"McDonald's!" The twins chimed in excitement.

Jenny looked at her dubiously. "How are we going to get there?"

It was definitely time to have her car delivered. "We'll call a cab."

"To go to McDonald's?" Jenny asked in surprise.

"Absolutely. We'll arrive in style."

Jenny continued to stare at her.

Katelyn tried to appear as though she had everything under control. As though it was a normal, everyday thing to take a cab to McDonald's for breakfast. "Okay, you guys have to get dressed." The twins started scampering down from the table. "Hold it! I'll help you two."

Their room was still a disaster, with only the beds cleared. She'd told the cleaning company to send a crew of three. Looking around, she wondered if that would be enough. Actually, she could have let the twins dress themselves this one last time. She doubted they could destroy the room any further.

Erin and Eric pulled off their pajamas and were now scrabbling through clothes, each coming up with a wild combination.

Katelyn stared at the ill-matched outfits. "You probably should wear something else."

Their little faces dimmed.

Would it really be that awful to let them wear what they wanted? "You know, green-and-blue stripes don't really go with orange-and-pink flowers. But do we care?"

"No!" they shouted in unison.

Katelyn laughed. "I doubt the fashion police will be at McDonald's and if they are, we'll tell them we're making a conscious fashion statement—not to match."

Erin chose her red tennis shoes and yellow socks to complete the outfit and held them up for her approval.

Katelyn chuckled. "You two are going to look like little rainbows." She thought it sounded kinder than "clowns."

Eric grabbed his cowboy hat as well.

"Good choice," Katelyn told him. "Anyone gives you a hard time, you can ride off into the sunset."

He smiled toothily. This was the first time she'd definitely been able to tell them apart. That might have something to do with the fact that they'd shed their pajamas and she could see which one was the boy and which one was the girl. But she had to admit it didn't seem like a practical method for the majority of the time.

"Okay. You picked your clothes, now let's get them on, okay?"

It didn't take long to dress the twins, who were happy to put on their wild choices.

Jenny popped in, dressed rather messily in a pink shorts set. Her hair was wild and her lower lip trembled.

Katelyn took one look at her and knew there was a problem. "What's wrong, Jenny?"

"It won't *do!*"

"What won't do?"

"My hair." Her lower lip trembled even more. "I want braids."

Katelyn reached out to smooth the tangled hair. "I think we can do braids. Do you have barrettes in your room?"

The lip was still quivering, but not as wildly. "Uh-huh."

"Let's go to your room, then."

Katelyn glanced around the child's room and immediately saw that while Finn provided well for his children, it was in Jenny's room that she could most see the absence of a mother. The room was neat and efficient, but not very girlish. It cried out for lacy, feminine accessories—things a mother would be sure her daughter had. But then Jenny had been very young when her mother died. Her room was decorated in clowns, something she had grown out of.

"So you want braids?" Katelyn asked. "One long thick braid or two?"

Jenny considered. "One, I guess. But with a ribbon."

"Okay." Katelyn gently combed through Jenny's hair, carefully untangling it and smoothing it into a braid. It didn't take much time to make a long, thick braid and then fasten a ribbon to the shining dark hair, so much like Finn's.

"Do you know how to French fry braids?" Jenny asked, twisting her face in the mirror to examine her new hairdo.

Katelyn blinked, then coughed to cover her chuckle. "French braids? I think I could manage one next time."

"Cool," Jenny declared.

Lips still twitching, Katelyn then straightened Jenny's clothes, helping her find socks and shoes and making sure they, too, were put on correctly.

Although Jenny appeared to be an extremely self-sufficient child, Katelyn suspected she was crying out the most for a mother's attention. Katelyn guessed the twins demanded the majority of Finn's time and Jenny, by being the little mother, got the least attention.

With Jenny and the twins ready, Katelyn phoned for a cab, knowing it would take a while for a taxi to reach the suburbs. Glancing at her watch, she saw that the cleaning crew should arrive before the cab.

She'd given the cleaning company a run-down on the special projects—like reassembling the twins' room and reviving the flooded carpet. Now she jotted down a few more things, ending with a general "If it needs to be done, do it."

It didn't take long to get her troop together. The cleaning crew arrived plenty of time before the cab and Katelyn breathed a sigh of relief, knowing they could put things back to rights.

The jaunt to McDonald's was incredibly successful.

Katelyn had no appetite for a fast-food breakfast, but she was relieved that the kids had a meal that was edible and that she didn't have to cook.

Afterward they took another cab to her condo and retrieved her Jag. The kids weren't particularly impressed with the car—which impressed Katelyn. She'd forgotten about innocence. And clearly McDonald's had impressed them far more than her expensive car.

Then Katelyn decided to do the one thing she did best, other than her work. She took them shopping.

First, she purchased car seats for the twins. Then she bought practical, everyday clothes for herself and a new outfit for each of the children, adding a few frilly items for Jenny and her room. A ballerina lamp and matching jewelry box cried out to be taken home with them and Katelyn couldn't resist. The wheels clicked as she discovered that Jenny liked feminine furniture and canopy beds. It might be time for some redecorating.

Because she'd bought Jenny so much, Katelyn took them to the toy department and let the twins pick out some new toys, adding a doll for Jenny as well.

Then Katelyn headed for the gourmet shop, avoiding a regular grocery store, knowing all the food there had to be cooked. After filling a basket with delectable goodies, some of which didn't even require heating before serving, Katelyn realized she'd never truly appreciated the value of takeout. She now had enough food for lunch and dinner without a pan in sight.

Next they stopped at the bakery. Each of the kids picked a sweet while Katelyn chose a magnificent dessert and fragrant loaves of bread to serve with dinner. She might not be able to cook or bake, but she knew how to shop!

It was a pity she didn't know of a store that sold scrambled eggs. But she suspected the intelligence that had propelled her career could take her through the pitfalls of a home and kids as well.

Couldn't three-year-olds learn to enjoy croissants, Gouda and melon just as well as scrambled eggs?

FINN GINGERLY OPENED the front door, not quite sure what to expect. Instinctively, he believed Katelyn had the children's best interests at heart. But she wasn't in her element.

Still the living and dining rooms looked calm and clean, everything in place. Tentatively he approached the kitchen, wondering what the newest disasters might be.

Taking a deep breath, he pushed open the door. The room was empty. Miraculously, it was clean as well. Disbelieving, he opened the microwave oven and saw that even it sparkled. In fact, the entire kitchen gleamed. It was as though it had never been under assault. He hadn't imagined that Katelyn's talents included housekeeping. He had fully expected to spend the evening cleaning.

Now he wondered where Katelyn and the children were. The house was awfully quiet.

He felt a moment's pure panic. Had something happened? Had he entrusted his children to the wrong person?

On a dead run, he galloped up the stairs, frantically darting into every empty room. She said she desperately wanted to be a mother and then he'd handed her his children. Had she taken off with them?

He pounded down the stairs. Noticing that the drapes flanking the patio doors fluttered in the evening breeze, he walked closer, seeing that the doors were slightly ajar. Following that lead, he bolted outside and stopped dead in his tracks.

The patio was lit brightly, the torchère lights shining in the growing dusk. A multicolored tablecloth was draped over the plain patio table that was set for dinner. An interesting-looking array of food was also laid out. Quite a change from soggy eggs and burned cheese sandwiches.

Hearing the dog bark, Finn glanced around the yard and spotted Katelyn. She and the kids were jumping up and down on a trampoline as Snuffles circled them from beneath, barking. Where had a trampoline come from?

His gaze narrowed. Clean house, gourmet food, expensive toys—whipped up no doubt by Katelyn's credit cards. And he'd almost begun to think she was some sort of miracle woman. The only miracle was that he hadn't heard the nuclear fallout from her credit-card purchases all the way across town.

His jaw clenched, Finn guessed he was choking on his own envy. He had hoped to parlay his limo service into a lucrative business that would provide the same luxuries. Katelyn had simply beaten him to it.

Just then the children spotted him.

"Daddy!" they shrieked, still jumping up and down on the trampoline.

"Come jump, Daddy!" Jenny called out.

"Oh, no, I don't—"

"Daddy, *please!*" All three begged, their faces flushed with excitement.

"Just for a little while." Feeling more than a little awkward, he climbed up and joined them. Katelyn grinned as he began jumping.

The children giggled as they chorused out shouts of "Watch *me,* Daddy, watch *me!*"

He obliged, watching each one, making sure not to jump too forcefully and bounce them too high. Still, they all giggled and shrieked.

Katelyn continued grinning and Finn found it hard to resist all the combined hilarity.

As they shifted around the trampoline, Finn found himself facing Katelyn. He watched her long legs as she jumped easily. He remembered how they had looked in the thigh-high slit of the long evening gown she'd worn just a couple of nights ago. And also in her short, stunning skirts.

Though he knew it was only accelerating already frustrated desire, his gaze traveled upward, skimming the gentle curve of her hips, the narrow expanse of her waist, then landing on the tight, thin T-shirt. Her full breasts bounced with her every movement, the casual cotton coverup doing little to disguise them.

Throat suddenly dry, Finn knew he should stop looking, stop thinking....

Yet he didn't. And each thought ricocheted into another. Finally he jerked his gaze upward and met Katelyn's.

And looked straight into awareness.

Today her changeling eyes were blue. As he stared, her eyes darkened, taking on a mysterious hue.

He really hadn't thought this whole thing out.

"Daddy! Watch *me!*" Jenny demanded, momentarily tearing his attention away.

"And me!" Erin chimed in.

Eric, the sole male sibling, chose to jump higher instead.

Seeing a potential disaster, Finn reached out to calm his son's exuberance. A domino effect was set in motion as Eric backed into Katelyn, disrupting her balance and tipping her into Finn. Belatedly, he reached out to straighten them both. Jenny chose that moment to jump higher.

Katelyn and Finn crashed into each other. She landed first, on her back. Finn came down on top of her. At the last moment he put his arms out and avoided completely crushing her. But only one arm connected with the trampoline.

And his body connected with hers.

Sensations hit him with a near painful intensity—a pain born of incredible pleasure. His chest was pressed against hers and he felt her nipples harden against him. A flame flickered, licking between them. Then her shapely legs were trapped beneath his and it didn't take a lot of imagination to suppose how they would feel wrapped around him, the heat between them burning out of control.

Looking into her eyes, Finn saw the reflection of his own desire. Then around him, waves of giggles penetrated his fogged senses.

Jenny and the twins were rolling around the still heaving trampoline. He supposed, in their eyes, the fall was hilariously funny. Two adults downed by a three-year-old.

Then Katelyn held out her hand.

And left the choice up to him.

Chapter Eight

Finn finished the last of his dinner, not certain what he'd eaten, just relieved to be off the trampoline. Not that he was sure he was anywhere near solid ground yet.

Katelyn thumped her forehead suddenly. "I meant to buy your favorite beer today." She stared at him. "What *is* your favorite beer?"

"You have more important things to deal with," he said. "Remember, I've been a self-sufficient bachelor for quite a while."

Her face softened. "But I haven't been a wife before."

Finn reached for her hand. The phone rang stridently. Reluctantly, Finn rose to answer it.

"Hello. Yes, she's here."

He handed Katelyn the phone, recognizing it was another business call.

She listened for a while, then the unsettled Katelyn resurfaced. In moments, she was on her feet, briskly pacing the length of the room.

"Look, Daniel. Just tell them it *has* to be a video conference. Jump through hoops, promise them anything, but do it. I can't be in the office tomorrow, I told you that. And messenger over the Randall files. Tonight, of course—since the meeting's tomorrow." She clicked off the phone.

"You have a meeting tomorrow?" Finn asked.

"Yes." Distracted, she handed him an uncut pie she had purchased for dessert. "And I've got a lot of work to do to prepare." With her fingers, she ticked off items. "I didn't even check my e-mail today, I've got a stack of faxes to catch up on, and I need to sketch out some new ideas for the Randall campaign. Not to mention going over their files as soon as they get here."

"Good thing today went so well, then," he commented innocently, thinking of her credit-card extravaganza.

Katelyn's head shot up, a trace of the old fire lurking in her expression. "Yes, it is." Then the fire faded, replaced by concern. "The kids have to be bathed, and put to bed." Quickly she rose and called the children. "When I get done I'll run a hot bath for you as well."

From siren to 1950s wife to mother to career woman and back. At this rate she was liable to be a victim of spontaneous combustion. He wondered what kept pushing her buttons.

He wasn't sure why any man wanted a woman who hovered. It gave him the distinctly uncomfortable feeling that his mother was looking over his shoulder. He half expected Katelyn to offer him warm milk next.

Still, as he watched her walk away, Finn noticed the gentle sway to her lithesome curves. And that caused discomfort of another sort. He sighed. But Katelyn had just told him she needed to spend the evening working. And that wasn't at all what he had been hoping for.

KATELYN CURLED UP with the Randall files and a diet soda. It had taken her hours to sift through her faxes and e-mail. And that was after bath and story time with the kids. Plus a little extra time with Jenny, brushing her hair, helping her try out the new barrettes, distributing the new items around her room. Finn had repeatedly offered to help, but Katelyn was determined to become a good mother.

Katelyn rubbed at tired eyes. How did women manage this day after day, balancing their careers and families? Two days, and she was exhausted. And today she hadn't devoted a fraction of the time she should have to the Randall campaign.

Still, her attention kept wandering.

To the empty side of the bed.

Where was Finn? And why hadn't he come to bed? She glanced at the folder in her hands. Could he be working overtime, too? But what kind of overtime did drivers put in?

Katelyn shook her head. She didn't need to be thinking about Finn's work—she needed to be thinking about her own. She wanted a fresh, new idea for the Randall television commercials. So far all she'd done is recycle stale ones that wouldn't excite someone who hadn't watched television in years.

Yet, her eyes slid toward the other side of the bed again. Where *was* he?

She fiddled with her papers for a few more minutes, then threw the folder down on the nightstand. Telling herself she needed a refill, she grabbed her nearly full glass of diet soda and headed downstairs. The living room was empty, as were the kitchen and den. She glanced outside, but the patio was unoccupied as well. Where could he be?

Katelyn mentally searched through the house's floor plan, rethinking the rooms she'd just walked through. The bedrooms were upstairs....

She paused. She hadn't really been through the entire upper floor. Retracing her steps, she headed back upstairs, passing the master bedroom and the children's rooms. Then she spotted a narrow wedge of light in the hall. Another room?

Walking quietly, she approached. The door was slightly ajar and Katelyn pushed it open a little more. She didn't know what to expect, but a study was the last thing she would have thought of.

However, from the desk, file cabinet and fax machine, it was clearly a home-office setup. She was surprised he needed one. She was even more surprised to see Finn stretched out on a lumpy-looking couch. But surprise quickly turned to disappointment as she realized Finn was asleep. Then she thought of the Randall files still in the bedroom waiting for her. She retraced her steps toward the master bedroom, reluctantly reaching for her work files, then tossing them down as quickly.

Katelyn paced in front of the oversized dresser. Did married women act differently than single ones? And how *was* that? Was she sending the wrong signals? She wiped nervous palms against her nightgown.

Belatedly, she glanced down at the practical garment. Should she have chosen something nicer? More alluring? The plain white cotton was both practical and comfortable. It occurred to her that those might not be the qualities she should have chosen since she was no longer sleeping alone.

She hadn't had time to unpack the things which had been sent over, but she doubted they contained anything more feminine. With a sigh, Katelyn stopped pacing, forcing herself to concentrate on the Randall presentation.

A LITTLE WHILE later the bedroom door pushed open and Katelyn forgot about her work. Finn dominated the room, seeming to fill it just by entering the doorway. Katelyn felt her mouth dry.

"I didn't realize I was so bushed. I sacked out on the couch and before I knew it, half the night was gone," he apologized.

Katelyn couldn't seem to tear her eyes from him. "What woke you up?"

"Snuffles. He reminded me I hadn't taken him for a walk."

"Oh," she replied quietly, thinking Finn looked even sexier when slightly rumpled. His thick dark hair was disheveled just enough to lend a slightly dangerous air. And his incredible blue eyes had darkened, seeming to match the languid mood of the night.

She watched as those eyes scanned the room, finally landing on the bed. "So," he said at last.

"So," she replied.

"You said you were tired...."

Katelyn attempted a smile. "I am...was..."

He clasped his hands together. Katelyn realized that they seemed larger and more muscular than she'd noticed before. *He* seemed larger and more muscular. All over.

And terribly, overwhelmingly male.

Finn grabbed a robe. "You're still working. I'll go take a shower."

Before she could protest, he headed across the room. Katelyn couldn't stop staring as Finn disappeared into the bathroom. Slim hipped, long legs encased in jeans, he made quite a silhouette. She felt her fatigue disappearing. Glaring balefully at the stack of files, she cursed the blasted things.

Soon, Katelyn saw steam escaping from the bathroom. Steam that continued for a lengthy time. Katelyn's nervousness escalated as the time passed.

When Finn emerged, she drew herself into a nervous ball. The opening of his terry robe revealed a hint of dark hair. Then he pulled the robe off and Katelyn drew in her breath. Clad only in boxers, she saw the body his clothes had hinted at.

Dark hair swirled over a chest full of muscles. His lean torso tapered into rigid abs that could have sold thousands of exercise machines. Muscular arms and long, equally muscled legs were worthy of body-builder status. Katelyn tried to remember that other qualities were more important, but at the moment she couldn't remember what any of those qualities might be.

A handsome face, she guessed, zeroing in on Finn's. She doubted that was it, but when she met his eyes, she realized she didn't care. Perhaps this was why she'd so impulsively suggested marriage. Had the sheer force of his looks made her forget everything else that used to matter? For the first time she could understand why.

He shoved a hand through damp hair, glancing at the piles of paper still surrounding her. "Do you still have a lot of work?"

Katelyn swallowed the excruciating dryness in her throat. "I can put it away for the night."

Finn's gaze locked on hers. "Good."

Hastily Katelyn shoved the files onto the nightstand, not particularly caring if they slid out of order, or if they disappeared entirely.

The mattress dipped beneath Finn's weight as he joined her on the bed.

Up close, Katelyn could see the lines around his eyes that spoke of frequent smiles. How had she initially missed that? She had been so quick to dismiss him because he wasn't a corporate player. She had failed to acknowledge that he was a rare breed—someone sure of himself—both in who he was and the choices he made. She had thought it was cockiness. Now she recognized the confidence, not born of arrogance but of strength.

She had underestimated the worth of a man who valued family and fidelity. And she had certainly underestimated the extent of his appeal.

But now every cell of her blood acknowledged the stirring. Especially when she looked in his eyes. Although darkened with seeds of passion, she recognized depth, that incredibly appealing confidence. Strength of body, mind and character was an intoxicating aphrodisiac.

Finn tilted his head, his lips sinking against hers. Again, the heat began. Not a slow growing warmth, but rather an explosion of scorching waves.

Katelyn realized the wonder of their first kiss had not been an overexaggerated memory. No wonder she had leaped into marriage.

Finn's hand cupped the back of her neck and the anticipation accelerated. Sighing, Katelyn reached for Finn's shoulders.

"Daddy!" Jenny's wail pierced the air, accompanied by pounding on the door.

Reluctantly they parted.

Finn's eyes conveyed frustrated regret. "Sorry."

Katelyn scrambled for composure. "No, it's okay." Yet as he headed for the bedroom door, she rubbed her lips, feeling bereft without his touch. But she couldn't fault Jenny. Clearly, the child was upset.

"Daddy, Erin's having a bad dream."

Finn sighed. "Okay, honey, I'll go see about her."

Jenny tugged at his hand. "She's in my room."

Finn ploughed a hand through already tousled hair. "Why is she in your room?"

"Your door was shut so she got in my bed. And now she's crying!"

Katelyn stared between them. "Can I help?"

Finn shook his head. "I'll take care of them." Then his eyes met hers. "It usually takes a while. Sometimes the dreams are contagious." His gaze landed pointedly on Jenny. More regret colored his expression. "So you'd better not wait up for me."

With a last longing glance, Finn left, Jenny's hand grasped firmly in his.

Katelyn looked at her empty bed. Marriage and motherhood were proving more complicated than she had expected. Certainly in more ways than she had anticipated.

KATELYN AWOKE, groggy and disoriented. She tried to turn over and found her body weighted down. It felt like a twenty-pound sack of...she opened one eye...*arm.*

Last night came back in a flash. Those first awkward moments when Finn had come to bed...her frustration...then the hours trying to fall asleep. And now... Apparently she *had* eventually fallen asleep—with Finn's arm trapping her almost beneath him.

Ridiculously, she felt a warm burn begin in her cheeks. This was normal, she guessed. Now all of her mornings would begin this way—sharing a bed with her husband. Somewhere in the back of her brain, something seemed to click on. A husband...someone to devote herself to, to lavish attention upon.

Finn stretched. And opened his eyes.

Katelyn blinked, looking into their blue depths.

Finn moved his arm. And realized where it was. And just what he was touching.

Chapter Nine

Katelyn's soft breasts were just beneath him, taunting his arm, beckoning his hands closer. Oh, God. What exquisite torture.

Leaning forward, Finn kissed Katelyn's nose. Then his lips traveled south, finally breaking away so that he could meet her gaze. "Morning."

She reached up to stroke his jaw. "Morning, yourself."

Finn smoothed one hand over the stubble on his chin, glanced at the clock and groaned. "I should have left twenty minutes ago. My timing stinks."

Katelyn acknowledged his regret, feeling her own. "I have a meeting, too, and you don't want to be late."

Stealing one last kiss, Finn grabbed his robe before escaping to the bathroom.

Katelyn stared after him at the closing door. "Welcome to married life, Mrs. Malloy."

KATELYN DRESSED in a bright coral suit, softening it with the ivory chiffon blouse she'd bought shortly before her marriage.

Marriage. It still seemed so unreal.

Yawning, she wished she'd gotten more sleep the previous night. Today was an important meeting and her first video conference. She wanted to get things off on the right foot.

Pushing open the door to the kitchen, she tried to re-member if she'd bought enough Egg McMuffins to last through today. If not, Daniel would find himself making a McDonald's breakfast run.

Breakfast fled from her mind as she stared in horror at the kitchen that had been spotless the night before. The twins sat in the middle of the floor, surrounded by mounds and mounds of white. The dog wandered between the piles, his dark coat now dusty white.

Katelyn blinked, not trusting her vision. It looked as though it had snowed in the middle of the kitchen. Fairly unlikely in Houston. As she walked closer, she realized the white stuff was flour and sugar. All the canisters were up-ended. And the trail began somewhere near the pantry.

Along with a corresponding trail of apple juice. The flour was congealing at a rapid rate and sugar was dissolving nearly as fast.

"Eric! Erin! What have you done?"

They squealed happily in response, plastering each other with the gooey mixture. Bending closer to look at them, she realized they were already covered in the goop. Erin smiled and reached for her skirt.

Before Katelyn could dodge the sticky little fingers, her skirt had a new design—white handprints. Briefly closing her eyes, she realized the coral suit might not have been the best choice, considering the twins.

What were they doing unsupervised in the kitchen?

She had assumed that Finn would keep them contained while she dressed. He must have assumed she was doing the same thing since he had to leave in a rush. And the twins were taking full advantage of their crossed wires.

Katelyn glanced at her watch. The twins were up at about the right time—but she'd taken time to dress. Apparently leaving them unsupervised for even a few minutes wasn't wise. She stared in dismay at the terrible mess. No, not wise at all.

Katelyn groaned. She had a meeting in less than thirty minutes. So much for getting off on the right foot.

Jenny trailed into the kitchen, yawning and dragging the doll Katelyn had bought her. "Where is everybody?" she grumbled. "I can't find Daddy."

"He's already left for work," Katelyn explained, unable to pull her gaze from the mess on the floor. She felt the knot in her stomach growing. She'd planned to spend the time before the meeting going over the client's files, not grappling with breakfast and...a ton of goop in the middle of the floor.

Katelyn glanced down at her once-immaculate suit. She could hardly tackle either without ruining her appearance and her meeting was a *video* conference. Her skirt would be out of sight under the desk, but her jacket and blouse would be in full view.

"Oh." Jenny stared at the twins and the mess they'd made. Then she turned to Katelyn, with all the philosophical casualness of a child. "What's for breakfast?"

The doorbell rang unexpectedly. Not pleased with the interruption, Katelyn wasn't smiling as she opened the door. But her expression changed when she saw that it was Daniel.

Immediately, she pulled him inside. "I was wondering when you would get around to visiting."

Daniel glanced around cautiously. "Is this a good time? Or am I interrupting?"

"Your timing's perfect. Finn has an early morning and I have that video conference. Tell me you're here to help."

"Depends. What do I have to do?"

She smiled hopefully. "Just keep the kids out of my hair until I get through the meeting."

Resigned, Daniel nodded. "Don't get me wrong. I like kids, but in small doses."

"You big faker. You're practically the Pied Piper to half the kids in your Big Brother group."

He waved away her words. "If you want my help you'd better have coffee."

"It's even hot!"

"Already the gourmet cook, Katelyn?" But he smiled to take the sting from the words. "Good. I haven't had my quota of coffee today."

Katelyn grinned, enormously pleased to have some contact with the outside world. "Have two cups, maybe three. It won't kill you to let loose once in a while. You're too hard on yourself."

He lifted his brows skeptically. "Um."

They entered the kitchen and Katelyn poured the coffee.

Daniel followed more slowly, picking through the chaos. "Rough morning?"

Her gaze followed his. "Something like that."

As she turned around, Daniel placed a gift-wrapped package on the counter.

"What's that?"

"Your wedding gift," he replied accepting a mug of coffee.

"You didn't have to do that." Yet, she was pleased. By skipping the traditional wedding service, she had also missed the fun of showers. Ignoring her coffee, Katelyn ripped into the delicate white and silver wrapping to reveal a compact stereo. "This is great!"

"I was worried that you might not be keeping up your campaign to stop smoking, so I combined sentiment with practicality."

"It has been difficult the last few days," she admitted. "I guess it's the stress of adjusting to a new situation."

"Well, now you have no excuse to put off listening to

your tapes,'' Daniel replied. ''This model is smaller than the one you had at the condo, so it can fit on your bedside table. But just like the larger model, you can program it to turn on automatically every night while you sleep. That way you won't have to take time out during your busy day to listen. And it comes with an earplug so you won't disturb Finn.''

''Sounds like a good idea,'' she agreed. ''I'll have to get around to reading the instructions so I can set the timer.''

''Setup is included with the wedding gift,'' Daniel improvised. ''Just head me toward the bedroom. In fact, I even brought along the tape.''

Her expression softened. ''You're so thoughtful. You know I miss having you boss me around all the time.''

''Oh, I don't plan to give up on that,'' he replied with a smile. ''Now, which direction is the bedroom?''

''Upstairs. First door on the right. But you don't have to do it right now.''

He gave her a stern look. ''You know it makes me crazy to procrastinate. Besides, I want you to enjoy my gift and this way I can be certain you will.'' He glanced at his watch. ''And I have time before the conference.''

''You really are a treasure,'' she said with an affectionate smile. ''I could find the biscotti while you're setting up the stereo.''

''Now that's an offer I won't refuse. Almond?''

''Of course. Instinctively I stocked your favorite. I was hoping you'd be coming by soon.''

Daniel's expression relaxed a bit. ''We're like a bad habit—hard to break.''

''Don't get all mushy on me,'' she retorted wryly. ''You know I would be lost without you—as a co-worker and a friend.''

This time his expression softened unexpectedly. ''You

too, Katelyn.'' Then he turned before the emotion got the better of him, heading back toward the stairs.

Watching him as he retreated, Katelyn realized she was lucky to have him for a friend. At least with Daniel everything was up-front—no hidden agendas. And that was a relief.

Her gaze drifted toward the unfed children and the disaster lurking in the kitchen. Mentally, she lined up her morning calls—knowing she would start with the cleaning company. Then she glanced toward the stairs. She had more in store for him than he realized.

FINN HEARD the phones ringing as he entered the house late that afternoon. It was a wonder they didn't drive Katelyn bonkers.

He walked by the alcove she'd made into her office. Shaking his head, he glanced at her desk—was that a crayon drawing taped to the computer screen?

Even stranger, at lunchtime he'd seen Katelyn conducting a video conference, with Jenny in her lap, brushing her hair, fastening her barrettes. But she didn't seem concerned about what it would do to her image.

Who'd have ever thought? It was still hard to believe she was the same woman who had once given barracudas a bad name. She seemed as determined to become the perfect wife and mother as she once had been to rise to the top of her profession.

Jenny staggered through the kitchen door, lugging a basket that was clearly too big for her.

''Whoa.'' Finn lifted the heavy basket from her. ''What'cha got there?''

''We're going on a picnic, Daddy. Just as soon as you got home. I'm glad you gotted home.''

''Me, too. What's this about a picnic?''

The kitchen door swung open again. ''Jenny, that's too

heavy..." Katelyn's words trailed off as she saw that Finn had taken the basket. She smiled. "We thought a picnic might be a nice change. The kids have cabin fever."

He glanced at her, seeing lines of fatigue. "They the only ones?"

"It has been a busy day." She glanced at the still ringing phones. "I just put them on the service. And Daniel's alerted. He knows he can reach me on my cell phone." She pushed her hair off her forehead. "But I warned him not to call unless it's critical."

"So where are we having this picnic?" Finn asked.

"I thought at a park," she answered.

"Any one in particular?"

Katelyn frowned. "Isn't there one close by?"

Somehow he doubted she planned her business with the same lack of foresight. "Not too far. Do we need anything besides this basket?"

Katelyn searched her mind. She'd had Daniel messenger over the picnic basket. What else was necessary? "I don't think so."

"What about the cold drinks?" Finn asked.

She frowned again. "I didn't think about that."

"It's okay. After I change clothes, I'll grab the cooler and we can stop on the way for ice and drinks."

Katelyn brightened. "Excellent. But everything else is in the basket." She'd been explicit—a supper basket for five people. And she needed this break. Trying to be wife, mother and executive was exhausting. Between juggling work, the kids' needs, and her attention to Finn she wanted nothing more than to escape.

Katelyn was surprised when Finn drove the limo, but then it occurred to her that it was his only vehicle—and her Jag would be crowded with the five of them.

It seemed rather elegant to arrive in the park in the impressive car. For a moment she imagined the same scenario, minus the children. It would be a romantic moment. She glanced back at the three endearing faces. But this would be fun—of a different variety.

The kids piled out of the car, spotting swings and slides. Since she was close enough to keep an eye on them, Katelyn didn't protest.

Finn shouldered both the heavy basket and cooler and she enjoyed watching the play of his muscles in the short-sleeved shirt he'd chosen to wear. His long legs were bared by shorts as well. Katelyn sucked in her breath, again realizing what an impressive-looking man he was.

He turned back just then. "This table okay?"

It looked like all the others to her, but she nodded. "Fine."

They let the kids run off most of their energy before deciding to eat. While Finn collected the children, Katelyn opened the basket, taking out the tablecloth on the top. She smoothed it over the table, then found plates and silverware. The table was set when Finn and the children returned.

As the kids scrambled up on the benches, Katelyn began unpacking the food, the kids watching eagerly. Crusty baguettes, pickled quail eggs, artichokes, Brie.

Katelyn continued to unpack the basket, catching the disbelieving look on Finn's face. It occurred to her suddenly, a jar of caviar in hand, that this wasn't exactly kid-friendly food. She kept digging into the basket, coming up with a stick of highly spiced salami, sharp, dry cheese, green-peppered mustard, truffles, rum balls, and amaretto cheesecake. Reaching the bottom, she held up a bottle of wine, feeling like an idiot. "Excellent year."

Finn looked at the exotic array of food and didn't comment.

"How come the eggs are in this?" Erin asked, poking at the jar.

"It's a fun way to have eggs," Katelyn improvised, desperately hoping the novelty would appeal to the kids. Twisting the jar open, she placed an egg on each of their plates.

"How come they're so little?" Eric asked, picking up the small quail egg.

"It smells funny," Jenny contributed.

"They're pickled," Katelyn explained. Gamely, she picked one up and popped it into her mouth. She enjoyed the piquant burst of flavor, but then she'd had years to acquire such tastes.

Always braver than his twin, Eric followed her example, his little face twisting at the unfamiliar taste. "Doesn't taste like eggs," he announced.

Jenny and Erin still stared at theirs. Katelyn quickly broke off chunks of bread. What she wouldn't give for a jar of peanut butter....

Finn reached for the Brie. "Umm, my favorite."

Jenny looked at her father. "What is it?"

"Cheese—*really* good cheese."

Katelyn glanced at him gratefully, knowing the children thought anything he did was wonderful. The Brie *was* mild. Maybe... She handed him a knife and he spread the soft cheese on Jenny's bread.

She tasted it carefully. "It's okay."

That was enough for Erin who accepted a piece of bread and cheese.

Eric climbed up farther on the table, examining the row of other foods. He pointed to the jar of caviar. "I want some of that."

Katelyn realized the expensive roe looked much like the jelly she used to make their peanut-butter-and-jelly sandwiches. "I don't think this tastes like what you think it does."

Eric set his jaw in a stubborn line, placing his small hands on the table. "Want some of *that,*" he insisted.

"But it—"

"Let him have some," Finn's amused voice broke in. "Then he'll know just what it *does* taste like. Trust me, it'll be worth the cost."

Eric enthusiastically dug into the jar. Katelyn tried not to think of the caviar's price as it dripped from his spoon. But Finn was right. Watching Eric was priceless. If she had thought he'd made a face with the pickled egg, this expression was light years funnier.

As soon as the salty, fishy taste registered, his face screwed up while he shook his head from side to side in an automatic response. Before they realized his intent, Eric spit out the offending caviar, spewing it on his sisters, who immediately squealed in protest.

"You'll live," Finn told them between bursts of laughter.

Jenny and Erin looked as though they had matching cases of black measles and they huffed as they stared at their father.

Although Katelyn was equally amused, she reached out with a linen napkin to clean their faces. "Men just don't understand that ladies want to look pretty all the time."

Eric wiped his mouth with the back of his hand. "Yuck!"

Katelyn wasn't sure if that was a commentary on the caviar or her remark. "I told you you wouldn't like it," she reminded him. "Maybe your father could give you some bread and cheese."

But Eric still stared at the row of intriguing jars. "Uh-uh."

Finn picked up the jar of artichokes and opened them. "You might like this."

But, after only thirty minutes, Katelyn could see that the

children were still hungry. Although they'd survived well for the past week on takeout, combined with delivered Chinese and pizza, she knew the picnic basket had been a bust.

Finn stood up, withdrawing the car keys. "Can you keep an eye on the kids for a little while?"

"Sure, but—"

"I'll be back in a few minutes."

The kids stared at her and she stared back. As she'd been learning all week, there was far more to this mother business than she'd realized.

True to his word, Finn returned quickly, his hands full of paper sacks. When he withdrew hot dogs and buns, the kids hooted with excitement.

He also had some wire hangers in one sack. "I always keep a few extras in the trunk—you never know what a client will bring along that might need to be hung up." He untwisted one and fashioned it into a roasting stick.

Watching him, Katelyn rather awkwardly duplicated Finn's efforts while he put the charcoal he'd bought into one of the park's concrete pits. Although it took her longer than Finn, she untwisted two more hangers. When the children each had a roasting stick they jumped up and down in excitement.

"You mustn't run with the sticks," Katelyn warned them, remembering she'd heard that somewhere. That and something about putting out an eye. She slid hot dogs on each of their converted hangers. "Okay?"

They nodded their heads solemnly.

Finn motioned them over and all three poised to run.

Katelyn halted them. "Remember! Walk, don't run."

They all walked in stiff-legged imitation of speed walkers, just keeping from breaking into full-fledged running. She saw Finn's grin and suspected he guessed the instructions she'd given.

His quick save for dinner was an unqualified success,

especially when the bottom of the grocery bag revealed marshmallows and the rest of the makings for s'mores.

Coated in marshmallow and chocolate, Jenny licked her lips as she looked up at Katelyn. "Ummm. I like your ideas."

She glanced ruefully at Finn. "But I didn't do so good with dinner. Luckily your father saved the day."

"But you're fun," Jenny insisted. Ever since Katelyn had bought her the feminine things, Jenny had opened up to her more and more.

"Thanks, I think you're fun, too."

Jenny licked at her gooey dessert. "You're different than our other baby-sitters."

Katelyn cocked her head, wondering how to explain just how different a stepmother was from a baby-sitter.

"Yeah, different," Erin agreed.

"Uh-huh," Jenny added, taking one of the last bites of her dessert. "The other baby-sitters didn't sleep with Daddy."

Katelyn choked on her own s'more, the graham cracker suddenly feeling like a two-by-four in her mouth.

Finn was glad he'd swallowed the last of his own dessert, considering he thought he might choke on his own tongue. Kids might say the darnedest things, but...

"Jenny, I don't think that's something we discuss over dinner," he tried.

"How come?" she asked, licking at her fingers, determined not to miss a drop of chocolate.

"Well, because..." He stared helplessly at Katelyn, the heat between them he'd managed to push into the background, demanding to be brought front and center.

"Because I'm not just a baby-sitter," Katelyn attempted, knowing one of them had to explain. She saw the doubt on Finn's face, but plunged on. "Your father and I are married. Do you know what that makes me?"

Three heads shook from side to side.

"It means that I'm your stepmother now."

Jenny stared at her father, then at Katelyn. "Really?"

"Of course," Katelyn assured her. "That's not something we'd tease you about." She kept her face in a proper motherly expression, but a telltale trace of red betrayed her. "That's why it's all right that your father and I sleep together."

Finn looked at his children. "I told you we got married when you met Katelyn. Don't you remember?"

"You didn't say she was our new mother," Jenny pointed out.

He cleared his throat. "Why don't you guys finish your s'mores. It's getting late."

"Can't we swing more?" Jenny pleaded.

"Five minutes—but that's all."

The kids didn't need any more encouragement, running toward the swings as soon as the words were out of Finn's mouth.

"Why did you send the kids away?" Katelyn asked quietly, having noticed his discomfort. It had been impossible to miss.

"Katelyn, we haven't discussed our future—more to the point…yours. I don't want to build up the kids' hopes. They know we're married, but I didn't want to emphasize your role as their mother in case…" He met her eyes. "In case you decide not to stay."

Her jaw jutted out in signature defiance. "We said we'd see how things go."

"And I also offered you an annulment, no hard feelings."

"No hard feelings? Is this a marriage or a poker game?" Pride, her worst failing, flared. He acted as though she considered this a lark. Her chin lifted along with her determination. She wouldn't admit defeat if the house fell in on them. ''It sounds like you're the one who wants the annulment.''

''I didn't say that,'' he protested.

''No, but you act like it,'' she retorted.

His eyes narrowed. ''What's that supposed to mean?''

The art of the deal roared through her veins and it was time to swoop in for the kill. ''We haven't consummated our marriage yet.''

''And you think that's because I want an annulment?''

''Isn't it?'' she retaliated, unable to back down.

Iced fury settled in his eyes. ''No. But until we decide whether this will work, I think we should keep things status quo.''

''Fine!' she retorted.

''Fine!'' he echoed.

The humid air throbbed with tension, but Katelyn's pride refused to relent. Clearly Finn's pride was equally strong.

Yet, she was unable to let him have the last word. ''So, you're suggesting a marriage of convenience? That would meet my needs.''

''If that's what you want,'' he responded evenly.

''I wanted marriage and children…''

''Then this is especially convenient for you—no nasty emotional attachments. And I get a baby-sitter.''

Her head jerked up, her eyes blazing. Was he being truthful or just pushing her buttons? Unable to decide, she nodded stiffly. ''Then we'll both have what we want.''

His eyes connected with hers once more and what she saw there made her shiver. As the children ran back to join them, Katelyn realized that for once her forceful nature might not win. Belatedly, she also realized she had just forced them into an impossible standoff.

Chapter Ten

What a morning. Finn had left in silence and the kids had already spilled grape juice all over the kitchen.

The doorbell rang. *What now?*

Wiping purple-stained hands on a dishtowel, Katelyn yanked open the door, prepared to rip into whoever stood there. "Stefanie!" Delighted, Katelyn pulled her friend inside. "What are you doing here?"

"I could ask you the same question. I had to practically shove bamboo under Daniel's fingernails to find out where you were hiding." Stefanie glanced around. "This is a charming slice of suburbia, but what are you doing in it?"

Katelyn laughed, delighted with her friend's candor. "I thought you were the one pushing me in this direction."

Stefanie pulled her sunglasses down a fraction as she glanced around the typical home. "Did you have to go so *middle class,* darling?"

Katelyn smiled wryly. "You didn't specify when you kept pointing out that the hands of my biological clock were spinning."

"True." Stefanie glanced again at the suburban home. "I thought that was a given."

Jenny peeked from around the dining room corner and Katelyn hoped she hadn't heard Stefanie's remark. "I love you, Stef, but don't be a snob."

"Ah...so that's how it is." Stefanie raised one brow. "Tell me, why didn't I know you'd fallen in love with this man?"

Katelyn glanced again at Jenny. "Later. Right now, I want you to meet Finn's kids. This one, hovering in the doorway, is Jenny."

Jenny walked forward reluctantly, staring at Stefanie, who was outfitted in a wild leopard-print suit with matching hat, purse and shoes.

Katelyn looked between the child and her friend and could see why Jenny was intimidated. "Can you say hello to Stefanie?"

"Sure she can," Stefanie answered for her. "Hey, kid. So, you into Barbie or Barney?"

Katelyn stared at her friend in surprise.

Stefanie shrugged. "I've got nieces and nephews coming out of my ears." She shook her head. "Now that's quite an image. You learn the lingo or they plow you down like *that*." She snapped her fingers. "Right, Jenny?"

Jenny grinned, obviously liking this exotic woman.

"And I bet you know where they keep the coffee," Stefanie continued, directing her words to Jenny.

"Uh-huh. I'll show you."

"And then you could take the twins to the TV room for cartoons," Katelyn suggested, wanting a few moments alone with her friend.

Jenny looked between them. "Okay. Can we have some candy?"

"Nice try," Katelyn responded. "Even I know it's not for breakfast."

Jenny shrugged philosophically and disappeared.

"Nice save," Stefanie commented.

"I try." Katelyn glanced across the kitchen bar at Stefanie who was practically inhaling her coffee. "Would you like some more?"

"At least a gallon." She yawned. "Or we could just inject the caffeine intravenously. I might wake up sooner."

Katelyn refilled Stefanie's mug and pushed it across the counter. Then she picked up a mug of her own, thinking of the disastrous ending to their picnic. A week had gone by and they were still at an impasse. Why in the world had she pushed them into a situation of no return?

"Earth to Katelyn," she heard her friend say. "Hey! I thought I was the one with the morning grogginess. You looked like you were... I don't know...channeling?"

Katelyn laughed. "Hardly. If I was going out of my body, I'd have thought of someplace more exciting to visit."

Stefanie glanced around the sunny kitchen. "I thought you were in love with suburbia."

Katelyn laughed. "That's not it. It's...well..." She exchanged a frank look with her friend. "There's just no break from it. I know I said I never wanted to get married or have children, but now I can see what I was missing." She lowered her cup, thinking of Finn, wondering if he regretted their situation.

"What do you mean—no break?" Stefanie asked.

"Just that—the children are here twenty-four hours a day. I'm learning how to juggle the kids and my work, but still..."

Stefanie stared at her in disbelief. "Don't tell me you haven't made arrangements yet?"

"What kind of arrangements?"

"Preschool, mother's day out, baby-sitters..."

Katelyn shook her head. "They've had nothing but baby-sitters since their mother died—that's not an option."

"Not full-time, you goon. Just when you—or you and Finn—want to go out. That hardly warps kids."

"I guess not...."

"And I take it you haven't signed them up for preschool?"

Katelyn stared at her friend, her eyes lighting up. "You mean there's school *before* school?"

Stefanie laughed. "That's one way of putting it. Preschool is for younger kids. Sort of a school to get them ready for real school. All kids go now. In fact, it puts them at a disadvantage if they don't go."

Katelyn looked at her skeptically. "Really?"

"Hey! Would I make this up?" She tossed her head, allowing her perfectly cut hair to settle attractively. "Okay, so I would. But, I'm not. I learned all this from my prolific siblings. Kids who don't go to preschool or daycare are behind other kids their age—mostly in social situations."

"You make it sound like they're going to a country club instead of kindergarten."

Stefanie waggled her brows. "It might as well be. If they don't learn how to interact with other kids by the time they get to school, they're helplessly behind."

Katelyn brightened. "Really?"

"Hey, there are people who put their kids' names on lists to get them into the 'best' preschools before they're even born."

Katelyn's face fell. "Then I don't have a chance of getting them in."

"Of course you do, unless you insist on the Harvard of preschools." She took another healthy swig of coffee. "Although, with a little more caffeine, I might even be convinced to go to battle with one of them." She smiled. "The average preschool should have plenty of openings. I'll get a list for you from one of my prolific siblings."

Katelyn gripped her own mug. "So, how long do they go to preschool?"

"Until real school starts." Stefanie glanced up from inhaling her caffeine. "Oh, you mean every day. Usually three or four hours."

"Three or four hours to myself." Katelyn stared at the T-shirt and jeans that had replaced her coral suit—a suit that was indelibly stained by grape jelly.

A week ago she had insisted on dressing for her video-conference meetings. Now she was thrilled simply to keep the kids entertained for the duration of the meeting. But if they were at preschool a few hours a day…

"And don't forget about the baby-sitters, either," Stefanie advised. "You and Finn need time for yourselves without the urchins." She held up a hand at the anticipated protest. "Nothing personal—I actually like your little curtain climbers, but you two have to have a little time alone to keep the fire burning. Nothing worse than a gutted blaze."

"You do have a way with words," Katelyn replied. "I'll try to make sure we don't gut ourselves."

"So…Katelyn. Am I finally going to get the details on Finn…your elopement…this hot romance?"

Katelyn smiled, using the mask she'd perfected in hundreds of corporate meetings. "Details, huh?"

She called on the same creativity that had taken her up the ladder. *Details.* God, she wished she remembered them.

FINN CREPT QUIETLY into the bedroom. He had left his planner on the dresser when he had changed clothes that afternoon. He needed it to complete his billing. He had taken to sleeping in the study since their confrontation. There hadn't much point in sharing a bed.

His glance strayed toward that very bed. Unable to stop himself, Finn stared at Katelyn's still form. Although a light cotton blanket covered her legs, he could still picture them—long, lean, beckoning. Her pristine gown more than hinted at her generous curves.

If he moved closer, he could almost feel the softness of her skin. As if of their own accord, his feet moved forward. Her pale skin, without makeup, was dusted with just a dash of freckles, her mouth free of lipstick, still the color of rose.

And her reddish-gold hair fanned out across the pillow. His pillow.

Finn's throat was suddenly dry. He could take a few steps closer. Accept the invitation he had once seen in Katelyn's eyes earlier.

Reaching out, he almost touched her cheek.

He remembered the tenuous nature of their relationship and he drew his hand back. But would it be so wrong? Perhaps she was ready for more from their relationship, too…

Finn whirled around.

He had never begged a woman, and he didn't plan to start now. Katelyn had what she wanted from this marriage—an instant family without the messy complications of love.

Remembering the intense bond two people could share, Finn felt a sharp pang of regret. But then he had never expected to find that again.

Involuntarily, his gaze wandered back to the woman who shared his house, but not his life. Who was she? The corporate shark or Carol Brady? Or was the real Katelyn someone in between?

Abruptly turning around, Finn vacated the bedroom, knowing he would find no answers, only more questions. Lost in thought, he closed the door behind him, the planner forgotten.

KATELYN PACKED the kids in her car, firmly putting the dog back in the yard, realizing the Jag really wasn't very practical with all the extra little bodies. But nothing would deter her this morning. Having checked on nearby preschools, she was armed with an address and determination. She had been told this preschool was practically guaranteed to have available space.

Katelyn knew that if she intended to maintain her career, she simply had to find time to attend meetings.

Spotting the preschool, Katelyn felt a sudden protective urge. What if the kids didn't like it? What if they cried and begged her to take them home? Feeling as mushy as a bowl of freshly cooked oatmeal, Katelyn parked and helped the kids out of the car.

Shepherding the kids inside, Katelyn quickly found the tiny office where three harried-looking women were crowded.

"Good morning," she greeted them.

The one at the desk nodded absently as she picked up a stridently ringing phone. The second didn't even glance up from the clipboard in her hands. Katelyn read her badge, seeing that her name was Evie Johnson and that she was the director. The third woman was deep in conversation with the director.

The first one completed her phone call and focused on Katelyn. "Can I help you?"

Katelyn read her badge and gave the woman her most winning smile. "I hope so, Ms. Carstairs. I'm here to enroll…" she paused, feeling a warmth as she said the words aloud "…my children. Jenny's five and the twins are three."

The woman's face turned downward in a concerned frown. "I don't know. We're very full."

"Full?" She had been assured by Stefanie that this was the preschool with the most slots for new students.

The phone rang again and Ms. Carstairs grabbed the receiver. Katelyn glanced at the second woman, the one she'd noticed was the director. She was still talking with the third woman, and Katelyn brazenly eavesdropped.

They were discussing a school fund-raiser and from their conversation, the event wasn't going well. In fact, it sounded as though it might be a complete bust.

Katelyn took a few steps closer to them—virtually the last remaining space in the office—and smiled at them. "I'm sorry, I couldn't help but overhear your conversation." She gestured to the obvious lack of space and privacy. "I'm here to enroll my children, but it sounds like you could use some help on this fund-raiser."

The director appeared resigned rather than annoyed at Katelyn's interruption. "I'm not sure our fund-raiser *can* be helped."

Katelyn felt a familiar surge of determination. "Oh, but I think it can." She whipped a card out of her slim purse and handed it to the director. "Promotion is my business."

Evie Johnson read the impressive card and looked at Katelyn with new respect. "So I see. But can this translate to a preschool fund-raiser?"

"Certainly. You just have to make it appeal to adults. The plans I heard you discussing are fine for the under-five crowd, but they're not the ones you're targeting." Basic rule, know your market. Katelyn warmed up, just as she did in any creative meeting. "You have to bring in the parents—and other adults—who'll open their wallets. Tailor the fund-raiser to them—including activities that involve their children—and you'll have a winner."

The director actually smiled. "It sounds like you have a wealth of ideas."

Katelyn shrugged modestly. "It *is* my work."

"And if we can find room for your children, will we benefit from that expertise?"

Katelyn didn't see the trap until she'd walked straight into it. Still, she kept the smile on her face. "Of course, I believe all concerned parents should be active participants."

"An attitude we wholeheartedly endorse," Ms. Johnson agreed, the shrewd light in her eyes signalling victory.

Having savored that same feeling of success enough times herself, Katelyn admired the woman's finesse. And wouldn't the extra time for her work be worth the contribution?

Eric tugged on her. At the same time, she noticed that Erin was perilously close to tipping over a papier mâché elephant perched atop a bookcase. As she tried to keep them contained, Katelyn filled out the necessary paperwork.

Ms. Johnson looked over the forms. Apparently satisfied, she smiled. "Why don't we get the children into their classes?"

Katelyn couldn't stop a sigh of relief. It had worked. "Good, I'd like to see where they'll be." Concern filled her again. She'd worried about the children protesting her departure. Now, Katelyn wasn't sure she could leave them.

It was silly, she told herself. Stefanie had assured her the kids *needed* this, would be disadvantaged without preschool. Still…

She knelt down, at eye level with Jenny and the twins. "We talked about preschool and this is it. Are you okay about staying?"

Jenny made an impatient noise. "I want to see my room."

Eric and Erin were more interested in the box of Lego beneath the table than replying, so Katelyn gave up. Disengaging their little fingers from the blocks, she took one twin in each hand and faced the school director. "Lead on."

It didn't take long to locate their rooms and introduce the kids to their teachers. Although Katelyn was feeling more pangs than she could have anticipated, Jenny and the twins were immediately drawn into the fun new atmosphere. And she had to admit the other children all looked happy.

Katelyn instructed Jenny to stay with her brother and sister after school was over until they got into the car. Hugging each of them fiercely, she finally left. The car seemed incredibly quiet without their childish chatter. Ridiculous, she told herself, knowing she needed this time for her work, to pull everything together.

Still, she was fifteen minutes early picking them up. Her Jag stood out among the cars parked along the circular drive. Katelyn noticed several curious stares. Well, it wasn't a mommy car, but she was feeling plenty of mommy anxiety.

When Jenny and the twins joined the group of children heading outside with their teachers, Katelyn breathed a sigh of relief. She'd known they were safe and being looked after, but there was something scary about knowing they were in an impersonal building...

"Katelyn, look what I made!" Jenny called out to her, waving what looked like a wreath.

Dried flowers were glued on at odd angles, but Katelyn shared Jenny's enthusiasm. "It's beautiful! And the perfect colors for your room."

Jenny grinned. "Tomorrow we're making pencil holders!"

The school was obviously a hit with Jenny. Katelyn looked from Eric to Erin, noticing matching colored mustaches on their faces.

"We had grape juice," Erin announced.

"So I see."

"Liked grape juice," Eric added.

"Did you like anything else?"

"They got lots of toy trucks," Eric told her.

"And paints," Erin told her.

The teacher smiled at Katelyn. "They did just fine. Fit

in as if they'd been here for months. Jenny's teacher told me that you'd instructed her to walk out with her brother and sister.''

''Yes, thank you. I feel better when they're all together.'' Although she herself was an only child, Katelyn knew that Jenny and the twins felt more secure as a unit.

The young teacher smiled again. ''Fine. Then that's what we'll do.'' She waved to the children, who responded eagerly.

''So, you had a good time?'' Katelyn asked again, needing reassurance.

Jenny answered, since the twins were occupied with trying to outdo each other in making handprints on the windows. ''Uh-huh. There was art…and we did letters. And we did snack time…and we went outside. Is real school like this?''

More uncertain territory. It had been a long time since Katelyn had been in kindergarten herself. ''Pretty much. So, you think you'll like real school?''

''Uh-huh. I liked today.''

Katelyn felt more of those warm fuzzies. While Finn hadn't objected to preschool, he hadn't seen a need for it, either. Although she couldn't take credit for the idea, she had implemented it. ''I'm glad. I want you to be happy.''

''Katelyn, are you ever going away?''

''Why should I do that?''

''Sometimes people do.''

Katelyn realized Jenny was referring to her mother.

''That's only when they don't have a choice. But I'm not going away.''

''You promise?''

Katelyn met Jenny's serious eyes, reminded of her still uncertain future with Finn. ''You don't need a promise.''

''Yes, I do,'' Jenny insisted. ''Unless you don't like us well enough to promise.''

Katelyn's heart constricted. ''That's not it!'' she protested, not wanting to hurt this vulnerable child.

''Then promise.''

Katelyn hesitated, realizing she had a choice. She could
hurt Jenny…or swallow her pride and try to make things
work with Finn. ''I promise.''

''Then I'm happy you married Daddy.''

Oh, those warm fuzzies were running wild. ''You are?''

''Uh-huh. And so it's okay if you sleep with him.''

Katelyn managed not to choke. ''It is?''

''Uh-huh.'' She waggled the wreath in her hand. ''So
when are you going to make a baby?''

Chapter Eleven

Stefanie stared over the pile of folders on Daniel's desk. "I don't believe I've ever seen your desk looking so messy. In fact, it's usually compulsively neat. What gives?"

"My sanity," he replied briefly, thinking of the stack of work he hadn't yet unsurfaced.

"Aren't things working out with Katelyn's telecommuting?"

Daniel frowned, not wanting to sound disloyal. "Actually, it's not bad. I get more input and frankly I like that."

"So Katelyn's impromptu wedding benefited you?"

Daniel flinched. That hadn't been his intent. And he was feeling guilty for enjoying his role of greater responsibility. "I hope it benefits her more," he replied stiffly.

"Don't get bent out of shape," she cautioned. "I didn't mean anything negative. I'd like to think that some good's coming out of her marriage."

Frowning, Daniel studied Stefanie's face. "What do you mean?"

She shrugged. "I'm not sure exactly. But I don't get the sense of a great love match." She lowered her voice as though not quite believing her own words. "If I didn't know better I'd think it was some sort of arranged marriage."

Daniel made a choking noise.

"I know it sounds ridiculous. Why would she arrange to be married to her driver of all people?"

"But that doesn't mean they can't be happy," he protested.

Stefanie tilted her head in contemplation. "I suppose you're right. I was encouraging marriage—I thought she was a natural for the whole white-picket-fence experience. Now I just hope Katelyn can forget for a while that's she an executive and remember that she's a woman."

Daniel's expression cleared somewhat. "You think she needs a gentle push?"

Stefanie snorted indelicately. "Gentle? No. But she definitely needs a push."

Daniel smiled at the outspoken brunette. When he had set up Katelyn's compact stereo, he had put in a new tape. And this one promised to encourage loving thoughts and ways. Perhaps that was all the push Katelyn needed. Daniel knew that deep inside, she possessed those feelings. But they had been locked away while she scrambled up the corporate ladder. They might be dusty, but Daniel expected with use they would become fully functional once again.

Stefanie smiled in return. "If I didn't know better, I'd think you were up to something."

Daniel decided to divert her suspicions. "Just thinking that maybe all Katelyn needs is some quality time for romance. That's not so easy with three children always underfoot."

Stefanie tapped her fingers on her chin. "You've got something there, my friend. And if we work together, the newlyweds can have all the time in the world."

He glanced at his unwitting accomplice. "Whatever you say, Stefanie."

"I don't want to brag, but I think I know what Katelyn needs. And she needs us to help orchestrate this romance."

Daniel managed to restrain a full-blown grin. "When you're right, you're right."

Stefanie leaned in a bit closer, her voice dropping to a conspiratorial whisper. "And if we play our cards right, Katelyn never has to know."

Losing the battle to hold back his grin, Daniel met her eyes and nodded. "It'll be our little secret."

FINN PUSHED THE remote on the garage-door opener. He started to pull the limo inside when he spotted a strange car. In the place of Katelyn's Jag was a gleaming new Jeep Grand Cherokee, dealer tags still attached. For a moment he wondered if he could have pulled into the wrong driveway.

Despite the dark of the moonless night, all the other garage paraphernalia looked familiar. Yep, that was his fishing pole, toolbox, and ten-speed bike. This was his own cluttered garage, all right.

If the Jeep hadn't been so *new* he would have thought it was a loaner—that Katelyn's Jag was in the shop.

Muttering to himself, Finn closed the garage and headed into the house. Although the porch light shone brightly, when he pushed open the front door, the interior was nearly pitch-black. He tried to adjust his eyes, stumbling in the darkness. Swearing beneath his breath, he grabbed his shin.

"Katelyn? Jenny?" Not hearing an answer, Finn tried to navigate a little more carefully. It was peculiarly quiet. Even the dog hadn't barked.

In the other room he could see the flicker of candlelight. Was the electricity out? But that didn't make sense. The garage door opener had worked and the porch light was on.

He searched his head for birthdays or holidays—none that he could think of. Were Katelyn and the kids up to something? He bumped into another low table. *Like kill Daddy before he can make it to the dining room?*

Soft music poured from the speakers—he recognized the Rachmaninoff tape he'd once played for Katelyn.

"Erin? Eric? Jenny? Daddy's home," he called out.

Finn heard the satiny swish of material, along with the subtle hum of music. "Katelyn?"

"Yes, Finn." Her voice was unusually throaty.

For a moment he wondered if she was coming down with a cold. Then his eyes focused on the candlelight and Katelyn's chiffon-clad body and he realized what she had was far more deadly.

Her movements were slow and deliberate as she glided toward him. He realized the chiffon she wore looked like layered scarves—and little else. Finn felt the groan building in his throat. What game was she playing?

Katelyn smiled nervously. "You're late."

"Traffic," he replied, easing backward and nearly tripping over an ottoman in the dark.

"Careful," she cautioned, the white of her teeth flashing in the darkened room.

"Maybe if we turned on a few lights..." He reached toward the wall, searching for the switch.

But Katelyn snagged his hand. "I thought you might like the soft lighting."

Cautiously, Finn looked for the trap. "Are we having dinner by candlelight?"

"I thought it might be nice," she replied, still looking uncertain.

"What about the kids?" he asked, glancing around the darkened room. "It's too early for them to be in bed—"

"They're with a sitter—my friend Stefanie." Katelyn's hands fluttered before she thrust them in the folds of chiffon.

Finn tried to be discreet as he inched toward the wall, planning to add a touch of light with the dimmer switch.

But he forgot about the low, slim hall table until he crashed into it.

"I didn't think the dark would be a problem," Katelyn apologized.

He rubbed bruised shins. "It's not really."

She crossed over to the dining room table. "I'll light another candle."

As she turned, he caught the scent of her perfume—subtle, mysterious, beckoning.

Yet her voice was still tentative. "You act like you've never seen candlelight before."

"Lately only on birthday cakes—five candles and under."

She smiled, still looking jittery. "But there are all kinds of candlelight, Finn. Some to read by. Some to share a gently lit dinner for two."

His gaze encompassed the beautifully laid out table. "So I see." Then he lifted his eyes. "Very nice. Are we celebrating something special?"

She fidgeted, glanced away, then reluctantly met his gaze. "I thought we might begin again."

The candlelight flickered between them as Finn studied her face, searching for the truth. "We could try," he replied cautiously. He wouldn't mind a new start—but still he was suspicious. What had brought this on?

She retreated into the kitchen, returning with a platter of steamed cockles. "Appetizers." Again her smile was tentative. "No home cooking, but I do a mean takeout."

"If you'd wanted to cook, you could have tried Jenny's specialty—peanut-butter-and-jelly sandwiches."

Her smile widened. "I very nearly did. The delivery boy arrived only a short time before you did."

Finn tried to relax, hoping to discern her motives. "Didn't I notice a new car in the garage?"

She nodded, breaking the crusty bread into cubes to dip into the garlic-and-wine-laced broth.

"What happened to your Jag?"

"I traded it in for the Jeep."

"Why?"

"You might not have noticed, but the Jag wasn't exactly a family vehicle, so I traded it for something more practical."

"Just like that?"

Katelyn stepped even closer. "Just like what?"

Surprised that she had traded in her car, Finn frowned. "Did you get a good deal on your Jag?"

Despite the low lighting, he could see the frustration playing over her face. "Is that what you want to talk about? The deal I got?"

"I just want to make sure you didn't lose a lot of money. The Jag's a valuable car."

"I'm aware of that." She pushed at her hair, left long, loose and heavy. "Actually, I got a great deal. And the whole transaction was very kind to my bank account."

The enormity of what she'd done struck him—the commitment she'd made. Was she sincere about a fresh start?

"No minivan?" he questioned, a smile surfacing.

Katelyn shook her head. "Not my style." Then she grinned too. "But the Jeep *is* safe for the children."

Had she grown to care that much? To change her lifestyle because of the children?

Finn leaned closer, staring deep into her changeling eyes. Now they resembled the dark that surrounded her—a deep, bluish-gray that nearly blended with the night. How much of all this—the commitment, the desire—was genuine? Was it simply fallout from an overactive biological clock? Or was it Katelyn? Perhaps a Katelyn he hadn't known existed?

A picture of her home office flashed into his mind. Covered in the artwork the children brought home from pre-school, it resembled a child's play area more than a cor-porate workplace. Could she have changed that much?

The phone rang suddenly, startling them both.

"It's not one of my office phones," she muttered. "I put them on the service." She stared at him, regret mixing the colors in her eyes. "That must be the home line. We don't dare not answer it—the kids…"

She didn't have to complete the thought. He hadn't let a phone go unanswered since Jenny's birth. A parent never knew… Suddenly he wondered about this friend of hers that was baby-sitting the kids. He'd met Stefanie, but he didn't really know anything about her.

That thought propelled him to follow Katelyn into the kitchen. But she was already replacing the receiver. "Stef-anie has a work emergency. She apologized, but her career comes first."

Relief sagged through him. He realized that lately he hadn't worried about his children with the same degree of intensity he had since his wife, Angela, had died. Then, he had felt the full brunt of that responsibility—sole parent, sole concern. Unconsciously, he'd allowed Katelyn to share some of that since she'd been here.

Not that first week or so. Not when he wondered if she could struggle through each day without a disaster. But sometime since then, he'd relaxed a fraction, allowed some-one else to worry about his children, too. To take a part in the decisions that affected them.

Something thawed deep inside—a part of him that he had kept locked away since Angela's death. Something that affected him more than Katelyn's silken-clad body or the seductive setting. And Finn realized with lethal clarity that this quality was far more dangerous. He could handle can-dlelight, evocative words and mood music. He wasn't sure he could say the same about a woman who genuinely cared. One who wanted to take the place of his late wife.

KATELYN COVERTLY READ the book's back cover. *How to Interest Your Man—a Modern Woman's Guide to Passion.* Peeping over her sunglasses, she could see that Stefanie still had the kids in the children's section of the bookstore. But she knew her friend was too restless to stay there long.

Quickly, Katelyn took the book to the cash register and paid for it. Ridiculously, she felt as though she should request a plain brown bag. Especially when the clerk smirked knowingly at her.

Katelyn snatched the bag from the young man and marched back to the children's section.

Stefanie took in her flushed face. "So, did you have to battle someone for the last copy of *War and Peace?*"

"Close, but no booby prize. Why don't we take the kids for some ice cream?"

"Lest you forget, I can eat my weight in ice cream. This is unjust, excessively brutal enticement."

"Ice cream!" the kids were chorusing.

Katelyn held up her hands. "If you can fight all of us…"

Stefanie sighed with great exaggeration. "Oh, fine. But if I can't get into my new designer pants Saturday night, you're dead."

"I'll risk it. I can almost taste the hot fudge.…"

Katelyn linked arms with her friend. "I hear they have a dessert they call the Carmen Miranda. Besides the hot fudge, there's caramel and butterscotch, bananas, whipped cream, strawberry sauce, streusel topping…"

Stefanie groaned. "At this rate I won't get in those pants with an industrial-strength shoehorn."

It didn't take long to order and eat the ice cream. Then the children begged to play in the enclosed area filled with slides and a merry-go-round.

Stefanie barely waited until they were gone before she demanded the low-down. "You've been clutching that book as if it's the last copy of *The Sensuous Woman*. Now, what gives?"

Katelyn felt an unexpected blush warming her cheeks.

"It's not really *The Sensuous Woman?*" Stefanie asked in disbelief.

"Not exactly." Reluctantly, Katelyn pulled the book from the bag.

Stefanie scanned the title, then stared at Katelyn. "But why do you need this?"

"To...well, you know...spark some interest."

Stefanie frowned and drew her brows together. "You mean you actually are having to create interest?"

Katelyn didn't answer directly. "Isn't that normal?"

"Are you kidding? You two are newlyweds—hell, you're practically still on your honeymoon. No, it's *not* normal."

"Oh." Katelyn's voice was uncharacteristically small. "Even with the kids around and all?"

"That would make it difficult—interruptions and such— but not impossible." She leaned forward. "Katelyn, is there something you're not telling me?"

Katelyn thought uncomfortably about their impulsive elopement, and their subsequent agreement to not consummate their marriage. But, somehow, it seemed disloyal to Finn to divulge that. And she already felt as though she'd told Stefanie too much.

Katelyn shook her head.

Stefanie's eyes narrowed sagely. "Has Finn gotten over his wife? Or are his feelings still tied to her?"

Katelyn considered this. "He loved her and her death was a terrible shock."

"It's possible he thinks he's being unfaithful when he makes loves to you." Stefanie suggested.

Katelyn drew her mouth into an 'oh' of surprise. "I hadn't thought of that. I'm not sure if that makes me feel better or worse."

Stefanie cocked her head. "What do you mean?"

Katelyn stared at her friend. "Don't you see? How can I fight a ghost?"

Chapter Twelve

Nervously, Katelyn fussed with the table linen. Tonight's dinner was special. She'd ordered it from one of the area's finest restaurants. Although the kids never tired of pizza, she had expected Finn to burst into a rendition of "O Solo Mio" the last time she'd had a pie delivered. They ate pizza as often as most people did vegetables.

And Katelyn knew that her cooking hadn't improved. In a desperate moment that afternoon, she'd considered taking cooking classes, but knew she wouldn't be able to prepare a gourmet meal by evening.

And this evening was going to be a special one. She wasn't going to try the tricks the book suggested or the few she could think of on her own. Tonight was about resolving Finn's past—so they could embark on their own future.

Hearing the front door open, she wiped her hands against the flowered skirt she'd chosen…and remembered to smile.

Finn entered the dining room, a wary look on his face as he spotted the table set for two. Since the moment he had realized Katelyn was trying to replace Angela, Finn couldn't shake the guilt. Logically, he knew he was over-reacting. But that didn't stop the feelings.

Maybe it was time to tell her—to call off their uncon-summated charade, let Katelyn return to her real life, to who she really was. He paused. Why did that cause a pang somewhere so deep he didn't want to acknowledge it?

Finn's eyes scanned her feminine, but demure appearance. She wore a simple silk blouse and flowered skirt that flowed around her long legs.

Her makeup was light enough for him to see the dusting of freckles across her nose and cheeks. She'd left her magnificent hair down, creating a bounty of loose waves. And her eyes today reflected the rainbow of colors in the artwork of her alcove—bluish-green with tawny highlights. She was an absolute knockout. And that made him feel even guiltier.

"Hi," she greeted him.

"What's up?" Finn asked, gesturing to the table.

"Nothing, really," she replied, a different note in her voice.

She was nervous, he realized. And that was rare for her. "The kids?"

"Stefanie offered to take them to the movies."

Finn stepped closer. "I wouldn't have taken Stefanie for the sort of person who likes Disney films."

"She's a surprising person in a lot of ways."

Finn watched the play of emotions on her face. "There's a lot of that going around."

Her hands darted skittishly toward her skirt again. "Really?"

"Really."

Their gazes met, hers tentative, his filled with desire tempered with doubt. The moment lingered, a poignant echo in the stillness.

"Why don't we have a glass of wine in the living room?" he suggested finally.

"That sounds good," she replied in relief. "Dinner's in the warming oven."

While Finn didn't own an impressive wine collection, he

did have a few decent bottles put away. He retrieved one, along with a corkscrew and two glasses.

Katelyn stood in the living room, looking out the window at the dark night, her thoughts apparently a galaxy away. As he watched her, it occurred to him that something might be wrong. He frowned. If that was the case…

Katelyn turned just then. "Did you know that you can see all the stars from here?"

"We keep them in the same place out here in the suburbs as you do in the city." Traces of a smile ghosted over his lips. "They don't get lost that way."

"At my condo, there are so many other lights I never see the stars." Her gaze met his. "But then I didn't spend much time looking for them, either."

Finn opened the wine and poured them each a glass.

Katelyn accepted hers. "How did you know I prefer red?"

"Good guess."

She sipped the wine, her fingers tracing a pattern over the stem. "How was your day?"

"Not too exciting. It isn't as much of a challenge driving around Mr. Mathison as it was with you."

He saw something light up in her expression. "You're just saying that."

"No, there was never a dull moment chauffeuring you." He realized that was true. Katelyn had kept him thinking and guessing the entire time.

She was still doing it.

"I miss that," she confessed. "I'm getting most of my work done from here, but the challenge of each new meeting—well, that's different now. It's not the same as being there in person, feeling the rush of adrenaline."

The light dawned. "Is that what you wanted to talk about?"

She stared at him, obviously dismayed. "What makes you think I had something special to talk about?"

He nodded toward the dining room table. "The dinner for two. The way you're behaving."

Her dismay increased. "I'm acting differently?"

Finn nodded.

"Well, I guess I do have something I want to discuss with you." She took a deep breath. "I've been thinking about us...about our time alone together."

He frowned.

Katelyn clasped her hands, then shoved them behind her. "I guess I mean...our intimate time."

Finn's grip tightened on the wineglass.

She tried to smile, but her flush merely deepened. "And I've been thinking. I know you loved your wife and you must still miss her a lot. And, well, I can see why it's difficult for you to *bond* with someone else...in all aspects." She took a deep breath, her face now a rosy pink. "I can see why that might even make you feel unfaithful to your wife." She cleared her throat. "I mean in making new *bonds,* that is."

Finn stared at her. So she had guessed his conflicting feelings. Her perception surprised him.

However, Katelyn wasn't through. "So, I was thinking that if I had known Angela and she had known me...well, I think we would have liked each other. In some ways I think I *do* know her. Through the children, I mean. I know there's a lot of her in them. And well, couldn't we all be friends—you, me and Angela? Isn't there room in your heart for both of us?"

Stunned, he couldn't answer. His gaze rested on and caught hers.

He felt incredibly, amazingly touched. Katelyn had obviously done some deep soul-searching to come up with her conclusions. So she thought Angela would have liked her. Funny, he thought so, too.

FINN SEARCHED the refrigerator for something to feed Eric. Katelyn had taken Eric to the doctor for a rash and his son was now undergoing allergy tests. Katelyn had told him some of the foods Eric couldn't eat, but Finn couldn't remember which ones they were.

And Eric dogged his every step, slowing down his progress even more. Katelyn was in the middle of a video conference—one that had been unplanned. But maybe he could interrupt just long enough to ask her if Eric could have peaches.

The kids were hungry and chaos filled the kitchen. He'd grown accustomed now to Katelyn handling the mornings, and Finn wished the conference call could have been postponed.

He sighed. Make that one for the macho pigs, none for the working mother. The phone rang, adding to the commotion. He was surprised to hear Daniel's voice.

"If you'll call Katelyn on one of her business lines, she'll pick up," Finn told her assistant.

"She's already started the meeting," Daniel replied. "I'm hoping you can slip her a note. I need the signatory page on the Atlantis deal—there are over fifty people on hold until they get it. I need to know whether she has it, or if she put it in the mail."

Finn sighed. Now he was becoming Katelyn's gofer. He wrote the note, adding one of his own about Eric and the peaches. Stumbling over Snuffles, Finn pushed open the swinging door and slipped her the note, but she didn't have a ready response.

So Finn headed back to the kitchen, knowing he had to find something for Eric to eat. He started to open the refrigerator, then paused, staring at the door. Atlantis. The name was emblazoned across the paper held by a bunny-shaped refrigerator magnet, amidst the art gallery Katelyn had tacked on the refrigerator door.

He plucked the paper from the refrigerator. It was the signatory page Daniel wanted. Retracing his steps he took it to Katelyn, then scribbled another note: "Should I call Daniel and tell him you'll send this today?"

She shook her head violently, then abruptly put her phone on hold. "No. Daniel can't have that page. Tell him to get another one signed."

"When you already have this one?"

"Turn it over," she instructed.

"What?"

"Turn it over. Erin drew that for me. I can't give it away."

Finn stared at her. What had happened to the corporate crusher?

She pushed the button on her phone and rejoined the meeting.

Still stunned, Finn returned to the kitchen in time for the phone to ring again. It didn't surprise him to hear Daniel's impatient voice.

"I gave her the note," Finn replied when Daniel questioned him about the signatory page.

Daniel's hesitation was brief. "If you could ask one more question—Katelyn's supposed to have made a crucial decision on the Falk campaign. I need to know what her decision is."

Promising to ask, Finn replaced the receiver. Balancing all this had to be tricky when Katelyn was alone with the kids. No wonder she'd enrolled them in preschool. She must have been tempted to check out military schools for toddlers.

Still, he took her another note: "Crucial decision—need your answer now."

Katelyn read the note and placed her hand over the receiver as she answered him in a distracted voice. "Yes, Eric can have the peaches." Swiveling her chair, she turned back to her video meeting.

So crucial decisions these days were peaches for Eric?

Finn hadn't known what to expect from Katelyn. But he hadn't anticipated such a radical change.

The kitchen phone was ringing again.

But all Finn could see was Katelyn and the office she'd decorated in toddler art and preschool sculptures. She was impressively capable, handling this meeting like a cakewalk. But he knew from Daniel's frantic calls that she was juggling several critical deals.

This incredibly competent woman had been nervous approaching him about Angela—and his reluctance to let go of the past. It flattered him to think that he could make her nervous about anything.

Finn retraced his steps to the kitchen, remembering not to plow into the dog this time. Erin and Jenny were finishing their breakfast as Finn spooned out some peaches for Eric.

He wondered if toast was on the approved list. Returning to the alcove, he opened his mouth to ask when Katelyn turned around suddenly. She put the meeting on hold as her red line phone rang—the one Daniel used only in a true crisis. She listened for a moment, her face exasperated, then grim.

Clicking off, she didn't return immediately to her meeting. "Finn—this morning's getting out of hand."

He didn't know what to tell her. He didn't have a ready-made solution, although he wished he did. "I'm sorry, Katelyn, but I have to leave in less than half an hour. I see how busy you are, but the Mathison contract's too important to screw up."

"Can't they send another driver?"

Finn's rosy visions of Katelyn scattered. He clenched the notepad in his hand, angry that he had to explain, even angrier that it embarrassed him to tell her the truth. "I'm it, Katelyn. Malloy Enterprises. One driver. One car. There's no one else to *send*. It's a struggling, one-man operation and if I lose this contract, it'll put me out of business."

She stared at him, her mouth dropping open in shock. "But…I thought…"

"I'm not sure exactly what you thought, Katelyn, but this is it." His overwhelming guilt blended with frustration and embarrassment, transforming into anger. "Sure, someday I'd like to expand, add more cars, hire some drivers. But in the meantime, I can't afford fancy gourmet food, or an extra car that's not the limo to drive the family around in, or a lot of other things you're used to. I don't have a dozen credit cards to whip out to solve my problems."

Her mouth thinned into a line. "That's not how I solve all my problems, either, but I'm not going to apologize for dealing with them the best way I know. I wasn't flaunting *fancy* food—in case you hadn't noticed, I don't know how to cook. And I traded in the Jag because it wasn't practical. If you'd told me we had money concerns, I could—"

"Have what? Thrown me a bone? My finances aren't any of your concern."

Her eyes widened in shock. "None of my concern?" She stood up, leaving her meeting forgotten. "Finn Malloy, am I your wife or not?"

Chapter Thirteen

Finn stared at her, realizing he'd blown it. He hadn't accepted Katelyn as his wife, despite his impulsive proposal. And now she knew it.

Her red emergency line rang. Katelyn ignored it.

Finn opened his mouth, wondering how to explain. How to make her understand. Then Eric screamed. A long, bloody wail that pierced through the swinging door to the kitchen as though it wasn't there.

Finn and Katelyn both ran. Eric was perched on a stool next to the counter, his face red from crying, the tears flowing nonstop. Finn reached him first and Eric held up his little hands. Finn reached for them as he bent to pick him up.

"Stop!" Katelyn yelled, almost in his ear.

"What—"

"His hands—they're burned." She turned on the cold water and tested it. "Quick, put them under the water."

Finn complied. Although Eric continued howling, his wails reduced in volume. As Finn held the small hands beneath the faucet, Katelyn found a large bowl and filled it with cooler water from the refrigerator.

"We need to switch his hands quickly to the bowl so not much air hits them," she told Finn. "Then you can sit somewhere with him until he calms down."

Following her instructions, Finn made the switch without any additional pain to Eric. Sitting at the kitchen table with him, Finn smoothed his son's brow, feeling him settle a bit, his cries winding down into an occasional hiccuping sob.

Katelyn grabbed a book from the shelf near the cookbooks. Finn angled his head so that he could read the title: *First Aid for Children.*

Quickly she flipped through the book, obviously reading the section on burns. ''Aloe vera,'' she murmured.

Finn frowned. ''I don't have an aloe vera plant.''

''No, but we have some gel.''

''We do?''

''I bought everything on the suggested first-aid kit list when I bought the book. I read through everything so I'd basically know what to do. Burns—treat immediately with water. Poisons, choking, drowning. The basics.'' Katelyn dug into a cabinet and lifted out a clear plastic box. ''Once the worst of the stinging's past, I'll put the gel on.'' She glanced at her watch. ''When the doctor's office opens, I'll call, but it doesn't look that bad.''

Finn stared at her, not hiding his admiration. ''How'd you know he was burned?''

''He was on a stool by the counter. The coffeepot's on the counter and Eric always reaches for anything shiny. Not that difficult, Watson.''

''Apparently not for you, Sherlock. And apparently I need to buy a different kind of coffeepot. This old stainless-steel percolator makes such good coffee I hated to give it up, but I guess I'll get a plastic drip model so there aren't any more burns.''

''That, or find a safer place for the coffeepot.'' She ran a hand over Eric's plump little leg. ''Someplace where Eric can't drag a chair over to.''

''Maybe. Or maybe I'll just retire the percolator until

he's older." He stared ruefully at Eric's reddened hands. "Nothing's worth hurting him."

Jenny and Erin were staring at their brother, waiting to see if he shrieked anymore.

Finn glanced at the girls. "Thank God he didn't jerk the coffeepot over on them." He shuddered. "This could have been a lot worse."

"But it wasn't," Katelyn said calmly. "Every day is filled with potential accidents and disasters. You can't dwell on them. You just have to deal with them."

"The best way you know how," Finn responded softly, echoing her words. "Katelyn, I'm sorry I—"

"It's forgotten. It's been a crazy morning. I should never have agreed to this early meeting. Normally I schedule them when the kids are in preschool, but the client insisted." She shook her head. "And I should have insisted more strongly."

Finn stared at Katelyn, his eyes widening. "Are they still on hold?"

She blinked. "I suppose so. I wonder if they worked everything out."

Finn was torn between grinning and apologizing "I'm sorry if this messed up things for you."

Katelyn waved her hands in dismissal. "This deal is a collaborative effort between two firms to promote both their ideas in a movie-related campaign. We're months behind because they couldn't agree. Maybe without me to run interference, they battled it out and made a decision. Could be the best thing that happened to them. If not, they'll get over it." Glancing at her watch she picked up the cordless phone and dialed. "Isn't it time for you to be leaving? I'll call Daniel and have him smooth out the edges."

"I can't leave you with Eric and—"

"We'll be fine." Katelyn shifted away, talking into the phone. When she clicked off, she quickly dialed the service and transferred the phones. "Daniel reset the meeting—told them I had an equipment failure. If Eric needs to see the doctor, we'll go while his sisters are in preschool." She held out her hands for Eric. "Now, you'd better get moving."

Reluctantly Finn released his son, feeling as though he was deserting them. "I should be home early."

She glanced at him absently, soothing Eric as she held him, unconsciously swaying in a gentle rocking motion. "Don't worry about it."

But he did. Suddenly he realized it was more than time to worry—about giving Katelyn something back.

FINN TURNED DOWN an extra outside assignment and got home shortly after five o'clock. He could hear Katelyn and the kids upstairs as he headed toward the kitchen. Relieved, he saw that she hadn't begun dinner—and he hoped she hadn't ordered anything either.

Unloading the groceries he'd stopped to buy, he pulled down the pans he needed from the overhead rack and then tied on an apron. He spent the next several minutes chopping and slicing.

When Katelyn pushed open the kitchen door, dinner was well under way. She stopped in surprise.

But Finn spoke before she could. "How's Eric?"

"No change since you called at noon, two, and four o'clock. He's just fine." She looked at the stove, the groceries spread out on the counter. "What are you doing?"

"Cooking dinner," he replied, as though he'd done so every night since she'd been there.

"But why?"

"Because I can. In fact I'm good at it. I'm a progressive kind of guy—why shouldn't I cook dinner?"

Katelyn slowly released the door, letting it thump closed behind her. "No reason, I guess." She glanced curiously at all the pans. "Are you sure you know how to do all this?"

"Of course. My mother taught me to cook when I could barely reach the stove. She said every man needed to know how to cook and take care of himself." He caught Katelyn's gaze. "Mother was right."

She shoved her hands in her jeans pockets. "Too bad my mother didn't share the same philosophy."

"I don't know. Sounds like your mother pushed you toward success. Can't fault her for that."

"I hadn't thought about it that way."

"A lot of people can put together a meal. Not many can put together the deals you do," Finn reminded her.

"But every wife and mother should know how to cook," she protested. "I even bought some cookbooks, but they're like reading a calculus text."

"I think you've taken on enough without trying to be Julia Child." Finn stirred the sauce, offering her a taste.

She accepted, instantly recognizing that Finn was more than just a capable cook—the sauce was delicious. "Your mother was quite a teacher."

"I liked cooking." He tapped the spoon against the pan, not quite meeting her eyes. "I'm not sure why I didn't offer to cook from day one."

"You probably thought you'd married a normal woman," Katelyn lamented.

No, he hadn't. He'd known she was special from the start. But not just how special.

Katelyn frowned suddenly, staring at the dinner he was preparing. "I almost forgot." She gestured toward the cookware. "We have a problem…"

The doorbell rang. He wiped his hands on the oversized chef's apron he wore. "Can it wait while we see who that is?"

She nodded and together they answered the door.

Stefanie's impudent grin only scarcely eclipsed her wild clothing. "Hi guys! Am I interrupting?"

Slightly flustered, Katelyn glanced between her friend and her husband. "Of course not, come in."

Stefanie strolled inside, her gaze drifting over Finn. "Nice outfit."

His glance mimicked hers. "Ditto."

Stefanie's gaze roamed around the hall. "I could swear I'd seen chairs in one of these rooms…"

Rattled, Katelyn apologized. "Let's go in the living room. I don't know where my mind is."

Stefanie's brow rose slightly. "I think I can guess."

When Katelyn pinkened, Finn decided he liked her friend's irreverent honesty. "We'll be having dinner soon. Will you join us?"

"That's a tempting offer, but I've come to ask a favor."

Katelyn's glance strayed toward Finn, before refocusing on her friend. "Sure. What is it?"

"I'd like to borrow some little people."

"Excuse me?" Katelyn questioned.

"Curtain climbers, rug rats." She blew out an exasperated breath. "Kids, you know, the short people who live here."

"What do you want with the children?" Katelyn asked in disbelief.

Stefanie rolled her eyes. "I haven't gone off the deep end, so there's no need for the straitjacket just yet. My niece is coming for the weekend. She's going to be bored senseless with just me for entertainment. So I thought maybe I could borrow your kids for the weekend."

"They're not exactly a cup of sugar," Katelyn reminded her.

"No, they're much noisier and messier than your average cup of sugar," Stefanie agreed. "But generally lots more fun."

Finn met Katelyn's gaze. "Three children are quite a lot of bother."

"I have scads of nieces and nephews," Stefanie replied airily. "One weekend I had eight at once. But Brianna's coming solo. And the poor kid's had a pretty rotten year. The family house burned down and all the pets were lost in the fire."

"I remember!" Katelyn exclaimed. "You practically bought out the toy store to replace her doll collection."

Stefanie shrugged. "But they couldn't replace the ones her late mother had given her."

Finn sized up the woman and found himself warming to her even more. Although Stefanie had taken the kids to a movie once, he wanted to be sure she was competent to watch four children for a weekend. "Katelyn, can you help me for a moment in the kitchen?"

"I'm not sure what help I can be."

"It's the sauce," Finn told her, finally catching her eye.

"That's married talk for 'we need to discuss this alone,'" Stefanie told her in a stage whisper.

"Oh, right." Katelyn rose, sending her friend an apologetic glance.

Once in the kitchen, Finn met Katelyn's eyes. "Would you trust the kids to your friend? A movie's one thing. A weekend is another."

"Actually, for all her eccentricities, Stefanie is very capable with kids. Her nieces and nephews adore her. There's always a fight for who gets to visit Aunt Stef. And she always returns them in one piece."

"I thought so. But there's a more important question. Do you want to spend the weekend alone with me?"

Katelyn cleared her throat. "I told you I wanted a new start."

Finn made up his mind. "Then Stefanie has a deal. The munchkins are hers for the weekend." *And remarkably, Katelyn was his.*

Chapter Fourteen

"A benefit dinner?" Finn looked at Katelyn as though she'd suggested bungee jumping into shark-filled waters with a frayed rope.

"I know this is our first weekend alone and the last thing I wanted to do was spend part of it at something work-related, but I don't have a choice. Lancaster Works is one of our largest customers and this is a command performance. It won't be a total bore. The food will be great—no rubber chicken. And there's an art auction to benefit For Kids' Sake—Lancaster's pet charity, I might add. All the proceeds go to help kids at risk. It's really a worthwhile cause."

Finn rubbed one hand across his jaw as he reluctantly agreed. "I've heard of the charity—and I know they do good work for the kids." He glanced down at the jeans he was wearing. "I just hadn't planned on having to wear a monkey suit."

Katelyn shook her head. "It's dressy casual—the art will be displayed outside and with the heat no one wants to broil in tuxes and long gowns." She glanced at her watch. "But we need to get moving."

Finn turned off the burners beneath the dinner he'd been cooking.

She looked ruefully at the food they wouldn't eat. "I'm

sorry about dinner. The benefit is what I started telling you about when Stefanie dropped by.''

''I suppose it's a good thing she didn't accept my invitation to dinner,'' Finn replied wryly.

''I hope this doesn't mean I'll never taste your cooking,'' she added.

''Of course you will. It'll still be here tomorrow. You *have* heard of leftovers?''

Katelyn had, but she'd rarely eaten them. Still, she smiled. ''Of course.''

It didn't take long to dress and then drive in the Jeep to Tuscany, the upscale restaurant where the benefit was being held. Finn had expected a hotel ballroom. Instead, For Kids' Sake had chosen a more intimate setting. The restaurant, styled after an Italian villa, looked as though it should be sitting in the rural countryside of Italy rather than in the midst of a metropolitan city.

But Finn was looking at the people. Dressy casual, Katelyn had said. Apparently that was what the privileged called thousand-dollar informal outfits. He spotted plenty of women in little black dresses that revealed lots of skin.

Katelyn leaned close. ''I need to circulate. Do you want to come with me?''

Finn shook his head, realizing this was her showtime. ''I'd like to take a look at what's up for bid in the silent auction.''

''Okay. I won't be too long.'' She strode off confidently and Finn paused to admire her. Katelyn fit in instantly, clearly in her element, surrounded by other successful, powerful people.

Finn tried to resist the feeling that swamped him—of being an outsider, welcome here only because of Katelyn. He strolled through the display of paintings, prints, photographs and sculptures.

He couldn't fault the quality of the art—some was crashingly modern, the sort of thing he never understood. But there was an equal number of representational pieces.

Finn felt himself stiffen uncomfortably when he noted the beginning bids on most of the artwork. Most would cover the cost of running his limo service for months.

Waiters circulated with trays of drinks and appetizers. When one approached, Finn smiled at the man. "Any beer?"

The waiter looked down his long, thin nose. "Wine only, sir." Did he imagine the inflection on "sir?" "Red and white. There's a full bar inside." The man looked at him as though he were instructing someone beneath his notice. So, even the waiter was feeling superior.

"Then I'll go inside," Finn responded evenly, watching the waiter gravitate toward small cliques of the beautiful people.

Finn turned away. Searching the crowd, he spotted Katelyn and watched as she blended naturally with these people. He observed her technique as she glided effortlessly from one group to another. High-level schmoozing, Finn concluded, was one of her many talents.

Glancing at a particularly high-priced bronze, he also knew that Katelyn could bid on the artwork without blinking. An instinctive feeling burning in his gut told him he was in over his head.

At that moment, Katelyn reached his side. Her lips were still upturned in a smile and irrationally it angered him to see her having a good time.

He picked up two glasses of wine from a tray on a nearby table, handing her one. "Did you see everyone you needed to?"

She tipped her head back in an unconsciously regal motion. "Ah, but it's not important who I *see*…but that I'm *seen*."

Finn's gut clenched again, suddenly remembering that to

this crowd he was merely the hired help. Hired help looked down on by *their* hired help.

He took a healthy swig of wine. "I don't guess this is a beer crowd," he finally muttered.

She glanced toward the bar. "I'm not sure."

"I am."

Katelyn glanced at him curiously, then touched his arm. "The buffet line's open. Are you hungry?"

Finn's appetite had dried up along with his interest in the entire event. *See and be seen.* He doubted that included being seen with her chauffeur husband. "Aren't there more important people you should have dinner with?"

She cocked her head. "Are you angry about something?"

He swallowed the truth along with the last of the wine in his glass. "I thought who you ate with was part of the game."

"The tables are reserved. Ellington sponsored an entire table. From what my boss told me, our firm's table is going to be pretty empty. I thought you might like that."

"So we don't have to test out my social skills?"

Her smile faded. "Actually, I thought you might want to be alone with me."

Finn glanced around, knowing he was in a room of players. People who could hire and fire him without a second thought. Still, this was her work—something he knew she had to do, something she had to excel at. That she did so without an effort shouldn't anger him—he'd known that about her from day one, minute one.

He drew a deep breath. "I hadn't thought about it that way."

Relief filtered over her face. "And the food here is always wonderful."

That was something he wouldn't know. Pricey restaurants like this didn't fit into his budget—nor was it the sort of place he'd likely bring three small children. But he made an effort for Katelyn. "Any rubber chicken and I'm out of here."

She laughed, a silvery tinkling sound. "Cold poached salmon with capers and dill sauce is more like it." Seeing the surprise on his face, she confessed, "I came inside earlier for a drink and I peeked, which is probably why I'm dying to get to the buffet."

She was right about the food, but Finn didn't have much appetite.

"The live auction starts soon," Katelyn told him after they'd eaten, consulting her program. "That's when they really raise the money."

Finn's brows lifted. So the pricey things he'd seen at the silent auction were just the small stuff. *Wonderful.*

"Having a celebrity auctioneer helps," she continued, not catching the irony in his expression as they headed back outside.

Silk banners fluttered in the breeze as the live auction proceeded. Finn listened in amazement as an in-home gourmet dinner for eight prepared by an executive chef went for thousands. Finn couldn't imagine that any chef coming to his house to cook could be worth such an outrageous sum. But as Katelyn continued to remind him, it was all for a good cause.

However, even that reminder couldn't stanch the resentment he continued to feel. Especially when Katelyn excused herself to circulate again. To be seen, no doubt.

Outclassed, outpowered, he nursed his anger along with the coffee he'd switched to. His chauffeur's license would be yanked in a second if he was cited for driving with even the slightest hint of intoxication.

Unable to stop himself, he watched Katelyn's every move. She was sure, confident, classy. As he watched her interact with the power brokers, he reminded himself whose bed she was sleeping in. And that tonight, no one else—powerful or not—would be between them.

THE RIDE HOME was quiet—far too quiet for Katelyn's peace of mind. She'd sensed Finn's discomfort, but she hadn't understood it. Nor did she understand the anger she saw laced through that discomfort. It had been a pleasant, successful evening. What was wrong with him?

Finn strummed his fingers against the steering wheel as he waited for the garage door to open. He wanted out of Katelyn's car, the one she'd insisted they take. No doubt she'd thought it would have been difficult to explain that her escort and limo driver were the same person.

The house was ominously silent and dark as they entered. Quickly, Katelyn reached for the bank of switches that controlled the lights and stereo.

"I'm not in the mood for music," Finn said from behind her, far closer than she'd realized. "Or lights."

Reluctantly she dropped her hand, swallowing a nervous laugh. "What *are* you in the mood for?"

"You tell me."

She tried to read his expression in the darkness, which was relieved only by the moonlight glinting through the large picture window. "I can't shake the feeling that you're angry."

"Just because we spent the night catering to a bunch of pretentious snobs?"

Her mouth opened in surprise. "We spent the evening attending a benefit for at-risk kids. To raise money, they tend to invite people who can afford to spend money."

"Which is why your name was on the invitation, not mine." He waved away her next words. "I know you were there because your firm sponsored a table, but I also know that even if they hadn't, I wouldn't have been at a five-hundred-dollar-a-head dinner because I can't afford it. I also can't afford to waste an evening with people whose idea of a good time is who and how they can impress.''

Katelyn felt her tolerance disappear and a slow burn begin. ''Since you didn't spend two minutes talking to the other guests, how could you possibly know whether they were trying to impress anyone?''

He barked out an unpleasant laugh. ''I'm neither blind, nor deaf. And it doesn't take a mental giant to figure out what was going on there.''

Her slow burn escalated, speeding straight into overdrive, the flames scorching her temper. ''What's that supposed to mean?''

''Just that tonight was a trumped-up excuse for the haves to pretend they care about the have-nots. All they really care about is that the benefit provided a good photo op.''

''Are you lumping me in with the haves?'' Katelyn asked in a dangerously low voice.

''I wouldn't put you with the have-nots,'' Finn replied in an equally dangerous tone.

Katelyn realized in some part of her brain he had moved closer. ''No? Then just what would you call me?''

He wasn't just close, he had stolen all of the space between them. His voice scraped across her raw nerves, pulsing with hidden messages. ''What do you *want* me to call you?''

Want, a word they hadn't discussed. A need they hadn't fulfilled.

Katelyn leaned a fraction closer to him. ''What is it *you* want?'' Voice husky, the words were something between a challenge and a promise.

Finn's breathing deepened ''I won't be a lackey—not yours, not anyone's.'' His hands grasped her arms.

Even though his fingers felt like steel against her skin, he didn't hurt her. She sensed his control was nearly shredded, but some fragment of it remained. Recklessly, she wanted to destroy what was left.

Deliberately, she pushed. "Are you telling me you're a man?"

"Damn straight," he replied, his face so close to hers that she could feel the whisper of his breath.

"Because you're afraid to *show* me you're a man?" she taunted.

She'd only *thought* his fingers felt like steel. Now his entire body told her what steel really felt like. From his demanding mouth to the rigid line of his hips as they pressed against hers.

She wanted to gasp, to shout...to melt into him. But the battle still raged between them, adversaries locked into a fight neither could win.

But as Finn forced her mouth open, she felt her resistance slipping. Then called it back, willing herself to remember her anger...her incredible anger....

He tasted much as she'd remembered—all male, all power. Their war of words translated to their bodies...to their fused mouths...and the passion that had been building between them.

Relentlessly, Finn explored her mouth, dueled with her tongue, released the passion he'd been holding back for weeks. Passion he could no longer deny.

Anger had created heat. Heat had created fire.

And now it threatened to burn them as they grappled for control, superiority...and for each other.

Finn thought briefly of the tasteful, expensive dress she wore. As he ripped the buttons free, he knew it was worth every penny the damage cost.

Katelyn gasped as a cool rush of air-conditioned air struck her exposed skin. Then the heat beneath her skin drove away that shock. Shoes thudded around them unnoticed.

Repaying the favor, she pulled at his shirt, careless of the buttons that flew, the tearing sound of cloth. The tangle of clothes that separated them were pushed aside in a frenzy of motion.

Motion that carried them to the carpeted floor, still half-dressed. Then Finn overcame the essential barrier, ripping away her delicate lace panties.

Fingers curled into his back, Katelyn welcomed each movement, craved more when he sought entry. Gasping when he plunged inside, she eagerly met each thrust.

Raw need was in command.... Passion denied screamed for release.

Despite the coolness of the air, Katelyn felt the slick perspiration that slid between them, the heat they generated.

The impossible heat that increased...seeming to bubble beneath taut skin.

Katelyn wanted to scream at the intensity as he filled her. Her fingers laced into his thick, dark hair, then dropped to grasp his muscled shoulders.

The rawness of their need shocked her...delighted her...excited her beyond anything she'd ever imagined. Nothing in her previous relationships had prepared her for this...or for this man.

Each movement showed her he knew it. Answered her challenge...fulfilled her promise.

Her climax burst around them like blue lightning.

Finn shuddered against her, lost in the explosion of his own release.

Their heaving chests pressed together, and the rapid pace of their breathing echoed in the quiet room.

Finn pulled back, finally looking at her face, drowning in the color of her changeling eyes...the color of mystery. "So...anything else you'd like me to show you?"

Chapter Fifteen

Katelyn had thought it would be impossible to smile after the intense experience they'd shared. Yet she couldn't help it. "I like what I've seen so far," she said, her voice husky. "What else did you have in mind?"

It was her smile, Finn decided. It turned her aristocratic face into something touchable, approachable. It turned her into someone he could call Katie.

He stood abruptly, pulling Katelyn up with him, then lifted her easily into his arms.

Automatically she linked her arms around his neck. "What are you doing?"

"Let's take this to the bedroom."

"That's upstairs. You don't have to carry me—"

"Let a man do his work," he interrupted.

"You telling me you're not weak with passion?" Her sultry smile was enough bait to make him bite.

And he did, reaching down to nip her neck, eliciting a groan of pleasure.

"You still questioning what a man can do?" he muttered.

"No. Anticipating."

He took the stairs quickly, reaching their bedroom as though she weighed nothing, his breathing still even. Not bothering with the light switch, he carried her confidently to the bed, knowing the path well in daylight or darkness.

Trapping her with his arms, Finn rose above her, seeing in the flush of satisfaction the seeds of new desire. The drapes were open, and moonlight spilled across the room, illuminating Katelyn's high cheekbones, the curve of her mouth, the slash of her smile.

"I think I like show-and-tell," she told him in a come-hither voice, arching her brows, widening her smile.

She reached to pull off her remaining clothing, but Finn stilled her hands, his voice husky. "Let me." Seeing the surprise in her eyes, he kissed her hands. And the surprise deepened into something more.

Slipping the destroyed dress off her body, he paused, his gaze lingering on the wispy camisole, on the delicate hollows of her throat. The camisole followed, revealing the promise of her full breasts, covered by her last piece of clothing. Despite what they'd just shared, he felt his throat grow dry in anticipation as he unfastened the front hook of her bra. Her breasts spilled into his hands, surpassing all his expectations.

Finn took time only to shed the remainder of his own clothing. Then his lips traced the path his hands had taken in removing her clothes, starting with the gentle slope of her shoulder, the valley of her waist, the curve of her hips, then moving upward to suckle each breast.

Katelyn felt the tremors begin, the wonder of his touch. She'd nearly burned from the heat of their first joining. Katelyn wondered that she didn't incinerate from the sensations he was generating.

Then he waged a double assault, his mouth and hands roving over each inch of sensitized skin. Straining against him, she wondered why they hadn't shared this before.... Marveling at his control, she realized hers had taken flight.

Finn felt like a starving man at a banquet. Her skin was

as soft as he'd imagined, her body as lush and beautiful as he'd guessed. Why had he denied himself this feast so long?

Nibbling a trail over that skin, he took the time neither had had the patience to take before. Their frantic need hadn't been dulled. It had grown into something far larger, far more complex…something that had entrenched itself, taking hold of his heart, entwining it with hers.

Finn's hands roamed over her body, knowing he couldn't discover enough, touch enough. When he met the soft folds of her slick heat, he felt her arch against his hand, moan into his throat. He found that he was ready for her again, surprising himself.

But this time, the urgency was tempered with something greater, something he couldn't name. Yet he acted instinctively, exploring her body, giving her the pleasure she deserved, at the same time multiplying his own.

Her hands journeyed over his body, seeking each point of arousal, finding undiscovered ones. When she stroked the skin of his inner thighs, he felt himself tremble beneath the onslaught. Her mouth proved to be a wicked tool of wonder as she nibbled a path to his arousal. Then she reached for him, cupping and exploring—testing the last of his control.

Finn could wait no longer. When she was sheathed around him, she was at once both familiar and new, accepting his more controlled movements, responding to each one, deepening his desire, causing him to abandon all reason.

Each stroke built into a new awareness. Her legs wrapped around him, urging him on. Signalling pleasure, her every reaction fueled his hunger, goaded his passion, took him to a different plane.

Then her body rode the wave of explosion after explosion, her cries whipping around him, her pleasure spelled out against him. Wild, frenzied, their joining was duplicated by the runaway beating of caged hearts. Hearts that yearned toward each other, as their bodies played out increasing desire.

Katelyn couldn't restrain the depth of her longing, craving Finn's fullness, seeking his heat. Another climax slammed through her, a torrent of immeasurable passion. Reaching for him, curling her fingers into muscled shoulders, she felt his answering shudders deep inside as though he'd reached her very womb.

Clinging to him, she cherished each moment, reveled in the feel of his body—velvet over steel. When he pulled back slightly, she reluctantly released her grip, wishing they could remain joined forever.

Finn's gaze locked with hers as he gently swept her cheek with the back of his hand. Then his lips met hers, tenderly, almost sweetly, and Katelyn could only look at him with wonder.

He had expected the passion, the fire, but not the tenderness, nor the wealth of feelings unfolding inside. This woman had willingly taken on mothering his children…and becoming his lover.

How could he have thought he knew her? A woman of incredible talent, mysterious layers, and a tenderness he'd never suspected. And what did he have to offer her in return.

The truth?

By MORNING, Finn wondered if he had dreamed the magical night. But Katelyn greeted him with warm kisses, ones that led them into a shared shower.

A postponed breakfast turned into hours of lovemaking. Rumpled and satisfied, Finn agreed that a delivered pizza sounded far better than anything they'd have to leave the house for.

The hours sped by as wrapped in a cocoon of their own making, they laughed together, learned about each other, and shared secrets.

Katelyn confided that she enjoyed working from home—that she'd felt a new burst of creativity. In fact, her campaigns were fresher, more enjoyable than they had been in years.

She showered him with kisses, then convinced him to make love beneath only a blanket of stars. As he'd suspected, hidden under her proper exterior was a banked fire, one that now blazed with abandon.

When he was with her, it was easy for him to forget their beginnings, the reasons he had resented her money and position.

And when the children returned home at the end of the weekend, Finn enjoyed watching Katelyn interact with them, occasionally catching her eye, seeing the promise that lurked there, now knowing how well she could fulfill that promise.

FINN POKED his head into Katelyn's downtown office, looking for Daniel who hadn't been in his own office. The room looked eerily vacant without her dominant presence. In many ways, he wondered how she had made such a complete change from corporate crusher to domestic goddess. The thought made him smile.

"Hey, Finn," Daniel greeted him. "What are you grinning about?"

"Just thinking about how changed Katelyn is."

"In a good way?" Daniel questioned.

"Absolutely. That's why I'm smiling. But I still can't help wondering if she misses all this, being in the thick of the action, instead of the suburbs."

Daniel frowned. "Aren't things going well?"

"On the contrary. Things are going so well I can't help

wondering how she made such a complete transformation. It's almost as though she had been programmed to become the perfect wife and mother.''

Daniel tried to squelch his grin.

Noticing, Finn smiled himself. "Okay, give. What's so funny?''

"I guess it's all right to tell you now," Daniel replied, choking back a laugh.

Finn laughed as well, caught by Daniel's infectious humor. "What?''

"Actually she *was* programmed," Daniel admitted.

Finn's grin faltered. "What do you mean?''

"I knew Katelyn wouldn't consider marriage on her own, so I gave her a little nudge.''

"Nudge?''

Daniel nodded. "So to speak. You know what a control freak she is. And she hated that she wasn't in control of her smoking. So I gave her some tapes that were supposed to help her quit.''

"And?'' Finn prompted uneasily, remembering the label to a tape about femininity. He hadn't thought about it since.

"Instead they were tapes designed to push her biological clock into overdrive...make her want marriage, children, the entire package.''

Finn warmed with fury. "Is that what you call it? A package? What did Katelyn think of your plan?''

Daniel laughed uneasily. "She doesn't know. No sense ruining a good thing.''

"But you've told me. How am I going to explain that to Katelyn?''

Daniel's smile faded. "Katelyn's happy. She'll be grateful you met, regardless of the method.''

Finn met his eyes grimly. "I wish I could believe that.''

Daniel's voice was equally sober. "Despite what you might be thinking now, I did this because I care about Katelyn. She was headed down a lonely road, so caught up in her corporate climbing that she'd arbitrarily dismissed having a relationship or a family. You can't tell me she's not happier now.''

"No," Finn admitted. "But I hope it doesn't crash down on our heads when she finds out."

Daniel frowned. "I still think you're underestimating her."

But Finn wasn't mollified. "That's not the point. I'm afraid she'll think this was all my idea and that I've known about the tapes from the beginning."

"Then don't tell her."

"And have Katelyn believe I knew all along? No, that's not an option." Finn sighed, unable to hide his frustration. "Damned if I do, damned if I don't. Some choice."

KATELYN HUMMED as she dressed, pulling out her now daily work outfit—T-shirt and jeans. She frowned when she found that the button of her jeans didn't want to fasten. Tugging, then sucking in her breath, she still couldn't fasten them. She tried to remember if this pair had recently been washed—perhaps shrinking in the dryer. Then she laughed at herself.

The last several months Finn had done as he'd promised—cooking wonderful dinners every night he could, unless his work kept him too late. Face it, she told herself. Too much rich food, coupled with the chocolates she'd been craving, had piled on the pounds.

"It's diet time," she told the mirror. "And that means no more chocolates!" She frowned at her own image, having recently discovered that she could add chocolate chips to the pancakes Finn had taught her to prepare. She'd had them in mind to make for breakfast.

"No wonder you've gained weight," she told her image, wagging her finger in disapproval. After all, she didn't want

Finn's attention to wander. Well aware that he was a handsome man, she intended to keep his interest at home. And only at home.

Finn slipped up behind her, encircling her waist. "Morning, Katie."

Why had she ever minded the nickname, she wondered. It was that much more special since only Finn called her Katie. Leaning back into his arms, she wished they had at least another hour of privacy, but the children would wake up any moment, and Finn had an early-morning assignment.

He'd spent that time with her both in the late evenings and in the early morning hours before the children woke, when their bedroom was an island of intimate privacy.

Finn kissed the soft skin of her neck. She could tell he was wishing he had more time to spend with her. She turned in his arms then, meeting his lips for a lengthy kiss.

He groaned. "You're not making it easy to leave."

"I don't *ever* want to make it easy for you to leave."

"That would never happen," he promised, cradling her close.

She sighed against him, instantly remembering their morning's passion. "The kids will be up soon."

He kissed her forehead. "Afraid so." His lips trailed down to the tip of her nose, then feathered over her mouth.

"Daddy!" Jenny hollered. "Eric locked himself in the bathroom again!"

Regretfully, Finn drew away.

"Reality check," Katelyn told him, already missing the warmth of his body.

He grinned ruefully as he retrieved a screwdriver from his dresser drawer, having learned to keep it handy.

Katelyn glanced down at her gaping jeans, glad that Finn hadn't noticed. They were still newlyweds—she didn't want him to think she'd let herself go already.

But she'd have to find the right outfit to wear to brunch with Stefanie, who never missed anything. And Katelyn didn't want to hear her friend's merciless teasing.

STEFANIE PROPPED HER CHIN in one hand. "There's something different about you. But I can't tell what it is. Any chance you'll clue me in?"

Katelyn laughed. "Trust me. There really isn't anything new. Same old me."

"No," Stefanie insisted. "Something's different."

Resigned, Katelyn shrugged. "Jeez, don't you ever give up? I hate to point out my own shortcomings, but okay, I guess I look a little different because I've put on a few pounds."

Cocking her head, Stefanie studied her. "Nope, that's not it."

Feeling uncomfortably like a bug under a microscope, Katelyn shifted in her chair. "Trust me. I had to search through my whole closet to find something to disguise it. If you'd seen me trying to put on my jeans this morning—"

"Katelyn." Stefanie stared at her. "Your *jeans* don't fit?"

"It's not a capital crime. I've already started a diet—no chocolate-chip pancakes this morning."

"When did you start eating stuff like that?"

"Don't knock it till you try it. Besides, I could eat chocolate for breakfast, lunch and dinner."

Stefanie made a strangulated choking sound. "Good grief, Katelyn, are you that dumb or are you just stringing me along?"

Stung, Katelyn straightened up. "I don't know what you're talking about."

Stefanie stared at her. "You really don't know, do you?"

"Know what?"

"Your jeans don't fit. You're craving chocolate. Did it

occur to you that something might be going on here? You are a *married* lady now.''

Katelyn blinked.

''We're getting you to an OB-GYN *now*. We'll call yours first. If he can't take you, we'll go to mine. This is a genuine, certifiable *emergency!*''

DAZED, Katelyn stumbled from her doctor's office. It no longer mattered that Stefanie had embarrassed her by bull-dozing past the receptionist, blatantly convincing the woman that it *was* an emergency.

She was going to have a baby. Finn's baby.

And from the dates the doctor calculated, she had conceived that first wonderful weekend four months ago. Never having been regular, she hadn't worried about a missed period. Truthfully she hadn't even noticed. Her days were a whirlwind of work and kids, her nights a whirlwind of an entirely different nature. The months had just slipped by.

Ever since the doctor had given her the news, all she could picture was Finn's face when she told him. They had created a new life, a new brother or sister for Jenny and the twins.

Another new Malloy. She could scarcely wait to hear what Finn would say when he found out.

Chapter Sixteen

Katelyn floated home in a cloud of euphoria. The children were on a field trip, so the house was empty. Thinking of the one spare bedroom that could be turned into a nursery, Katelyn ascended the first step of the stairs. Before she could climb on the second, the doorbell rang. Knowing she still had a silly grin plastered on her face, one she couldn't shake, Katelyn hoped it wasn't someone who would guess her secret. She wanted Finn to be the first one to know.

Opening the door, she stared in surprise. "Daniel! I wasn't expecting you, but it's great to see you." Grabbing his arm she pulled him inside. "Come on in. I was just telling Finn the other day that we need to have some sort of get-together. You know, an officially married sort of party. We're both so busy we haven't even considered entertaining, but now I think we should."

Daniel stared at her. "I don't mean to be rude, but it's not like you to babble."

She laughed. "You're right. It's just that I'm happy. So much that it's overflowing. Who'd have thought it?" Katelyn clasped his hand. "You did though. You were the only one who told me I'd be happier with a husband and family. I really am grateful to you, Daniel. You could say this was all your doing."

He grinned in relief. "So you do know. And I thought

Finn was going to keep the plan under his hat. But obviously I was right. You're clearly happy even though you know.''

Katelyn felt a warning pang, yet she managed to keep her expression noncommittal. "Know about what?"

"The tapes."

She blinked.

"You know," he continued, "the ones you thought were to help you stop smoking and instead they made you want to be the wife and mother of the century." He pantomimed a moment for her benefit.

"And Finn knew about them," she questioned quietly.

"Sure. You must have known that." He paused, his eyes widening. "You did know that, didn't you?"

Katelyn's expression tightened as she felt the knife of betrayal. "You and Finn conspired to make me believe some stupid subliminal tape?"

"I wouldn't say conspired—"

Katelyn cut off his words. "What would you call it? Just having a little fun at someone else's expense?"

"You're blowing this all out of proportion," Daniel protested.

Her gaze narrowed. "You think so? Based on those tapes I cut back on a thriving career I had sacrificed my entire life to build. You and Finn decided that marriage would fill any holes that were left in my life!"

"You just said you were happy!"

Katelyn ignored the searing wave of pain. "I was deluded. How do I know what I'm really feeling? Perhaps when this brainwashing fades, I'll resent the hell out of my decisions."

"But you and Finn—"

"The man who eagerly helped you put your plan in action." She retorted bitterly, turning to hide the sudden spurt of tears.

"Katelyn, I wouldn't have said anything if I'd known you would react like this."

Her eyes met his. "How long do you think I could have existed in this fog? At some point I would have wakened to the truth."

Remorse filled Daniel's face. "I only had your best interests at heart. There was no grand scheme to trick you, Katelyn."

Her face was bleak. "Then why didn't Finn tell me?"

"Katelyn—"

"Daniel, if you don't mind, I'd like to be alone now."

"But you have everything wrong—"

"Daniel, I appreciate your concern, but I don't particularly want to see you right now. I thought we had a special bond, one beyond reproach." Her betrayed eyes lifted. "I thought I could trust you."

"You can—"

She shook her head. "Goodbye, Daniel."

Quietly she shut the door, but the very air seemed to reverberate with all the unspoken emotions.

Daniel kicked the pillar flanking the door. With a muttered curse, he left, knowing he had to find Finn and warn him.

WEARILY, Finn pulled in the driveway. It had been a killer day, making impossible time deadlines, shuffling clients. He'd planned to be home in time to cook dinner, but that had been scrapped as well. And though he'd tried to call Katelyn to let her know he'd be late, the phone had been on the service all day. That had bothered him—it wasn't like her to use the service unless she was gone or in a phone conference. And it wasn't likely that she and the children had been gone all day. Then his cell phone had croaked and he hadn't been able to call again.

He breathed a sigh of relief seeing her Jeep parked in

the garage. If something was wrong, she would have called. Maybe she just needed a break from the phones. Remembering Katelyn's early-morning passion, he knew nothing else was wrong with her.

The house seemed quiet when he entered. A quick survey of the kitchen showed it to be clean and empty. Whatever she'd ordered for dinner must have already been stashed away. Strolling through the dining room, he glanced through the patio doors, but it was empty, too.

Hearing a thump from overhead, he guessed they must all be upstairs. He headed toward the landing, anxious to see Katelyn.

Despite the long day, he felt a new spring in his step as he climbed the stairs, whistling beneath his breath. He didn't venture down the hall toward the kids' rooms. He wanted to surprise Katelyn first.

Quietly he pushed open the bedroom door.

But the surprise was his.

Katelyn stood in front of the bed, throwing her clothes in suitcases. Designer suits were tossed together with jeans and T-shirts. A scattering of wickedly feminine lingerie was littered over the bed as well.

Finn could only stare in amazement at first. Recovering his voice, he strode inside. "Katie, what are you doing?"

She didn't turn to look at him. "My name is Katelyn."

He didn't register the words, as much as the inflection. Her voice could have frozen boiling water.

"I know your name. I want to know what you're doing."

"Packing. That should be clear even to you."

Her words stung, but he had to know what had caused this abrupt change. "Why?"

"I'm not sure we have enough time to go into *all* the reasons." Her changeling eyes were the color of cold steel—gray and accusing. "We could start with your ambush—the subliminal tape that made me want to leap into marriage and motherhood. Then, of course, there's your altruistic reason for tricking me—to pay me back for being such a heartless snob. After all, I had a high-paying job, while you were struggling to raise three kids alone.''

Shock silenced him momentarily. He felt a knot in the pit of his stomach, which told him what he'd suspected, since Daniel had revealed the truth about the tape. It was inevitable that Katelyn had to find out at some time—and he had let all of his chances to explain slip away. Still, he had to try. "I know it sounds bad with only the bald facts—''

"The truth you mean.''

Briefly Finn closed his eyes, hoping for a miracle. "All right, the truth. But not for the reasons you believe.''

"Oh, you mean now you no longer need a built-in baby-sitter?" she challenged. "Or is it that you're tired of having Carol Brady greeting you every evening?''

"You know that isn't true.''

"Which is why you told me everything, including the fact that I married you because of a subliminal tape.''

Finn shoved a hand through his thick, unruly hair. "I realize I should have told you. I put it off because I didn't know how to make you understand.''

Katelyn stared at him, her face filled with both anger and pain. "I understand all too well. You saw the perfect opportunity to both pay me back and get a free baby-sitter, one who couldn't quit.''

"That's not true, Katie.''

"Don't call me that!'' Her voice was close to a screech, the volume tempered no doubt only because of the children.

Finn saw everything they'd built crumbling. And knew he had himself to blame. As soon as he'd learned about the tape he should have told her. "I'm sorry that I didn't tell you about the tape. And as lame as this sounds now, it was because I was afraid you'd act this way. I'm sorry you didn't know the truth. But I can't wish we hadn't married. I wouldn't have gotten to know you…the children wouldn't have, either. And I don't mean as a baby-sitter. You've been the only mother the twins have known, and for that matter, Jenny, too. She lost her mother when she was so young. They care about you, Katelyn.'' His gaze sought out hers. ''So do I. Can you forgive me for not telling you as soon as I knew?''

But her eyes had taken on an unforgiving hue. And suddenly he knew the color of regret.

Katelyn clutched a forgotten nightgown in her hands. ''I thought you cared about *me*. Instead I find out that you and Daniel coldly manipulated me. You didn't care about me, or that you could be wrecking a career I spent my life building.'' Her voice resonated with raw hurt. ''I don't have that much forgiveness in me.''

''But you can't just leave!'' he argued.

Pivoting, she slammed the lid of her suitcase closed. ''Watch me.''

''Daddy!'' Erin shrieked just outside the bedroom, coming to a halt after running down the hallway. ''Jenny's got spots!''

Torn between the woman who had grown to mean so much to him and his daughter's words, Finn stared beseechingly at Katelyn. But she was walking toward Erin. ''What kind of spots?''

''Red. All over. She's sick.''

Katelyn marched down the hallway and after a heartbeat, Finn followed. But he paused at the doorway, watching her with Jenny.

''I feel icky all over and I itch,'' Jenny was telling Katelyn who had pressed her hand to the child's forehead. ''And I'm hot.''

''How's your tummy?''

''Yucky.''

"Would some ice cream make it feel better?" Katelyn asked.

"Uh-uh. I'm not hungry."

Katelyn frowned. Jenny hadn't wanted any dinner either. "Do you think maybe Sally Sue would make you feel better?" She reached over to the dresser to fetch Jenny's favorite doll.

"She might get spots, too," Jenny replied, obviously torn.

Katelyn shook her head. "Sally Sue's already had measles and chicken pox, so she can't get either one again."

"Which one have I got?"

"I'm not sure. Chicken pox, I think. But the doctor will know."

"You won't let him give me a shot, will you?" Jenny implored, her eyes widening.

Katelyn gazed at this child who'd grown so dear. As much as she despised what Finn had done, she couldn't take out her anger on Jenny. She reached for Jenny's brush. "Would it feel better if I brushed your hair?"

Jenny nodded, her eyes flickering. "No shot?"

"No shot," Katelyn agreed, fairly sure neither childhood disease required shots. "Unless the doctor thinks it's absolutely necessary."

"You make him say no."

Katelyn drew the brush through the child's dark, silky hair. "I'll do my best. After I brush your hair and we put some calamine lotion on your spots, would you like a story?"

"Uh-huh. The fairy-princess one." Jenny snuggled against her.

Katelyn continued brushing her hair.

And Finn continued watching her, feeling hope build.

Katelyn lifted her gaze just then. Her accusing eyes conveyed far more than words. And Finn felt his hope die. He should have told her.

Jenny turned her face toward Katelyn again. ''Will you stay with me tonight? Please?''

And a collective breath was drawn, fluttering through the room as they waited for her answer.

Chapter Seventeen

"Until you go to sleep?" Katelyn asked.

Jenny nodded.

Finn watched from the doorway, wondering how deep a hold the children had on her—if it was enough to keep her here. If Jenny's spots had been an answer to his plea for a miracle.

He had hoped from what Katelyn had said that she planned to take Jenny to the doctor, which would delay her departure. And now his daughter had bought him a few more hours with Katelyn.

Hours he didn't intend to waste.

Finn checked on the twins, warning them that they only had a few more minutes to play before bath time. Going downstairs, Finn grabbed a flashlight and headed into the backyard, stumbling over Eric's trike. After a few missteps, he found what he was looking for.

Taking out his pocket knife, he sliced through a stem, capturing a perfect peach rose.

Holding it carefully, he headed back inside to bathe the twins and put them to bed—which he knew would require at least one story per child.

Then he had favors to call in, from friends who could be pressed into taking all his late-night assignments for the coming days. He suspected he would only know hour by hour how long Katelyn planned to stay. But he didn't intend to miss any of that time.

KATELYN STRETCHED her stiff body, easing her arm from beneath Jenny's head. Reaching over, she turned the lamp off, leaving only the soft glow of the nightlight. Jenny had fallen asleep initially, then awakened twice. As restless as she was, there was a good chance she would wake up again during the night.

Pulling a blanket up over the sleeping child, Katelyn knew she couldn't abandon Jenny when she was sick. Her feet dragged as she returned to the master bedroom and reluctantly opened the door.

Dozens of flickering candles greeted her. They were nestled on the windowsill, atop the dresser, lined up across the vanity, stacked on the nightstands. And they gave off the scent of roses and magnolias. Suspiciously, she looked around but didn't see Finn.

Katelyn took another step inside. And then another. The bed had been turned down. On her pillow rested one peach rose. She wanted to reach out and fling the rose away. To throw away Finn's offering. Instead her fingers touched the velvet petals.

Slowly she picked up the rose, bringing it beneath her nose to inhale the sweet fragrance. The thorns had been trimmed away, leaving the stem smooth. She wished Finn could remove the thorns from their relationship as easily.

Why had he done it? Why had he let her take his children into her heart?

Why had he made her love him?

KATELYN HELD JENNY in her lap as they waited in the doctor's office. Normally independent, Jenny had become very clingy since the previous evening.

She had awakened shortly after Katelyn had gone to bed,

but not to sleep. Relieved not to have to confront Finn in the intimate space of the bed, Katelyn had taken refuge in Jenny's room. Knowing she wouldn't get any sleep, she'd spent the night in a rocker watching over the child.

Katelyn glanced over at the twins, who were settled in the play corner, engrossed in the box of toys, pulling out nearly every single one. She supposed she should tell them to only take out one toy at a time, but she didn't have the heart or energy to correct them.

In a few minutes, a smiling nurse came to escort them to one of the inner rooms. It didn't take long for the doctor to diagnose Jenny's chicken pox. He advised rest as he wrote out a prescription to stem the itching. Jenny didn't lose her anxious look until the doctor gave her a balloon.

Then he glanced at Katelyn. "Don't look so worried. Plenty of rest and your good care and she'll get through this just fine."

Katelyn managed to smile, despite the knot in her stomach. *Her good care.* The doctor couldn't know that she planned to leave, that the situation made it impossible for her to stay.

She glanced down at Jenny and a lump formed in her throat as she thought of leaving them.

Just then Jenny glanced up. "You can have the balloon, since you kept him from giving me a shot."

The lump in her throat thickened. "I didn't do anything, sweetie. You didn't need a shot."

"You fixed it," Jenny insisted. "'Cause you're my mommy."

Katelyn blinked away the tears that threatened. Kneeling down, she hugged Jenny, knowing what a precious child she was. Knowing she'd fallen in love with all of them.

KATELYN THUMBED through the first-aid book, checking to see if she should take any other precautions with Jenny's chicken pox. But the section on chicken pox reiterated the doctor's advice.

She was closing the book when a thought occurred to her. Precautions. She remembered what the obstetrician had told her the previous day—to consult him if she had any health concerns, since many things could affect her pregnancy.

Vaguely recalling having heard that measles could be damaging to an unborn child, she suddenly wondered if chicken pox could be, too. Panic fluttered and she knew she had to speak to the doctor. Glancing at her watch, she saw that it was almost five-thirty, leaving barely enough time to reach the office before it closed.

Anxiously she held the line for more than five minutes as the doctor finished with a patient. She filled him in on the situation quickly.

"Have you had chicken pox, Mrs. Malloy?"

"Yes, I'm sure I have. I remember what they looked like and how they itched—that's how I knew to put calamine lotion on Jenny. My mother tied gloves on me so I wouldn't scratch my face." Katelyn stopped abruptly, realizing she was rambling.

"Then there's no reason for concern, Mrs. Malloy. The fetus can't contract chicken pox from a third party—your daughter. And since you've already had the chicken pox, you have sufficient immunity in your system."

Katelyn clutched the phone closer. "So you're sure chicken pox can't hurt the baby?"

"I'm sure. Your diligence is commendable, but you can relax. I hope your daughter's well soon."

'Thank you, doctor." Replacing the receiver, Katelyn turned around. And met Finn's stare.

"I..." She steadied her voice. "I didn't know you were home."

"Apparently." He took a few steps closer. "Katie, is that what it sounded like? Are we going to have a baby?"

Katelyn wasn't sure there was a *we* in this equation. She lifted her head, firming her chin. "*I'm* going to have a baby, yes."

He closed the distance between them, grasping her arms. "That's wonderful." His smile dimmed for a moment. "When did you find out?" Then he shook his head. "It doesn't matter. All that matters is that we're going to have a baby."

"That's a rather simplistic attitude, don't you think?"

Finn didn't release her arms. "It's simple to me, yes. We've had a major misunderstanding, and I'll admit that I caused it by not telling you about the tapes as soon as I learned what Daniel had done. But, now that we're having a baby, doesn't this put a new spin on things? Let the past stay just there—in the past."

"No."

Finn glanced at her. "Just like that?"

"Me having a baby doesn't change anything. You didn't think enough of me to tell me the truth before. Why now? Because there's a baby? I don't think it's fair to the child."

"Katie, that's not the only reason—"

"I may be a victim of subliminal conditioning, but I'm not a completely gullible fool. You really think I'd believe whatever reasons you tell me?" Her eyes took on the hue of newly frozen ice. "I think not. And don't bother buying anymore subliminal tapes. I disabled the sleep timer on the stereo."

"You still intend to leave?"

"As soon as Jenny's better. I promised her I'd stay with her while she was sick." The child didn't know that she meant to leave the family. Innocently, she'd asked Katelyn to keep taking care of her and she had agreed, still choked up that Jenny had called her "Mommy."

Finn realized this was the only extension that he was going to get. Wisely, he didn't argue further. Another thought struck him. "Was it chicken pox or measles?"

"Chicken pox."

Briefly Finn closed his eyes, dreading asking the next question, knowing he had to. "Is it safe for you to take care of Jenny?"

"The doctor said it is."

Finn let out a breath he hadn't been aware of holding in. "This isn't the end of our discussion, Katie."

"As far as I'm concerned it is." She turned and Finn's eyes focused on her abdomen, thinking about what they'd created. Realizing they'd created even more. Now he just had to convince Katelyn of that.

KATELYN TURNED DOWN the lamp, watching Jenny sleep. The ache in her back told her she couldn't spend another night in the rocking chair. And she certainly couldn't spend the duration of Jenny's illness without sleep.

She would ignore him, Katelyn decided. Pretend he didn't exist. Stifling a yawn, she navigated down the hallway. Although she opened the bedroom door cautiously, no surprises awaited her.

Not knowing whether to be relieved or disappointed, she quickly changed her clothes, slipping into a simple gown. Reaching for a brush, she stared into the mirror for a moment.

Had her cleavage always been so generous? Katelyn stared down at her transformed body. It was odd that she'd managed to miss the changes for so long. Had she been so happy she simply hadn't noticed? She felt a new pang, a mixture of loss and discovery.

Resolutely she turned toward the bed, refusing to think about everything she'd shared in that space with Finn. Pulling the sheet and blanket up to her chin, she stared into the darkness. Several minutes later she sighed and reached over to flip on her lamp. Fiddling with the dial of her bedside clock radio, she found a station she liked, adjusted the volume to low, then clicked the lamp off.

She turned her back toward Finn's side of the bed, determined to offer him only a cold shoulder. Punching her pillow, she tried to find a comfortable position, one that would allow her to fall asleep. It would be the best way to ignore Finn when he came to bed.

But when he came to bed she was still wide-awake, her mind filled with everything she'd learned in the past forty-eight hours. She held herself stiff as she heard the rustle of his clothing as he undressed. Telling herself not to, Katelyn imagined him in the abbreviated boxers he wore to bed.

She clutched her pillow more tightly. Feeling the mattress dip with his weight, she rolled closer to the edge of the bed, hanging on as though it were the ledge of a cliff.

Finn sighed heavily and she knew instantly that she hadn't fooled him. He was completely aware that she was awake. Yet, stubbornly, she held her rigid position as unwanted memories assailed her, along with the heat of his body so close to hers.

Nights of unparalleled passion came to mind first, followed by images of how she'd tried unsuccessfully to seduce him time and again. Had it been such a chore to make love to her? Aggrieved, she flipped over and reached for her second pillow, punching it hard.

And connecting with Finn instead.

She heard his whoosh of breath, along with a surprised grunt. "What was that for?"

She didn't bother to try explaining it was a mistake. "Take your pick."

"If it'll work off your anger, you can take as many shots at me as you want."

"You don't have that much hide," she retorted.

He reached over, grasping her arm and shoulder and turning her to face him. "I don't know. We've shared plenty of skin."

She jerked back. "I hope you remember it well."

"It's burned in my brain."

"I hope the memories keep you warm, because I don't intend to." She shifted to turn away from him.

Finn's arm shot out to hold her in place. "Not so fast."

Chapter Eighteen

"Let go of me," she snapped.

"After you listen to what I have to say."

"A captive audience?" She gave an unladylike snort.

He didn't release her, instead shifting her to face him more closely. "If that's what it takes."

She wriggled against his hold.

"And apparently it does." But he was fighting for too much to give up. "I'm not the only one who enjoyed those 'memories.' Don't deny it, I wasn't alone sizzling in these sheets."

He sensed rather than saw the telltale betrayal of her pulse jumping in her throat. But instead of answering, she averted her face.

"Tell me you won't miss the children, Katie. Children who think of you as their mother."

"That was low," she retorted, turning her face back to stare at him. "It doesn't seem as though you thought out your plan. Didn't you consider how they would feel when I left?"

"Dammit. I told you this wasn't my plan! Admittedly, I made a mistake in keeping the truth from you. Tell me you never did something similar."

"Oh, I made a huge mistake. When I didn't fire you after your first screwup. I wouldn't be here now."

Finn released his grip. He'd forgotten how barbed her tongue could be. He also knew how raw her pain was. She was bound to strike back. But he intended to outlast her, to take every dart and quill she flung his way. And turn them into Cupid's arrows.

KATELYN STARED at Eric in dismay. A crop of red, widely scattered spots covered his face. Pulling up his T-shirt, she saw that the eruptions had spread over his body as well.

Not another case of chicken pox!

Jenny had started getting better, her clinginess easing somewhat, making Katelyn feel she would be able to leave soon. The past weeks had been a nonstop marathon, between caring for Jenny, keeping up with the twins, juggling her workload, and maintaining her hostile standoff with Finn.

Katelyn studied Eric, feeling her resolve melt. She couldn't leave him when he was sick, either. Although a growing, rambunctious toddler, he was scarcely more than a baby. One, she reminded herself, who had never known another mother. Holding a hand to his forehead, she felt the fever. Listless and doleful, he clung to her.

"I got spots," he announced, his face flushed, his warm body drooping.

Despite the video meeting she had planned, Katelyn lifted him into her lap. The phone rang and she proceeded with the conference. If her client thought it was odd that she held a spotty three-year-old, he didn't comment.

When the meeting concluded, she took Eric upstairs for a cooling bath. Then she tucked him into bed slathered with calamine lotion. Luckily the girls were still playing with their Barbie dolls in Jenny's room.

"How about some dinner?" Katelyn asked him. "I could order you something special."

He shook his head.

"Ice cream?"

"Uh-uh."

Katelyn smoothed his forehead. "Juice?"

Eric shook his head again.

"Anything you *do* want?"

"Just you, Mommy."

Katelyn's heart lurched. No doubt he was simply following Jenny's lead. Even so, she was overwhelmed. He reached out warm arms, and Katelyn cuddled him close, knowing she was lost again.

After he eased into sleep Katelyn slipped away to her bedroom to call the pediatrician. He reassured her that she'd taken the right steps and that he would call the pharmacy to order the same medicine Jenny had been prescribed.

Hanging up the phone, Katelyn braced herself for at least another two weeks. Time that she knew she would spend locked in the same battle with Finn that had been raging— primarily in their bed at night.

It was a battle of silence and accusations. But Katelyn couldn't fight the feelings of anger that flared each time she thought of the tapes that had pushed her over the edge. Although he claimed it was Daniel's plan, Katelyn was convinced Finn had collaborated with him.

She stood up, possessed with the need to learn more about the stranger who was her husband. Crossing to Finn's dresser, she pulled open the top drawer, ignoring the niggling sense of guilt she felt. She'd never touched his things, even leaving his freshly laundered clothes on the dresser top for him to put away.

Glancing inside, she nearly changed her mind, seeing a collection of what looked like his most personal things. Resolutely, she forced her reluctance aside. The children's newborn name bands from the hospital rested next to an antique pocket watch, one she guessed had probably belonged to his father or grandfather.

There were only a few pieces of jewelry—Finn's class ring, tiny baby rings, and... Katelyn picked up a simple gold band—no doubt his wedding band from his marriage to Angela. She palmed the ring in her hand, tempted to read the inscription but finally putting it back in the drawer, unread. This was not part of her battle.

Pulling open another drawer, she was relieved to see stacks of clothing. She didn't want to dig through any more of Finn's past.

But after a thorough inspection, the drawer only revealed T-shirts, boxers and socks. Thoughts whirling, she decided on another tack. It was time she listened to her programming.

Stalking over to the stereo, she plunked the tape in with greater force than necessary, knowing just how she planned to spend the next few hours.

FINN UNLOCKED the door, wondering if everyone was asleep. It was late—far later than he'd intended to be. But he had driven the Mathison Foundation van today on a special outing to Galveston. And a carload of loud, high-spirited kids had been difficult to control. Since Katelyn now kept the phone on the answering machine all the time, he had left a message, telling her that he would be late.

But his main concern wasn't whether she'd listened to the message, or even that he hadn't been there to cook dinner. Rather that his time was running out. Katelyn had made it clear that when Jenny was well, she still planned to leave. Since he couldn't wish his daughter to remain ill, he knew the days were numbered.

Finn opened the door quietly, not wanting the dog to start barking and rouse the household. He breathed a sigh of relief when Snuffles stayed quiet.

His relief was short-lived.

"You...you!"

He barely registered Katelyn's voice when he realized something was hurtling straight toward him. He ducked in time to see a tape hit the wall. "Katie, what are you do—?"

The last of his words were cut off as she chucked a plastic cassette holder at him. It bounced harmlessly behind him. "I'm not sure what—"

"How could you?" she demanded.

He glanced at the fallout. "First of all, *I* didn't. Besides, you already knew about the tape."

"But I didn't *listen* to them until today."

He winced. It was one thing knowing about the tape, another listening to it. Then he realized exactly what she'd said—*them*. Did that mean there had been more than one?

Another tape hurtled toward him and he realized there must have been at least one more.

"I suppose you thought you were real smart," she continued, the fire in her changeling eyes resembling heated amber. "And smug, and..." She pitched the tape's holder at him.

Finn moved to one side, wondering what else was in her arsenal. "For the hundredth time, it wasn't *my* plan."

"Then where did you get this tape label?" she demanded, tossing it at him.

Belatedly, Finn remembered finding the label, intending to return it to her, then forgetting about it.

"It's not what you think—"

"I think you men stick together," she accused. "Daniel wasn't the one to benefit from this deception. It doesn't take a genius to guess that you must have been the mastermind."

He sighed. "That's *not* true. But maybe now that everything's out in the open—"

"Like how you tried to turn me into a harlot?"

He stared at her. "What?"

"Don't play dumb with me," she countered, picking up another tape.

Vaguely he wondered if there was an entire collection.

"I truly don't know what you're talking about."

"Oh, really. And you don't know anything about the Modern Woman tape, I suppose."

Katelyn didn't wait to see if he would come up with an explanation. Instead she tossed the offending tape at him, throwing wide and high, hitting the wall above his head.

"Katie, I hope you're running out of ammo."

"I've only just begun." She flung the last remaining cassette holder at him. "And you'll think this was a pleasure excursion in comparison!"

"MOMMY!" Jenny ran down the stairs, back to her normal self now that Eric had broken out with the chicken pox.

After more than a month of the new moniker Katelyn was growing accustomed to it, but it still thrilled her to think the children thought of her that way.

"I'm in here," Katelyn called out from her study. She was trying to get caught up on a killer campaign—this one was for a jewelry company that wanted a romantic theme for their advertising. What actually came to mind was putting out all the eyes in their dreadful little Cupids and smashing all their heart-shaped jewelry into twisted pieces. But she suspected the client wouldn't be pleased.

With the children out of preschool so that they wouldn't infect their classmates, she'd gotten behind with everything. And, she acknowledged, the time together had allowed her bond with the children to grow even stronger.

"Mommy," Jenny repeated, skidding to a stop in front of her desk.

Katelyn glanced up from the computer screen. "Yes, sweetie."

"You'd better come look at Erin."

Katelyn hit the save key. "Why? Is something wrong?"

Jenny nodded her head. "Spots."

"Spots!" Katelyn's hands crashed onto the keyboard. "She can't have spots! I moved her into your room. I haven't let her near Eric—and I gave him an extra week to recover. How did she catch them?"

Jenny shrugged her shoulders. "I dunno. But she's got 'em."

Groaning, Katelyn followed Jenny up the stairs.

Chapter Nineteen

Glad to be home early, Finn strolled through the kitchen, relieved to see that Katelyn hadn't ordered anything for dinner yet. He planned to cook her favorites. Although Erin had wound up having the most severe case of chicken pox and the longest recuperating time, he knew that it wouldn't be long until she was well. Which meant it wouldn't be long until Katelyn would leave.

Going upstairs to change clothes, he was surprised that everything was so quiet. Poking his head into the twins' room, he saw that Erin was sleeping. Down the hall he found Jenny and Eric in Jenny's room. Finn couldn't prevent a grin when he saw that Jenny was playing G.I. Joe with her younger brother. Especially in the room Katelyn had converted to something very frilly and little girlish.

Despite the scalloped wallpaper, canopy bed, and the new lace bedspread, Jenny was deep into the game of war. It was interesting to watch the dynamics change when the twins were separated.

But where was Katelyn? His smile faded. For a moment he felt pure terror in his gut. Increasing his pace to a near run, he headed back downstairs and searched the rooms. She wasn't in any of them.

Running back upstairs, he paused at the master bedroom. The door was ajar and he pushed it open. His eyes darted around the room. He felt the relief whoosh through him when he saw Katelyn in a wing chair angled close to the window.

Finn stepped closer to her, but she didn't stir. He closed the remainder of the distance between them. Her fiery hair feathered softly from a wildly askew barrette, past her earlobes, trailing down her neck, curling in soft wisps.

Long lashes rested against translucent skin. No makeup camouflaged the sprinkle of freckles across her nose and her rosy lips were bare of lipstick. He had to stifle a powerful need to reach over and kiss each freckle, then capture her mouth.

Finn expected her to sense his presence and wake up, but then he saw the exhaustion on her face, the steady rise and fall of her breathing. She was sound asleep. Retrieving a light cotton blanket, he bent to cover her, but his gaze lingered on the changes in her body. Now that she was six months pregnant, her abdomen bulged slightly. With his baby.

Unable to resist, Finn reached out to stroke her cheek. Still she slept on. Knowing he was entering precarious territory, his hand moved downward to stroke her stomach, something he'd longed to do since he'd learned she was pregnant. A sense of possessiveness filled him and he knew he would fight anybody and anything to keep Katelyn and his baby with him.

Fuzzily Katelyn opened her eyes. Trying to focus, she blinked and wondered if she was still dreaming. She thought Finn was kneeling reverently in front of her, holding his hands over her stomach.

Rubbing one eye, she looked again. And met Finn's gaze as he glanced up. Something deep inside fluttered as she read the intensity in his eyes. It was something greater than desire, more far-reaching than passion. She fought to cling to her anger, knowing she needed the shell of its protection.

"You were sleeping," Finn told her.

She cleared her throat. "I was tired."

Finn didn't move his hands. "You're doing too much."

"No. It's just that my back's bothering me—"

"Where?" His eyes lit with concern. "It could be something serious."

"No, I just did a little too much bending." Katelyn indicated her lower back. "And my shoulders are stiff."

"Come get into bed."

She raised one eyebrow. "Excuse me?"

"I'm going to rub your back."

"There's no need to—"

"This is your health, Katie, and it affects the baby's health."

Katelyn knew she should refuse, but her back ached…and more importantly, she was drawn to the expression she saw on Finn's face, wondering just what the intense look in his eyes meant.

He grasped her hands, pulling her from the rocker, seeming to sense the low level of her resistance.

"While you slip on a robe, I'll make some tea," he told her.

Since that sounded inordinately good, she didn't protest his assumption that she would easily shed her clothes for a back rub. Katelyn frowned as she glanced at her changing body in the bathroom mirror. Finn hadn't seen her naked in months—not that he would today, either. She shrugged, knowing that what he thought shouldn't matter.

Reentering the bedroom, she saw the flicker of several candles. It was not quite the display he'd once put on, but still, their soft scent reached her. Along with a soothing yet oddly sensual feeling. Naked beneath her robe, she hadn't expected candlelight or…music. Finn had flipped the stereo on as well, and soft music played in the dim light of the flickering candles.

He reentered the bedroom just then, carrying a steaming cup of tea. "Chamomile with honey," he told her, lifting the cup slightly. "The water just boiled."

"You were busy while it was heating," she commented, gesturing toward the candles and stereo.

"For relaxation purposes."

She eyed him warily. "Um."

Finn placed the tea on the nightstand, along with a small dish. "Oreos."

For some silly, stupid reason the Oreos touched her more than the candlelight or music. She'd been craving chocolate for months and lately she couldn't seem to get her fill of the cookies. But she was positive they didn't have any and Finn hadn't had time to go to the store. "But I was sure we were out."

"We were. I stopped on the way home and bought them."

Katelyn bit her lip, hoping the pain would stop the ridiculous melting she was feeling. *Tapes,* she told herself. *Remember the tapes.* Trying to ignore him, she stretched out on the bed.

Katelyn also tried to ignore the press of his weight against the mattress…his very closeness. Then his hands gently kneaded the back of her neck. Initially stiff and rigid, she gradually relaxed as his hands moved between her tense neck and shoulders.

When he slipped the robe back to free her shoulders and upper back, she tensed up immediately.

"Relax. This is for therapeutic purposes only," he told her.

Then why was she feeling anything but therapeutic? When Katelyn nodded, even that movement was stiff.

But Finn's hands worked their magic, gliding over her upper back, finding each tender, sensitive spot. When he pushed her robe down even farther, Katelyn knew she should protest, but she couldn't resist the joy of his touch, the memories it evoked.

But when the top of her robe neared her waist she reached for it in a panic, thinking of her expanded waistline.

"Katie, this is the part of your back that hurts," Finn protested as she tried to cover up.

"I don't want you to see how fat I've gotten," she mumbled against her pillow.

"That's not fat—it's baby," he admonished her. "And both of you look beautiful."

Katelyn slowly swung her face so that she could peer back at him. "You don't have to say that."

"I know I don't," Finn replied evenly. He purposely touched the sides of her waist. From his vantage point, there weren't any obvious changes.

He longed to turn her toward him, to see and feel the changes in her body, from the small bulge in her tummy to the fullness in her breasts. Knowing she wouldn't welcome such a move, he slid his hands over the soft skin of her lower back, over the slope of her hips, remembering how often he had touched her at will...and how much she had enjoyed his touch.

Lost in his own memories, in the satiny feel of her skin, he didn't see that Katelyn's fingers dug into her pillow, clenching until they were white.

Katelyn remembered their first night of lovemaking—the desperate, urgent need they had slaked, then the tenderness they had shared. She had thought nothing could be better. But she'd been wrong.

Everything they'd shared after that time until she'd learned about Finn's deception had been even more wonderful. They'd grown, shared, and built something precious. And now the touch of his hands brought all those memories soaring to the surface. Part of her longed to turn over, throw herself in his arms and let him ease the burning. But this was no simple thirst to quench, no itch to scratch. Because this was for keeps...her heart was at stake.

ONCE SHE KNEW that Eric was fully recovered, Katelyn sat down with the children and explained that she would have to leave. It had been difficult.

"So, I'll miss you terribly, but—"

"You can't go!" Jenny blurted out, jumping to her feet.

"I just explained—" Caught up in the pain of telling the children, she didn't notice that Finn stood at the doorway.

"I don't care! You promised!" Jenny's voice trembled. "You said you'd never leave!"

With a sinking feeling, Katelyn recalled that promise. "But, sweetheart, sometimes things happen...things we can't predict or know about."

Jenny's gaze fixed on her. "Do you have a choice?"

"A choice?" Katelyn's dismay grew as her own words came back to mock her.

"Katelyn, are you ever going away?"

"Why should I do that?"

"Sometimes people do."

Katelyn realized Jenny was referring to her mother. "That's only when they don't have a choice. But I'm not going away."

"You promise?"

Katelyn met Jenny's serious eyes. "I promise."

Helplessly, Katelyn spread her hands. "It's not that simple."

"You said if people promise not to go away, they won't unless they don't have a choice. Do you have a choice?"

Finn watched her reaction tensely. Katelyn had a choice and Jenny, even at her tender age, sensed that.

Katelyn's eyelids flickered shut briefly.

"Don't go, Mommy," Eric implored, his lip trembling

as he reached his arms toward her, begging to be picked up.

"Where's Mommy going?" Erin asked. "Can we go, too?"

Jenny put an arm around her sister's shoulders. "Not if she leaves."

Erin's face twisted into a wail.

Katelyn stared between the three children, her eyes meeting and holding Jenny's heartbroken ones.

"What's everyone crying for?" She dashed a hand across her own moist eyes. "Nothing's been decided for sure." Katelyn glanced again at Jenny. "And I don't have time to worry about it now."

"Mommy's staying?" Eric asked.

"Yes."

Happy, he scrambled off her lap.

Jenny took his place, curling her arms around Katelyn's neck. "Don't *ever* leave, Mommy. *Ever.*"

Katelyn stared between them at the growing mound on her abdomen. She was in her final trimester. Soon there would be another child. How could she leave them? Yet how could she stay? How ever was she going to extricate herself from this mess?

And how was she going to live with Finn in the meantime?

Finn edged away from the doorway, his relief matching and overtaking the children's. For a moment he had thought she was going to walk away today. And he didn't think any of them would have survived it.

Chapter Twenty

Katelyn stared at her swollen belly in disgust. Rifling through the closet, she tried to find something that would disguise her bloated condition. Logically she knew that she'd always viewed pregnant women as lovely, but now that she felt as though she were carrying a baby elephant, her outlook had changed.

She finally just grabbed a loose smock, knowing nothing would flatter her. It didn't take long to dress. Her nerves were on full alert. Tonight was her first Lamaze class.

She hadn't really wanted to think ahead to the actual birth part—but she wouldn't be able to think of anything else while she was in the class. Katelyn reminded herself that millions of women went through childbirth, but statistics weren't very comforting. The fact that she would be doing this on her own made it especially scary.

Finn had insisted on knowing everything the doctor said and had wanted to accompany her on those visits. She'd refused, knowing she couldn't share that much intimacy with Finn.

She peeked in on the kids and saw that they were all occupied. Having told Finn about the Lamaze class, she knew he would be in charge of the kids for the evening.

Downstairs, Katelyn looked for her keys. Not finding them in their usual spot, she wondered if she'd left them in the kitchen. She headed that way but Finn stood in the doorway, leaning one hip against the doorjamb. He held one hand up—and her keys dangled from his fingers.

"I wondered where I'd left them." She held out her hand. "I need them to go to my class."

"I know," he replied. "That's why I have them."

She frowned. "I don't have time for games. I'll be late."

"No. *We'll* be on time."

Annoyed, Katelyn shook her head as she reached again for her keys. "There's no *we*. This is a solo expedition."

Finn deliberately held the keys out of her reach. "I respect your right to privacy for the doctor's visits. This is different. You need a birthing coach—and it's going to be me."

Exasperated, Katelyn glared at him. "I don't think so."

"I know so," he replied, meeting her glare and not flinching.

"You've conveniently forgotten about the children," she reminded him. "We can hardly leave them alone."

"That's why there's a baby-sitter in the living room," Finn replied.

Her smugness disappeared. "That doesn't mean you have to come with me."

He walked toward her until little space remained between them. "You're not going without me."

Katelyn glanced at the keys still held firmly in his muscular hand, knowing she could hardly wrestle him for them. "It seems I don't have a choice."

Finn's upper lip lifted into what looked suspiciously like the beginning of a grin. However, when she gave him a wary glance, his expression was even. Almost too even.

Knowing it was hopeless, Katelyn stalked into the living room, giving a litany of instructions to the baby-sitter.

Finn finally took her elbow and steered her toward the

front door. "We're going to be gone a few hours, not months."

"But—"

"Katie, the kids will be fine. The baby-sitter is competent and experienced."

Still she fretted, worried about leaving them in a stranger's care.

Finn slanted a glance at her. "If you're this worried about leaving them for an evening, how can you stand the thought of leaving them permanently?"

BY THE FOURTH CLASS, Katelyn was resigned to having Finn accompany her. She'd tried several of what she thought were ingenious methods to avoid him and all had failed. He was determined to be her coach, and short of skipping the class herself, she was out of options. She knew that even if she took a cab to class, Finn would simply drive there alone and sit with her.

Katelyn tried to pay attention to the teacher, but today's lesson was distracting. The coaches were being instructed on back massage, especially methods that could be used in the event of back labor.

But Katelyn wasn't thinking about labor. All she could think about was the feel of Finn's hands on her back, the sure, familiar thrill of his touch.

The teacher's voice continued, but it didn't penetrate her consciousness. She felt the restrained strength of Finn's hands as his fingers continued to deliver firm, yet gentle pressure to her back.

Aching to lean back into his arms, she struggled instead to hold herself stiffly alert.

Finn leaned close, whispering in her ear, "Brings back memories, doesn't it?"

Far too many memories. But she didn't reply, pretending to look terribly interested in the teacher's words.

Finn's hands drifted down her sides. Again he leaned close. "We could do a complete body massage when we get home."

She jerked upright, again focusing on the teacher. "I want to pay attention."

"She just told us to take a break," Finn told her with a grin.

"I'd have known that if you weren't distracting me," she replied, flustered.

"Oh, I *am* distracting you then?"

She pushed a hand through her hair, then tried to look collected. "It's break time, I believe."

Finn stood up, offering his hand.

Katelyn wanted to refuse, but getting up from the floor wasn't practical on her own. She accepted his hand, and he easily tugged her to a standing position as if she were weightless. She realized too late that he'd pulled her extremely close. For a moment she was paralyzed, their faces only inches apart.

Her breath came more rapidly, her pulse tripping into a runaway pace. His head slanted toward hers and she could almost feel the firm pressure of his lips on hers, his taste mingled with her own.

His lips opened and she swayed toward them.

"Let's share everything again, Katie."

She froze. She wanted the happily every after. Desperately. But she couldn't forget his deception, his willingness to sacrifice her for his own needs. How could she be certain he wouldn't do it again?

Confusion and sorrow tinted her eyes as she drew back.

Finn knew this was one color he could never put a name to. He also knew he wasn't going to give up.

KATELYN LOOKED at her friend in exasperation. "Stefanie, don't tell them it's okay to put grass in the sandbox!"

Stefanie shrugged. "Like you got where you are following all the rules."

Sighing, Katelyn instructed the children to keep the grass out of the park's sandbox. Then she settled back down, shifting on the bench to accommodate her girth. "Actually, I *did* follow most of the rules."

"Which makes it hard for you to understand why someone else doesn't."

"You planning on operating a psychic hotline in your spare time?" Katelyn asked, uncomfortable with the accuracy of Stefanie's guess.

"Nah, I'll just concentrate on my friends—like you. Am I close?"

"You're going to keep probing, aren't you?"

Stefanie buffed long, red fingernails against her purple silk suit. "Yep. I know something's up with you. Might as well come clean."

Katelyn told her friend everything that had transpired since she'd met Finn.

When she finished, Stefanie whistled, long and low. "Even though Finn only broke one rule—it goes against every grain in your very pregnant body."

"Exactly."

"And you really plan to leave?" Stefanie asked, angling her head toward the sandbox.

"That's what's so difficult." Katelyn stared over at the children. "Before I knew the truth, I promised Jenny I'd never leave."

"How do you plan to get out of that?"

"I don't know. I can't decide if my brain's turned to mush or if there really isn't a solution. Jenny told me that people leave even when they say they won't."

"Her mother?" Stefanie guessed.

"Exactly. I let her know that her mother didn't have a choice...."

"But you do."

"Right again. Which is what Jenny called me on when I wanted to leave." Katelyn stared ahead, verbalizing some of the thoughts that tormented her. "I want her to know that she can count on people...."

"How can she? Though it wasn't her fault, Jenny's mother left. She's a child—she felt abandoned. Now if you leave, Jenny will be convinced that when she loves and trusts someone, they'll abandon her."

Katelyn threw up her hands. The truth had been spinning through her mind endlessly, leaving her unable to make a decision. "So what am I supposed to do?"

Stefanie studied her friend. "Can't you get over those broken rules?"

"Could you?"

"Problem is, I'm not you." Stefanie threw back her head. "But, then I guess it depends on how much you love him."

"I didn't say—" Katelyn started to protest.

Stefanie gave her a rueful, understanding smile. "You didn't have to."

FINN PUT the last vase of roses into place. Standing back, he surveyed the limo with satisfaction. With the exception of the driver's and one passenger seat, it was filled with flowers. Even the console in the front seat was filled with fragrant blooms.

He also viewed the empty spot in the garage with satisfaction. He'd had the dealership pick up Katelyn's Jeep for a maintenance check and it was now long gone. Finn expected Katelyn to protest riding in the flower-filled limo, but she wouldn't have an alternative.

Nonalcoholic champagne rested in a cooler along with two chilled glasses. And this time he had a respectable ring

in his pocket, a diamond he'd gone into hock for, but one
that Katelyn deserved.

Hearing the front door open and then close, he quickly
stashed the picnic basket in the trunk and then opened the
passenger door.

Katelyn eyed the limo warily, since they normally drove
the Jeep to Lamaze class. But she stepped inside and Finn
shut the door, quickly skirting the hood to reach his side
of the car.

Sliding inside, he met Katelyn's suspicious stare.

"Did you drive for a wedding today, Finn?"

He smiled, turning the key. "No."

"Then I suppose you're counting on a funeral tonight,"
she countered.

"I don't think so."

"I do," she muttered, swiveling her head to take in the
abundance of flowers.

Finn glanced at her, seeing only the glow. She was so
incredibly beautiful, yet she didn't seem to know it. For all
her confidence in business matters, she wasn't aware of her
physical impact—even in her advanced state of pregnancy.

Katelyn glanced out the window as they drove along.
"Why are we going this way? The class isn't this direction."

"Tonight's class was rescheduled to Thursday."

"Then were are we going?"

"On a champagne picnic," he replied, smoothly switch-
ing lanes.

"I don't have time for this. Besides, it's nearly dark."

"Did I mention that it's a picnic beneath the stars?" Finn
asked, knowing how much she enjoyed gazing at the night
sky.

"I don't care if it's beneath diamonds, I'm not going on
a picnic with you."

At the mention of diamonds, the ring in his pocket

seemed to catch fire. "Since your half of the limo's going to the picnic with mine, I don't think you have a choice."

They rode along in silence until Finn turned in at an office complex filled with towering buildings.

Katelyn stared at him. "This isn't a park."

"It wouldn't be very comfortable for you to sit on the ground in a park," he explained. "But I think you'll like this just as well."

Once they had parked, Finn guided her toward the elevator, ignoring her protests.

"This is ridiculous," she complained.

"Everything can't be practical," he countered, meeting her eyes. "Or work out the way you want."

Once inside, Finn pressed the button for the top floor. Closing her eyes, Katelyn eased her back against the wall of the elevator. The bell dinged and the doors slid open. Finn grasped her elbow as they stepped out.

Katelyn stopped abruptly. "Where are we?"

Finn pointed to a door. "We're almost there."

"Where?" she continued asking as he guided her through the doorway. The door shut behind her and she stopped again, staring. "The roof? We're on the *roof?*"

He took her hand and led her to the garden terrace. Redwood chairs, benches and tables were scattered casually among the greenery and flowers. Dusk was approaching and soft lights lit the area, twinkling as though longing to be part of the night sky. Deserted now that the building employees had left for the day, they had the place to themselves.

Katelyn chose a bench, since the chairs looked too low to be comfortable. Finn placed the basket on a nearby table and withdrew the champagne and glasses.

Her brows rose when she saw both.

"It's nonalcoholic," Finn explained. "It won't hurt the baby."

"Or aid in programming me yet again?"

Finn winced. "You aren't part elephant, are you?"

She immediately glanced down at her ever-enlarging shape and then back at him with a hurt expression.

"I didn't mean your shape—you're gorgeous," Finn hastened to assure her. "I meant your memory. Can't you let *anything* go?"

"I don't rewrite history, if that's what you mean."

Finn handed her a filled glass. "I'm just hoping you can let parts of it fade."

Tentatively she sipped the drink, realizing it was exactly what he'd said it was. "A long time ago I realized it's wise to learn from your mistakes. Only a fool forgets about them and hopes they won't happen again."

Finn shifted, feeling the weight of the ring in his pocket. But first, he opened the basket and drew out the food.

When they finished eating, dusk had melded into darkness and the stars were out.

Katelyn tipped her head back. "I do love looking at the stars." Then she glanced around at the unique setting. "How did you know about this place?"

"One advantage to being a driver—I get to a lot of places most people don't."

"Any others? Advantages, I mean."

Finn gazed at the woman who had come to mean so much to him. "Every once in a while there's a chance of a lifetime. One you never expected, never looked for, never even hoped for."

Katelyn's gaze reluctantly slid to meet his.

"And never believed could be so wonderful," Finn continued, watching her eyes, now the color of blue velvet. He reached into his pocket, retrieving the ring. Seeing the pulse in the hollow of her throat jump to life, he felt a surge of new hope. "I've made some mistakes, but the biggest one I could ever make would be letting you go." He opened the jeweler's box and lifted out the ring. "Katie, can you forgive me?"

Sadly, she stared between Finn and his beautiful gift. "You destroyed what I cherish most—trust."

Frustrated, Finn wanted to rail out again that the tapes had not been his doing. Regretfully, he knew he should have told Katelyn about them as soon as he'd found out about them. Bleakly, he realized it might be the one mistake she never forgave.

Chapter Twenty-One

Katelyn compared this evening's ride to Lamaze class with the one earlier in the week that had turned into the rooftop champagne picnic. Both she and Finn had been unusually quiet tonight.

Of course that might have something to do with her repeated rejection of his apology. While part of her wanted to bend, a more insistent force remembered in vivid clarity that every step of their relationship had been carefully orchestrated. And she simply couldn't get the tune out of her mind.

Walking into the classroom, Katelyn jealously observed the tender closeness between the other couples. There was a big hole inside her that wanted that same closeness. She darted a glance at Finn, knowing the tenderness he was capable of.

The nurse practitioner looked ready to begin, so they quickly took their places. They started with exercises, something they usually closed with. As always, the interactive exercises with Finn were a torturous pleasure for Katelyn. Tonight, Finn's hands seemed to linger longer than necessary, sending ripples of yearning through her.

"You doing all right?" Finn asked, his face close to hers.

She nodded, unable to trust her voice.

"You're awfully tense."

Katelyn wanted to tell him he didn't know the meaning of tense. She was strung tightly enough to be on the high wire. "I'm concentrating," she said instead.

"Right," Finn muttered.

"Let's all grab some chairs," the teacher called out. "Sit where you can see the TV."

Finn carried two of the well-padded folding chairs to the front of the room. Katelyn trailed behind, hoping tonight's video wasn't the one she was dreading.

The instructor slipped a video into the VCR at the front of the room. "Tonight is the culmination of all our lessons—the goal we've been progressing toward." She smiled broadly. "Parents, we're going to watch birth films tonight."

Bingo. It was *the* video. Katelyn swallowed the anxiety she felt. She really hadn't wanted to watch this film. Frightened enough already, she didn't think she needed an actual visualization. It seemed that could only make it worse.

And a few minutes into the video, Katelyn knew she was right. Knots formed in her stomach—big, hairy knots that were choking her from the inside out. Motherhood didn't frighten her—she already knew she could handle Finn's children. But the actual birth was something else. Something that had her scared to death.

The film continued. Like a rat drawn to a perilous but enticing trap, she couldn't take her eyes from the screen. As her anxiety increased she dug her fingers into the arm of the chair.

"Katie," Finn whispered.

Eyes glued to the TV, she answered distractedly. "What?"

"Normally I wouldn't complain, because I love it when you touch me, but you're digging holes in my arm."

Horrified, she pulled back his hand, realizing it was *him* she'd been digging her fingers into. "I'm sorry."

"No problem, but why don't you try to relax?"

"Right," she muttered, missing the disbelieving expression on Finn's face.

"Next thing you know we'll be finishing each other's sentences."

"Uh-huh," she replied, not hearing him, already drawn back into the film, grimacing as she watched another birth begin.

When the film was over and the class dismissed, Katelyn's face was an unhealthy white. Finn glanced at her as they were leaving the room and automatically he reached for her arm, deciding she needed a steady support. When she didn't even notice his touch, he knew something was seriously wrong.

"Katie."

She kept walking toward the exit.

"Katie!" He jiggled her arm. "What's wrong? Aren't you feeling well?"

Her gaze focused on him "I'm okay."

"You don't look okay."

Looking offended, she adjusted her dress as though his comment referred to her appearance rather than her health. "I *am* pregnant, you know."

"So I hear. Maybe we should go back inside and have the nurse check you out."

"No!" She lowered her voice as she increased her pace toward the exit. "I mean there's no need. The class *is* over."

"Then what's bothering you?"

Katelyn stopped suddenly, her voice small. "The end of my pregnancy."

"That's natural. Most women are nervous about taking care of a new baby."

She shook her head. "That's not it."

Finn stared at her. "Then what else is there about the

end of..." His voice trailed off. Could it be she was frightened of childbirth? This woman who could chew up corporations and spit them out like toothpaste?

"Never mind," she said hastily. "You're right. I don't feel so good. I'm ready to go home."

If she didn't want to admit her fear, he could let it pass. "Do you want to stop for some coffee?"

"No. I just want to go home." Katelyn's hands tightened around the straps of her purse. "Now."

Finn saluted smartly. "Whatever you say...*ma'am*."

Her head snapped up. *Ma'am?* Suddenly she remembered the day she'd met him—how she'd treated him like a hundred other employees. Katelyn craned her head to look at him. Had there been any truth to his initial impression of her?

"Is it going to be a brother, or a sister?" Jenny asked.

"I want a brother," Eric announced, planting his feet apart in a totally male fashion.

Erin didn't state a preference, instead handing Katelyn a doll crafted out of Play-Doh. Studying it, Katelyn realized the crude doll had a bulging tummy much like her own.

Dodging their questions, Katelyn still wondered what she was going to do about these children of her heart. And they'd reminded her of something she'd tried not to think about. This child would be a brother or sister. She couldn't keep siblings apart.

"I'd prefer a handsome millionaire whose only fault is extreme generosity," Stefanie drawled.

Katelyn smirked at her. "Put it on your list for Santa. Then if you're a *very* good girl..."

Stefanie pushed her sunglasses up on her forehead. "If I'm that good I won't have to wait for Santa."

"Yes, you do," Jenny told her. "Everybody has to wait for Santa. And you have to give him milk and cookies."

Stefanie smiled at her. "Sounds like I could learn a lot from you. Milk and cookies, eh?"

"And carrots for the reindeer," Jenny added.

Stefanie lifted her diet soda. "Now, that's one I wouldn't have thought of."

Katelyn smiled between her friend and her children, delighted they got along so well. *Her children.* Had she actually thought that? She'd referred to them that way to their doctor and preschool teachers, but when had it become a natural assumption in her mind? And in her heart?

"Can we go on the swings and slide?" Jenny asked.

"If you'll watch out for your brother and sister," Katelyn replied, the words barely out of her mouth when they all scampered off.

Stefanie glanced at the Play-Doh doll. "Your twin?" She picked up the doll and poked the protruding stomach. "Good likeness. Won't be long now till it's show time."

Katelyn winced. "Don't worry about being indelicate."

"I never have before. Why should I now?"

"Good point. But then you've always played by your own rules."

"Just like you. After all, it's your obsession with rules that's keeping you and Finn apart."

Katelyn stared at her healthy drink, a combination of half a dozen juices. "I'd kill for a soda," she muttered. Then she raised her troubled gaze to meet Stefanie's. "Do you really think I'm too unbending?"

"Let me put it this way. Steel pipe has more flexibility."

"Really?"

"Haven't you ever made a mistake, Katelyn?"

"Sure, but not one that played with people's lives."

Stefanie lifted one brow. "Not even when you were commanding an army of employees? You never made arbitrary decisions that ultimately changed their lives?"

"That's different. That's business," Katelyn insisted,

wondering if it was true. "Besides, I never made a mistake as mammoth as Finn's."

"Men are programmed to make mistakes. But according to you, his was in the whopper category."

Katelyn had always enjoyed discussing things with Stefanie. She was painfully frank and never pulled any punches, stating things exactly as she saw them. Katelyn usually valued this quality in her friend. Right now, she wished instead that Stefanie possessed a little more blind loyalty.

"His mistake was in a category of its own," she retorted.

Stefanie shrugged. "If you say so." It was the closest Stef would come to blind loyalty.

Katelyn played with the straw in her drink. "Do you think I'm wrong not wanting to risk trusting Finn again?"

Sighing, Stefanie patted her shoulder. "That's a toughie. And only you can decide. I don't know Finn like you do. If he doesn't have any romance in his soul…"

Katelyn immediately thought of the flower-filled limo, the champagne rooftop picnic beneath the stars, the candles he'd filled the room with…the Oreos.

"…and if you're sure he's untrustworthy…"

Katelyn had only to glance over at the slide to see three well-loved, decently raised children—hardly signs of an untrustworthy parent.

Stefanie met her gaze. "Then it's still your decision. Look, kid, you've got to make this call. Pretend you're evaluating a client or a campaign. You know merit when you see it. Does Finn have any?"

MERIT. Katelyn listened to the silence in their dark bedroom as she debated the question. Finn's controlled breathing told her that he was still awake.

She thought of the long hours he worked to provide for his family, never complaining. Then there was his single-minded determination to make the limo service a success so that eventually he could hire additional drivers, allowing him to spend more time with the children. In spite of her hurt, she knew those were sure signs of merit.

Finn shifted in the bed, bringing him closer. She longed to share the warm heat from his body, the comfort of his touch.

"Having trouble sleeping?" he asked.

She shook her head, then realized he couldn't see the motion in the dark. "Sort of."

"Can't find a comfortable position?"

She wished that was really the problem. "There aren't too many positions that work."

He reached for the extra pillow beneath his head, then adjusted it beneath her abdomen, his hands gentle as he slid the pillow into place. Did she imagine that his hands lingered longer than necessary?

She knew she didn't imagine her response, her yearning to turn to him. Why had things grown so complicated? Remembering what they'd shared before she learned of his deception, Katelyn suddenly wished she could turn back the time and that things could be as they'd been before.

The baby kicked suddenly, insistently. Her hands reached to cup her abdomen. In that instant she knew her wish was foolhardy, that she would never wish away the wonder she held inside. Even to turn back time.

Finn's hand touched her just then, his fingers rippling over the length of her hair. His gentle strokes told her that he thought she was now asleep. Should she turn to him and let him know she was awake? Or keep her silence? And her heartache?

Finn sifted his fingers through hair soft as silk, wishing he could soften her anger to match it. He knew she was conflicted. He also knew that she was torn between being the unbending executive who would never say die and the gentler woman she'd become, one who adored his children. One who now carried his child.

One who held his heart in her hands.

Chapter Twenty-Two

Katelyn stared at the computer screen, but she didn't see the graphics of her latest ad campaign. Instead she kept remembering the morning as Finn left. As always, he had warmly hugged the children. But as he rose from a kneeling position, his gaze had caught hers. She had seen the longing, the caring.

A mockingbird's shrill cry broke the utter quiet. The house was very still when the children were in preschool. And, as much as she craved time to work through her ideas, she missed their giggles, the sounds of play. Especially now when her mind was so full, her thoughts so tortured.

She had once considered herself an excellent judge of character. It had been pivotal to her success. Sizing up people, then being able to guess what would please them. But in Finn's case, she had been so wrong.

First, dismissing him as though he had no value simply because of his occupation. Then discovering what a wonderful, caring parent he was. But never guessing he would trick her into marriage. And now, wondering which man he really was. A con-artist who had used her for his own purpose? Or a loving man who even now was telling her the truth?

The doorbell rang. Katelyn considered ignoring it, but

then realized any distraction from her thoughts would be welcome.

Opening the door, she realized that wasn't quite true. Daniel stood on the doorstep, his expression somber.

"Daniel," she greeted him coolly, not opening the door any wider.

"Katelyn," he replied evenly.

She was certain he noticed her unwelcome stance, but he didn't comment on it. "What brings you here?"

He held out a precise white envelope. "This is for you."

Automatically, she reached for the envelope. "You could have couriered it over."

"Not this."

Puzzled, she glanced at him.

But he spoke before she could question the contents. "It's my resignation."

The word ricocheted through her consciousness but it couldn't penetrate the shock. She was furious with Daniel, but she hadn't considered this possibility. It seemed like an equal betrayal. "What?"

Daniel made an impatient noise. "If we're going to discuss this, I'd rather not do it on the doorstep."

Reluctantly, Katelyn pulled the door open, then led the way to the living room, selecting one of the few chairs she could rise from. "So, talk."

"You made it clear you didn't believe me when I told you Finn had nothing to do with the tapes. There was no conspiracy, Katelyn. But your suspicion is wrecking your marriage. I've never seen you happier than you have been since you met Finn. I can't say I'm sorry I gave you the tapes because it brought you two together. But since the method is killing the result, I have to let you know how serious I am. I'm resigning so that you will see that Finn and I are not scheming. And never were. I'm sorry it has come to this, but I'd be sorrier to see you lose your first taste of happiness."

Tears pricked Katelyn's eyelids. Not only because of his words, but because she considered Daniel the brother she'd never had. He, too, was prepared to walk away. Yet, she felt the still undissolved kernel of distrust. "How do I know you're not just saying this to protect Finn?"

"Why would I do that? He and I are acquaintances, but you and I are friends. And friends don't lie to each other."

Katelyn swallowed. "But are you such a good friend that you're prepared to sacrifice your job to keep Finn's betrayal from hurting me?"

"Now, that's convoluted," he replied wryly. "Katelyn, the truth is I made a mistake. I should have told you what I'd done."

"Finn should have, too." She couldn't keep the bitterness from her voice.

"Once he knew, maybe so. But I think he believed you'd react just as you have. He was caught in a do or die situation. If he had told you when he learned what had happened, you would have questioned his part from the beginning. And if he didn't tell you, he risked your learning about it and still condemning him. Either way, he was doomed. He hoped this whole thing wouldn't come crashing down on our heads. Yet it has."

"I would feel that way, too, if I were about to be found out."

Sadly Daniel shook his head. "Clearly, there's no convincing you when you're determined not to budge."

Katelyn lifted her chin, wishing none of this had happened, that her marriage to Finn was what she had believed it to be. She also wished her friend hadn't tricked her. "It's difficult to see the truth, with everything else that's clouding it."

Daniel nodded. "As I thought."

Katelyn extended the envelope toward him. "But I'm not prepared to accept your resignation. I suppose your intentions were good, just terribly misguided."

Daniel didn't accept the envelope, instead rising from his chair. "No, I can't accept that answer. And, I can't allow Finn to take the blame for my actions. Unless and until you realize that I'm telling the truth, I can't work for you."

Shocked, Katelyn automatically rose as well. "You can't mean that!"

"Sadly, I'm afraid I can. The nudge may have been mine. But the magic was solely your own. You and Finn were meant to be together. For your sake, I hope you realize that, Katelyn. Before it's too late."

"MOMMY." JENNY tugged on Katelyn's sleeve. "Morrica said when her baby brother came home they had a new room fixed up for him. Where are we going to put our new baby?"

Katelyn disguised her flinch, unable to face the question since her future was so uncertain. Her mind was still filled with Daniel's visit and the resulting introspection. But she smiled tenderly at Jenny, reaching out to smooth back her hair. "We need to be concentrating on your room. We haven't got the matching curtains yet for your new bedspread. And I think we should pick up your blinds, too."

"Pink!" Jenny replied, clapping her hands.

"Yes, pink." Katelyn had ordered a pale blush to coordinate with the new accessories in Jenny's room. "Let's get your brother and sister and go shopping."

Jenny jumped up just as the phone rang. Katelyn answered it, not thinking about letting the service pick up the call.

Stefanie's irreverent voice greeted her. "Hello, sunshine. Got time for a friend?"

"Actually, I was just about to take the kids shopping."

"Great. I'll meet you there."

Katelyn frowned. Although she relished Stefanie's friendship, she didn't need her friend's too watchful and knowing eyes. Then she glanced at the clock. "Isn't this the middle of your workday?"

Breezily, Stefanie laughed. "Luckily, I penciled in time for you today."

"Actually, this isn't the best time. You know how shopping is with kids. They're off in separate directions and it's so distracting we can hardly talk."

"It's not that bad. I'll risk it," Stefanie persisted.

"We could go another time when they're in school," Katelyn suggested, wishing Stefanie hadn't chosen today to be so insistent.

"Don't you want to play with your old single friend?" Stefanie asked, sounding hurt.

Immediately remorseful, Katelyn shoved her own pain aside. "Of course I do. But don't say I didn't warn you." After setting a meeting spot, she gathered the children and headed toward the mall.

Stefanie paced the tiled corridor of the food courtyard, her heels tapping out the agitation she hoped to conceal. They had agreed to eat before hitting the stores. Stefanie had been delighted by the choice. With the children's attention on food, she would be able to talk to Katelyn.

Sobered earlier by a revealing call from Daniel, Stefanie knew she had to make Katelyn see the truth. Convinced that Daniel's motives had been pure, she agreed with him that Katelyn and Finn belonged together. And the impish side of her didn't totally disapprove of his methods. Unfortunately, her friend was far more determined to play strictly by the rules. However, Stefanie didn't want to see Katelyn sacrifice her happiness because of that.

Spotting Katelyn and her brood, Stefanie watched them

from afar as they approached. Katelyn had changed dramatically since her marriage. And it wasn't simply the pregnancy. She was softer, more caring. She had always been a good friend, but now there was a depth to her that she'd hidden before.

Prior to Finn and the children, Katelyn had made her career her sole priority. There had always been an edge to her personality. And Stefanie believed that edge had been a defense against the loneliness which Katelyn kept carefully concealed.

And until she'd learned about the tapes, Katelyn had glowed from her unexpected happiness. Now, as her friend approached, Stefanie searched for that happiness, seeing instead the carefully masked pain. It was just the catalyst Stefanie needed. She intended to help Katelyn see the truth.

Katelyn tried to make her smile believable. "I hope you haven't been waiting long. We had a few last minute costume changes." Pointedly, she glanced down at the twins who had chosen today to insist on wearing purple and orange shirts with their lime green pants.

"I like it!" Stefanie told Eric and Erin with a grin. "No wishy-washy colors for you." Then she turned to Jenny. "And I definitely approve of the hot pink."

Jenny brightened. "Mommy and me picked it out." She wiggled her tennies. "And my shoe laces match."

"So they do. I'll have to get Mommy to help me on my next shopping trip," Stefanie replied with appropriate seriousness. Then she glanced up at Katelyn as though expecting a tart remark.

But Katelyn only nodded, her mood too disheartened to comment. Then she smiled, seeing the concern on her friend's face. "Why don't we find a table?"

"Tell you what," Stefanie suggested. "If you'll order the food, I'll scout out a table. I'll even take the rug rats with me."

"Fine," Katelyn replied. "I promised them corndogs— their favorite."

"Mine, too," Stefanie agreed. "At least when I'm at the mall."

A short time later, loaded tray in hand, Katelyn searched for Stefanie and the kids.

Stefanie stood and waved. Approaching, Katelyn frowned. It looked as though Stefanie had set them up at two tables—one for adults and one for the children. Although the tables weren't far apart, Katelyn was accustomed to keeping the kids at her side.

"Wasn't there one large table?" she asked.

"The kids loved the idea of having their own grown-up table," Stefanie explained. "And they're only about two feet from our table. They can't get away from us."

Katelyn scanned the crowded food court. "Maybe if we keep looking we can find one big table."

"We want this one!" Jenny exclaimed.

"This one!" the twins chimed in.

Defeated, Katelyn distributed the food. And, sitting at the table with Stefanie, she realized the kids were scarcely more than an arm's span away. Just far enough away that they could talk but not far enough that the children could get into trouble.

Stefanie munched happily on her corndog. "You have to admit that the two tables aren't such a bad idea."

Katelyn nodded. "I guess I'm overprotective."

"You came into the motherhood game late. So you appreciate the kids even more and want to keep them safe."

"I'd like to think that I would have appreciated them either way."

"The way you appreciated Finn?" Stefanie asked.

The pain intensified. "It's not the same thing."

"No? Isn't he part of this family?"

"Of course he is." Katelyn lowered her voice. "But my feelings for Finn and the children are different."

Stefanie's cool, knowing gaze zeroed in. "And how do you feel about Finn?"

Katelyn glanced over at the children. "Not now."

"What better time? The kids can't hear us and they won't ever be more occupied than when their hands are filled with corndogs."

Reluctantly, Katelyn agreed. "I'm not sure how I feel. Until Finn came along, I never allowed myself to trust a man. I saw from my parents' marriage how unhappy a relationship can be. That's why I never wanted it for myself. Then to learn that Finn tricked me into marrying—"

"Hold it. How can you be sure of that? Finn told you he didn't discover what had happened until shortly before you did."

"Of course he'd say that."

"Now that's a lot of trust! How would you have felt if Finn had told you then?"

"Well, I..."

"Can you be sure your reaction would have been any different?"

Katelyn wanted to say it would have been, but she wasn't sure. "At least he would have come forward, instead of letting me learn on my own."

"And how would that have helped? Think about it, Katelyn. The man was damned if he did, damned if he didn't. No doubt he was very torn. He probably wanted to be honest with you but he guessed how you would react. If he claimed to have just discovered the truth, you would have doubted him. And my guess is he was afraid he would lose you. Katelyn, I know you play by the rules, but there's a more important barometer." Stefanie's expression sobered with uncharacteristic earnestness "And that's your heart."

The same heart that was fractured with pain and uncertainty. And the love she'd tried to deny. Katelyn lifted troubled eyes. "Everything's such a mess. My doubts about myself, the barrier between us that I'm not sure can be repaired."

"With love all things are possible, my friend."

With love. Katelyn desperately wished that were true. But their love, fragile and new, had been tremendously abused. And now Katelyn wasn't even certain she was the person Finn had come to love.

KATELYN REARRANGED the candles, wondering if they were too much. She had planned on a simple dinner for two since Stefanie had willingly taken the children home with her.

Somehow, the simplicity had disappeared when Katelyn had dimmed the overhead lighting, brought out the best dinnerware, and added flowers from the garden. And now she wondered if the table was too fussy, too obvious. It was only one of the many doubts she had been feeling.

Hearing the door open, Katelyn took a deep breath.

"Katie?" Finn called out from the hall. "Jenny? Eric? Erin?"

"In here," Katelyn replied nervously.

He stepped into the room, his face registering surprise when he saw the table. "Only set for two?"

"Stefanie has the kids." Katelyn fiddled with the lace napkins, then pressed her hands together. "She wanted to take them to the new Disney movie."

"Oh," he replied tentatively, obviously wondering what was going on. "I'm sure they'll enjoy that."

"I thought we might have a quiet dinner alone."

Again his gaze scanned the table. "You won't get any argument from me." Then he glanced down at his working clothes. "Just give me a minute to freshen up." He headed toward the doorway, then turned back. "Don't disappear on me."

Nervously, Katelyn smiled, but her expression dimmed as he left. She checked on the food which was in the warming oven, feeling a sense of self-derision. What normal wife counted on takeout and restaurant-prepared meals?

Opening the refrigerator, she removed the salad she had prepared, her only culinary claim to fame. And to think she had been convinced she could become the perfect wife and mother. That was the heart of her anguish. Much of her indecision was centered on self-doubt. Doubt that she could be what any of them needed...or wanted.

"Whatever you have planned for dinner smells wonderful," Finn told her as he stepped into the kitchen.

"It's the special from Tuscany's," she replied.

His eyes darkened, clearly remembering how their only evening at Tuscany's had ended. It had been the first time they had made love. "Then I'm sure it will be wonderful."

Shakily, Katelyn handed him the salad bowls. "I think we're ready for the first course."

"At the very least."

Their eyes met in the charged moment. Finn accepted the salad and together they reentered the dining room.

Tentatively, Katelyn picked at her food, not caring what she ate. "I ordered the fettucini for both of us. I hope that's okay."

Seated next to her, Finn placed his hand over hers. "Whatever you do is okay with me."

Katelyn felt the sting of tears and fought them back. "I wish that were true." Agitated, she flung out her hands, knocking over the tureen. Chilled basil tomato soup spilled over the tablecloth, pouring into her lap. For a moment she stared at the ruined table, then clumsily rose.

"Katelyn? Let me help!"

But she ran toward the stairs, unable to bear her emotions

or his pity. Once inside the bedroom, she halted in front of the cheval mirror, grimacing at the image of her stained dress.

Finn's footsteps sounded behind her. Reluctantly she kept her gaze trained on the mirror, knowing even before she lifted her eyes that his gaze would be locked on hers. Instantly, she remembered the first moment they had stood in just this position. Images of fevered yet tender lovemaking nearly obscured her vision. With a small sob, Katelyn brought her fist to her mouth, hoping to muffle the agonized sound.

Gently, Finn reached out and turned her to face him, his hand cupping her chin. "What did you mean just now?"

Katelyn attempted to keep her voice steady, but her lips quivered. "When you get to know the real me, you won't feel that what I do is okay."

"The real you?" he questioned, his brows drawn together.

"The one not programmed by a tape to be the perfect wife and mother," she admitted painfully.

"I know the real you." His fingers skimmed the gentle slope of her cheek. "And that's the one I love."

"But what if I revert back to being a cold workaholic, one who doesn't care about you and the children?" she questioned, admitting her deepest fears.

Finn pulled her even closer. "Katie, the tapes didn't change you. They only work if you *want* them to. The tapes simply allowed you to get past your fears and show the warmth and love that's always been there. The caring that you've kept hidden." He kissed her temples. "The tapes caused only two things. They made you realize what you had to give."

Hope, nearly extinguished, leapt to life. Could he be right? Could the tapes have only removed her inhibitions? "You said *two* things?"

''The tapes also brought us together. And I won't ever regret that.''

''How can you be sure about me when I'm not?'' she cried, unable to release the anguish which stalked her.

''Because I love you,'' he replied simply. ''I've come to know your heart, Katelyn Malloy. And it's a heart large enough to encompass three motherless children, their rogue of a father, and even more. Life isn't a Rockwell setting, Katie. It's chicken pox and burned toast and scraped knees. It's hugs and arguments and laughter. It's what we already have together. That is, if you can come to trust me again.''

The tears Katelyn had held back erupted. ''I think I had to hang on to believing you tricked me. I couldn't face that I wasn't what you and the children had come to love.''

Finn stroked the hair from her forehead, his eyes as tender as his touch. ''You are everything we love. You're smart and funny and kind. Each moment you've devoted to the children is engraved in my heart, making my love grow more each day. Don't ever doubt yourself, my love. I'm the one in your debt. And in your snare... I signed on for life, Katie.'' His hand reached to cup the gentle swell of her abdomen. ''All our lives.''

Katelyn's tremulous smile nearly eclipsed the joy in her eyes. ''I'm sorry I doubted you, Finn. I love you so much more than I ever knew was possible.''

Moonlight flickered over their faces, their lips joining in a kiss of promise...an affirmation of love. Sheer curtains rustled in the breeze, revealing the fullness of the rising moon. One beam seemed to linger, illuminating the tender embrace, then it shot skyward, carrying their dreams to the unending heavens.

Epilogue

Azaleas, resplendent in their showy colors of palest pink to fuchsia, bloomed in cultivated gardens. But in the fields that spread out from the city in great waving fans, bluebonnets and brilliant orangish-red Indian paintbrushes dotted the horizon. Spring was kind to the lush, far-flung land.

As fate had been the case, Katelyn acknowledged yet again. The smile that was never far from her lips bloomed as she gazed at her family. Hers. Truly and in every way.

They had chosen to picnic as a celebration. Finn had just finalized several new contracts—enough to purchase four more limos and hire drivers. The start to his fleet was a reality. And the time he'd longed for was now available. Time to spend with his family. Jenny, Erin and Eric, and their newest son, Matthew.

The baby gurgled as he reached across the blanket, hoping for a handful of his oldest sister's hair.

"No, no, Mattie," Jenny told him patiently, scooting out of reach. To distract him, she picked up the wand to her bubble mixture. Dipping it into the soapy liquid, Jenny waved the wand in the air, producing a profusion of iridescent bubbles.

Matthew chortled, reaching upward toward the display.

"Mommy!" Eric and Erin clamored in unison.

Anticipating their request, she handed them each wands.

Soon the air filled with hundreds of bubbles of all sizes and shapes.

Warm hands reached to cover her eyes. ''Penny for your thoughts.''

''They're worth a king's ransom,'' she replied, reaching up to cover his hands with her own.

Finn lowered their joined hands, turning her to face him. ''That valuable?''

A wayward breeze ruffled his thick black hair, and the blue of the sky paled in comparison to his eyes. Her pulse thrummed. How was it that he could steal her breath with just a look?

She sighed, a soft sound that lingered between them. ''Oh, yes. Riches beyond compare.''

Bubbles drifted by, dozens of circular rainbows. When they burst, fractured bits of color dissolved in the sunlight.

''They match your eyes,'' Finn told her quietly. ''I always wondered how to describe them. A rainbow of colors to capture your moods.''

Katelyn felt the catch in her throat. His words might sound like blarney to some, but she had learned he was a man of no artifice. She no longer doubted that trust...or herself. And she had Finn to thank for both. Her smile was tremulous. ''Can you guess my mood now?''

His fingers skimmed the length of her cheek, coming to rest on the fragile hollow of her throat. ''I can feel your heart, Katie. The pulse of everything that is you. The pulse that says you're happy...and well loved.''

A shimmer of tears glimmered in her eyes. ''Sometimes I still feel as though I will wake up and learn this was a dream, a wonderful, incredible dream.''

He clasped one hand, kissing her fingers. ''Sometimes dreams do come true.''

Katelyn's eyelids flickered shut briefly. ''In ways we couldn't begin to imagine.''

Finn tipped up her chin. ''Not in a thousand lifetimes.''
Ever so slowly his mouth sank against hers, a gentle brand,
but a claim nonetheless. One that had begun by chance and
now was sealed by love. Their union was as certain as one
single perfect calla lily, surrounded by the permanence of
stalwart violets.

The children's happy shrieks blended with the bubbles
that floated in the air, then disappeared to the winds. As
sure as the tides, as endless as the great canopied sky...they
echoed the sounds of joy. One hand...one heart...one
touch. And they were one.

**Starting December 1999,
a brand-new series about
fatherhood from**

HARLEQUIN®

AMERICA·N ◆ ROMA·N·CE®

THE **DADDY** CLUB

Three charming stories
about dads and kids...
and the women who
make their families
complete!

Available December 1999
FAMILY TO BE (#805)
by Linda Cajio

Available January 2000
A PREGNANCY AND A PROPOSAL (#809)
by Mindy Neff

Available February 2000
FOUR REASONS FOR FATHERHOOD (#813)
by Muriel Jensen

Available at your favorite retail outlet.

◆ HARLEQUIN®
Makes any time special ™

Visit us at: www.romance.net   HARDC

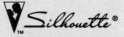